"YOUR GRANDMOTHER NEEDS YOU," JOE SAID

"I'm not sure that's true."

"How can you deny it?" Joe asked, incredulous. "She's over eighty years old. She's not going to live forever."

"Of course not," Susannah snapped. "But I can't step in and take over her life. I have no right to march in here and boss her around!"

"To save her life, you have the right to do a lot of things."

"I don't feel that way," Susannah said staunchly, wondering how she could have imagined Joe Santori was an attractive man. "My grandmother's life is hers to live, not mine."

"I suppose we should be grateful for small favors," Joe muttered. "Your grandmother is obviously living a full and happy life, while you're only worried about catching your flight to the Caribbean. It beats me how you ended up in the same family!"

"It beats me how you ended up in the human race. You're obviously a superior being—in your own mind at least!" She stormed up the stairs.

Special thanks and acknowledgment to Joanna Kosloff for her contribution to the concept for the Tyler series.

Published June 1992

ISBN 0-373-82504-8

MONKEY WRENCH

Printed in U.S.A.

MONKEY WRENCH

NANCY MARTIN

Harlequin Books

TORONTO • NEW YORK • LONDON
AMSTERDAM • PARIS • SYDNEY • HAMBURG
STOCKHOLM • ATHENS • TOKYO • MILAN
MADRID • WARSAW • BUDAPEST • AUCKLAND

TYLER

WHIRLWIND
Nancy Martin

BRIGHT HOPES
Pat Warren

WISCONSIN WEDDING
Carla Neggers

MONKEY WRENCH
Nancy Martin

BLAZING STAR
Suzanne Ellison

SUNSHINE
Pat Warren

ARROWPOINT
Suzanne Ellison

BACHELOR'S PUZZLE
Ginger Chambers

MILKY WAY
Muriel Jensen

CROSSROADS
Marisa Carroll

COURTHOUSE STEPS
Ginger Chambers

LOVEKNOT
Marisa Carroll

TYLER

American women have always used the art quilt as a means of expressing their views on life and as a commentary on events in the world around them. And in Tyler, quilting has always been a popular communal activity. So what could be a more appropriate theme for our book covers and titles?

MONKEY WRENCH

This distinctive pattern, which demonstrates how the simplest of shapes can be placed together to form an exciting, intricate design, originally went by more traditional names such as Snail's Trail, Indian Puzzle and Virginia Reel. The changing names reflect America's westward movement and the evolution from an agrarian, colonial society into the mechanical age.

Dear Reader,

Welcome to Harlequin's Tyler, a small Wisconsin town whose citizens we hope you'll soon come to know and love. Like many of the innovative publishing concepts Harlequin has launched over the years, the idea for the Tyler series originated in response to our readers' preferences. Your enthusiasm for sequels and continuing characters within many of the Harlequin lines has prompted us to create a twelve-book series of individual romances whose characters' lives inevitably intertwine.

Tyler faces many challenges typical of small towns, but the fabric of this fictional community will be torn by the revelation of a long-ago murder, the details of which will evolve right through the series.

Big changes are afoot at the old Timberlake resort lodge, which has attracted the attention of a prominent Chicago hotelier, a man with a personal interest in showing Tyler folks his financial clout, and a private objective in reclaiming the love of a town resident he romanced long ago.

Marge is waiting with some home-baked pie at her diner, and policeman Brick Bauer might direct you down Elm Street if it's patriarch Judson Ingalls you're after. Even television personality Susannah Atkins knows she can find everything she needs at Gates Department Store. She'll probably stop in when she makes an unscheduled stop in Tyler to check up on her Granny Rose. So join us in Tyler, once a month for the next nine months, for a slice of small-town life that's not as innocent or as quiet as you might expect, and for a sense of community that will capture your mind and your heart.

Marsha Zinberg
Editorial Coordinator, Tyler

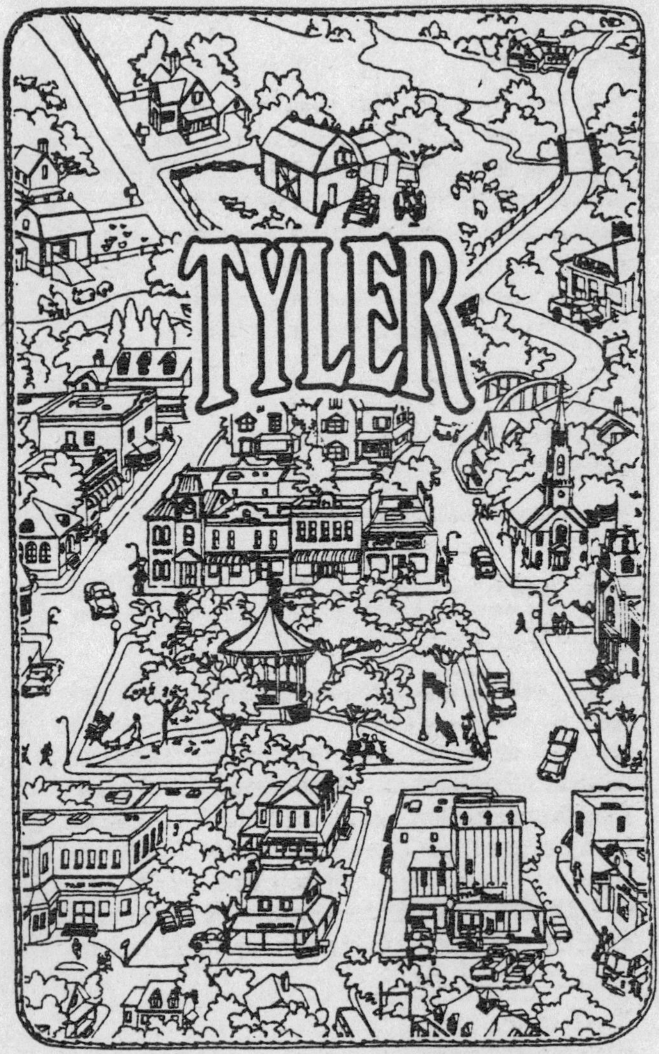
TYLER

CHAPTER ONE

"THAT'S A WRAP!" the director called. "Have a merry Christmas, everybody!"

Susannah Atkins blew a sigh of relief and stepped out of the spotlight that brilliantly illuminated the kitchen set of "Oh, Susannah!," the daytime household-hints program that was her claim to fame. Untying the strings of her apron, she draped it around the neck of her favorite cameraman, Rafael, and playfully tugged him close.

"Thanks for rescuing me when I missed my cue. And happy holidays, Rafe."

"Same to you, superstar."

Susannah laughed and gave the young man a kiss on his bearded cheek. Around them, the rest of the crew and production staff of "Oh, Susannah!" were calling cheery farewells and "see you next years" to each other. It was a pleasant sight. After six exciting years of working together, the team had become a close-knit family, not one of those squabbling gangs Susannah heard horror stories about when she visited other stations. Everyone connected with "Oh, Susannah!" was genuinely fond of the others, and Susannah felt a swell of pride at the thought. A relaxed and professional attitude of the star sometimes made all the difference.

The show's burly director, Pete Willard, made a detour around a camera to say goodbye to Susannah personally. "That was a good show, Suz," he said, pushing his glasses onto the top of his slightly balding head—a sure sign he was finished working for the day. He pinched the bridge of his nose to alleviate his chronic headache. "You headed someplace exciting for the holidays?" It was almost two weeks before Christmas. Somehow the taping schedule had worked out so that Susannah had nearly three full weeks of glorious free time before she had to be back at work.

Susannah grinned and began to rub the director's tense shoulders—the best way she knew to ease Pete's stress. "The Caribbean. I can hardly wait. We've got a condo right on the ocean."

The director groaned as she rubbed. "Sounds wonderful. I'd give my right arm to get out of Wisconsin this winter, but the kids...well, they think it's not Christmas without snow."

"I hear Santa visits beach houses, too."

"Yeah, well, tell that to my two-year-old! You don't know how lucky you are not having any kids, Susannah."

She kept her smile in place and released his neck. "I'll think of you on Christmas Eve when I'm dancing to steel drums—"

"And I'll be putting together that damned dollhouse I bought for my Jennifer. Ah, that feels great. You're the best masseuse I know, Susannah. Must be that Swedish ancestry of yours." Pete looked far from dismayed at the prospect of spending his holiday piecing together a toy for his child. He patted Susannah's arm and said, "Have a great time. Just don't get sunburned! We'll need that pretty face of yours back in front of the camera on January second!"

"I'll be here," Susannah called over her shoulder, half wishing she could be worrying about something other than her face this Christmas.

But she banished the thought quickly and waded into the studio audience—her faithful fans.

The audience always waited patiently for their favorite local star after the show taping. And Susannah had been careful from the beginning not to play the prima donna. Even in a city the size of Milwaukee, it never hurt to hang on to those small-town values that her public seemed to appreciate most. Susannah signed autographs and allowed her picture to be taken a dozen times.

"Miss? Susannah?" An elderly man tugged at her sleeve. "I really got a kick out of your pumpkin pie recipe. Who else but you would have thought of adding summer squash and pecans? You ought to write a book!"

"Oh, it's just an old family recipe of mine. I enjoyed the chance to share it."

"Would you mind signing my program?" he asked flirtatiously. "I want to prove to the guys at the bowling alley that I really talked to you."

"For a pumpkin pie lover, anything! How shall I write the inscription?"

"To Hank," coached the old man, leaning close. "What a hunk. With love, Susannah."

Susannah cheerfully obeyed. She liked the relaxed and genuine affection of her fans. It made up for a lot of things—things Susannah tried not to think about. After half an hour, she finally tore herself away and headed for her office, a small, unpretentious cubicle tucked at the end of a narrow corridor near the studio.

In the office, which was jammed with so many books and gadgets it looked like the lair of a mad wizard, stood Susannah's young secretary, Josie. Nearly six feet tall in her flat shoes and always dressed to the nines, glamorous Josie looked more like an up-and-coming television star than Susannah, who left her clothing choices to the studio wardrobe department and wore jeans in her off hours. Josie always looked elegant despite her youth. Susannah, on the other hand, looked elegant only when somebody else dressed her. Otherwise, she preferred to use her energy on more creative endeavors.

Despite their differences in personal style, Josie and Susannah were a perfect team. With a schedule as hectic as Susannah's was, she needed a good secretary more than she needed anything else. And Josie was worth her weight in gold. Her limitless energy had often saved Susannah when her own resources got low. With the telephone receiver pinned to her ear as Susannah pushed through the door, Josie was saying sweetly, "I'm sorry, sir, Miss Atkins is still taping a show in the studio. I can't interrupt."

Susannah mouthed, "Who is it?"

Josie shrugged elaborately and said into the phone, "I'm sorry, sir, but unless it's an emergency, I can't... yes, yes. All right, I'll double-check. I'll put you on hold for a minute, all right?"

Susannah was also thankful that Josie was unbelievably organized—a quality Susannah herself lacked almost entirely. And Josie took inordinate pride in her ability to fend off the hundreds of hopeful male viewers who called the station every week on the chance of getting in touch with "Oh, Susannah!" herself. The young black woman had turned the gentle letdown into an art form.

"Who is it this time?" Susannah asked, sliding into the comfortable swivel chair behind her antique desk. "Another senator who wants to meet me for lunch, like yesterday? Or someone trying to sell his mother's recipe for goulash?"

"Neither," Josie said, lighting a cigarette one-handed, obviously in no rush to get back to the caller waiting on the other end of the line. "He's a nobody. But he's got a voice that makes my blood tingle." She blew smoke and waggled her dark eyebrows lasciviously. "You know, the low and rumbly kind, a cross between Darth Vader and...oh, somebody sexy. Kevin Kline, maybe. Trouble is, the ones with great voices always turn out to be four feet tall with overbearing mothers."

"Josie!" Susannah laughed and kicked off her shoes. She put her stocking feet on the desk, noting lackadaisically that she had a run in her panty hose already, and leaned back in her chair to relax. "Do you mean to say you actually meet some of the men who call for me?"

Josie sniffed aloofly. "In the interest of science, that's all. Somebody ought to do a study on guys who call television stations. It might as well be me. One of the perks of my job is getting your castoffs. It's in my contract."

"Yeah, right. I think my contract says I *can't* date men who call here."

"You don't date anybody, honey," Josie remarked. "'Cept old Roger, and he hardly counts."

"What's wrong with Roger?"

Josie shrugged. "Too nice."

"Too *nice?*"

With a grin, Josie tapped cigarette ash into a seashell sitting on the desk. "You deserve more excitement. Want me to line up an appointment with this guy?" She wiggled the receiver. "Maybe his face matches his voice."

"I doubt it. Better get rid of him."

"Chicken. But you're the boss." Josie punched the hold button with one of her long, enameled fingernails. "Hello? Still there, sir? Good. Look, I'm sorry, but I can't seem to locate Miss Atkins at the moment. I could . . . yes, I can take your name."

Susannah closed her eyes and listened with only half an ear while Josie reached for a pad and pencil from her desk and began scribbling. "Will you spell that for me, please? S-A-N-T-O-R-I. Yes, I got it. Now, can I ask what this is in reference to, Mr. Santori? Who? From Tyler?"

Susannah sat up straight. "Tyler?"

Josie's gaze met Susannah's, communicating a new message altogether, and she said into the telephone, "Yes, I know Tyler is Miss Atkins's hometown. Who? Oh, you mean Miss Atkins's grandmother? Is something wrong?"

Susannah didn't waste another instant. She reached for the receiver and took it from Josie's hand. "Hello?" she said briskly as soon as she clamped it to her ear. "This is Susannah Atkins. Is my grandmother all right?"

A wonderfully melodic male voice said, "I thought you couldn't come to the phone."

"I'm here now. What's wrong?"

"Nothing's wrong," he said soothingly. "I'm butting in, that's all. I think you ought to come home for Christmas."

"Home? Why? Is my grandmother ill? Or—"

"Take it easy. She's not sick. At least, not yet."

"What's that supposed to mean?" Susannah found she could hardly breathe. Her grandmother was the most important person in her life, and the thought of Rose sick or in trouble was horrifying. Susannah's hand clutched the receiver with a clammy grip. "Please tell me what's wrong."

"Look, I don't want you to get all upset, Miss Atkins, okay? Your grandmother's not sick—at least she claims she isn't. But... well, in my opinion, she hasn't been up to snuff lately."

"Oh, dear heaven."

"It's not bad," the man assured her. "But she's disappointed that you're not coming home for the holidays, and I...well, I don't believe she's feeling as good as she pretends. I got to thinking—if it was me, I'd want somebody to call before I went away on a trip. And I'd want to check for myself. You're going to a beach, I hear."

Susannah frowned and tried to control her emotions. "My plane leaves tomorrow. I was going to see her when I got back, but—"

"Do you have time to drive out here this afternoon? You could take a look at her yourself before you go."

"Let me check my book."

"Your book?"

Most people did not understand Susannah's total reliance on the small, leather-bound datebook she kept within reach at every waking moment. With her many appointments and her busy work schedule, Susannah's life was very complicated. She had many obligations and responsibilities. What made things worse was her mental weakness concerning dates and times. Though talented in a hundred different ways, she absolutely could not keep her life on track without writing down every detail. Fortunately, Josie kept a duplicate book so that, between the two of them, Susannah ran on schedule.

But the man said peevishly, "You can't squeeze in a couple of hours for your own grandmother?"

"Of course I can," she retorted. But there were things to juggle, no doubt—like a public appearance at a department store that Susannah had promised to make that very afternoon. As she flipped open her datebook, her eye fell on the appointment at once.

Josie was checking her version of Susannah's schedule, too. In an undertone, she said, "I'll cancel the department store, if you want."

"They'll understand a family emergency."

"But listen," Josie said. "The store's on your way to Tyler. Why not drop in, make the appearance a short one and buy yourself that bathing suit you need for your trip?"

"I'm not sure," Susannah murmured uneasily.

"You could be in and out of the store in twenty minutes. I'll go along and make sure it goes smoothly."

"I really must get a bathing suit."

"May I suggest a bikini?" said the dry male voice in her ear. "In pink, maybe."

Susannah had forgotten that her voice was audible to her caller, but he probably hadn't heard Josie's side of the conversation. "Oh, sorry—"

"You look good in pink," he continued sarcastically. "A pink bikini sounds like the perfect choice. It'll make you forget all about your grandmother, I'm sure. Sorry to have bothered you, Miss—"

"Wait! That's not it at all. I'm just checking my schedule. Of course I'll come. I just have to make a quick stop along the way, that's all."

"For the bikini. All right, go ahead." Tartly, he added, "The right bathing suit might do you a world of good, in fact."

"I beg your pardon?"

"A lady as straitlaced as you seem on television—a lady who has to check her book before she goes home for a visit—well, that's a lady who needs loosening up, I'd say. Get a hot-pink bikini, Miss Atkins."

He was probably right, Susannah thought. Maybe her life *was* pretty strict, and she had allowed herself to forget the things that were truly important—like grandmothers and bathing suits. She found herself nodding in agreement.

Besides, it was hard not to be seduced by that marvelous voice. Glad he couldn't see her smile, Susannah said, "I'm hardly the bikini type."

"Who says so?"

"*I* say so."

"That's too bad." There was a slight pause, during which he must have decided he'd flown off the handle. His voice dropped another half octave and on that new note he said, "Maybe you ought to try something out of character for once."

"I like my character the way it is."

"An occasional change can be healthy. Buy a bikini and see what happens."

Susannah couldn't hold back her laugh. "Are you always so free with your advice?"

He laughed, too, and the tension eased. "When it's needed. And I think it's definitely needed in this case. I'll tell your grandmother that you're coming today, all right?"

"Fine." Susannah hesitated, then impulsively asked, "Who are you, anyway? A friend of my grandmother?"

"Yep," said the voice. "I'm Joe Santori."

"Well, I'm warning you, Joe Santori. My grandmother is going to be mad at you. She doesn't like people interfering."

"I can take it," he replied with a laugh.

He hung up without another word, leaving Susannah to stare, smiling, at the humming receiver. For a friend of her grandmother, he sounded very young indeed. Maybe he was one of those little old fellows who hung around Tyler's retirement home. She frowned again, trying to place his name. Was Joe Santori one of the old coots who played gin rummy every day at the hardware store? Or one of the gentlemen who sang in the church choir?

He didn't *sound* like an old man. Far from it. With that low, sexy voice, he could be—

"Well?" asked Josie, interrupting Susannah's runaway thoughts. "Who was he?"

"I haven't the faintest idea," Susannah replied, cradling the phone. "But I'm going to find out."

THE DEPARTMENT STORE was mobbed with Christmas shoppers, but Susannah and Josie managed to slip into the resort-wear section for a swimsuit before making Susannah's quick appearance in the kitchen appliances, where she had promised to demonstrate a new brand of food processor. She apologized to the store manager for cutting her stay short, but the woman was completely understanding.

"I look after my grandparents, too," she said sympathetically. "Sometimes I have to drop everything to take them to the doctor's office or to the grocery store. It's exasperating, but I wouldn't trade them for any promotion in the world."

"Thanks," Susannah said, relieved that she'd found a human being to deal with. "I'll make it up to you, I promise."

The manager smiled. "I'll hold you to that! Our customers love 'Oh, Susannah!'"

Josie took the manager aside to schedule another appearance, and Susannah began her presentation. It was fun and lighthearted, and she even managed to sell a few food processors to people who had gathered around the demonstration table to watch her chop, grind and puree.

Then Josie stepped in and broke up the event, making apologies on Susannah's behalf and hurrying her out of the store.

"You know how to get home to Tyler, right?" Josie asked, bundling her into her car in the parking lot. "You want me to follow you as far as the interstate?"

"I may be an organizational cripple," Susannah shot back cheerfully, "but I can find my way home."

"Okay. Then you'll come back early tomorrow, right? You need time to finish packing for your trip. I'll phone Roger to tell him what's happening."

"Thanks. What would I do without you, Josie?"

"You'd be a dismal failure, I'm sure," Josie said with a grin, kissing Susannah's cheek as they hugged. "Either that, or you'd be a network star making millions. Maybe I'm just holding you back."

"You're holding me together. Someday it will be your turn, you know."

"I can't wait. One more thing. You'll need this." Josie handed over the small suitcase she insisted Susannah always keep ready in her office, packed with a few essentials and a change of clothes. "Don't go off to Tyler unprepared."

"Oh, Josie, you're a lifesaver. And I appreciate it more than you can imagine. Give Marlon a smooch for me."

Marlon was Josie's temperamental cat. Josie laughed. They parted then, with Josie turning her car back to the city and Susannah heading west.

The drive to Tyler normally took more than an hour, but Susannah lost track of time and was surprised to find the sunlight slanting over the horizon when she finally pulled her station wagon into the town limits of Tyler, Wisconsin.

Tyler looked as pretty as a Christmas card, covered with snow that sparkled in the last flicker of afternoon light. Picturesque trails of smoke wisped from the chimneys of the neatly kept houses on Elm Street. The steeple of the Methodist Church pointed heavenward from a thatch of spruce trees, with snowflakes settling gently on the fluffy green branches.

Susannah's chest felt tight as she drew up to the curb in front of the tall Victorian house on the corner of Elm and Third streets. No matter how many years had passed since she'd left her hometown for college, she always got a pang of pleasure when she returned.

Pleasure mixed with regret. Susannah often thought of Tyler as the life she'd left behind. The lovely town was quiet, yet full of good people who lived rich, full lives. Tyler had a lot to offer. But, even though she visited occasionally, Susannah had turned her back on it somewhere along the line. She had never meant to abandon her roots so completely. Sometimes a hot career in the big city paled by comparison.

Her grandmother's house, with its gracefully curving front porch, its scalloped trim and its twin turrets, looked as welcoming as ever. Susannah knew every nook and cranny in the house, having lived with her grandmother after the deaths of her parents. Nothing had changed, as far as Susannah could see. It was comforting to know that life stayed the same in Tyler.

When she opened the car door, she could hear the soft croon of Bing Crosby singing Christmas carols from the loudspeakers in front of Gates Department Store, just a few blocks away. Across the street, Mr. Connelly was stringing colored lights in his shrubbery while his two small children watched, bundled in identical yellow snowsuits with pompoms on their hats. The children looked away from their father long enough to give Susannah happy waves of greeting.

"There's certainly a feeling of Christmas in the air," Susannah murmured, reaching into the back seat for her overnight case and a gaily wrapped jar of peach chutney she'd brought along to give to her grandmother. It was an old family custom to bring little gifts when visiting. Then she straightened and inhaled the fragrant scent of wood smoke that hung in the air. "That's the way life is in Tyler—it's always like Christmas. Oh, I almost wish I wasn't going to spend the holidays in the Caribbean!"

"Maybe you can get a refund," said the same wonderfully masculine voice Susannah had heard on the telephone.

She spun around, fully expecting to come face-to-face with one of her grandmother's friends—an old man with a cane, perhaps, or loose dentures. A lot of men came to visit Rose Atkins, because she was so lively for her age. Her vigor seemed contagious. But standing in front of Susannah on the snow-encrusted sidewalk was no withered senior citizen with a gleam in his eye. Far from it.

He was tall and lanky, with amazing shoulders, coal-black mischievous eyes full of improper suggestions, plus curly dark hair that tickled his ears and the back of his strong neck. His clothes were rough—a rumpled old parka over jeans, a faded flannel work shirt and heavy boots suitable for hiking the Klondike. The parka was unzipped, revealing a low-slung tool belt worn with the panache of a gunslinger.

"Let me guess," said Susannah when she could control her vocal cords. "Mr. Busybody Santori?"

His wide mouth quirked into a wry grin. He had a strong Italian face with prominent cheekbones, expressive brows and velvety black eyes that communicated volumes. "Am I going to get a lecture from you, too, Miss Atkins?"

"That would be cruel," Susannah shot back, smiling. "I bet my grandmother has chewed you up one side and down the other already."

"I'm still licking my wounds, in fact."

"She was angry at you for calling me?"

"Furious," Joe Santori pronounced. "She says I have spoiled your vacation by suggesting you come home, and I'll never be forgiven."

"It's not as bad as that," Susannah replied, hefting her suitcase out of the car and slamming the door with her other hand. "I'm sure I'll still be able to catch my plane. I'll bet she's mostly angry that you interfered. My grandmother prides herself on her independence."

"She has a right to be proud." Joe took her overnight case without asking and slung the strap effortlessly over one shoulder. "But we all need a little help now and then."

Looking up at him, Susannah doubted that Joe Santori believed his own words. He looked like a man who'd rather die than ask for help for himself. The arrogance that showed plainly in his face was tempered only by his lopsided grin. Obviously, he was perfectly at ease conducting the lives of people around him and felt justified telephoning a complete stranger to come home to check on a sick relative.

But there was something else in Joe Santori's expression, too—something Susannah felt she could trust. Along with his natural self-confidence, he seemed to radiate honesty. He had a few flecks of gray in his dark hair, and the laugh lines around his eyes also seemed to bespeak a certain amount of tragedy along with amusement. He had an interesting face. A trustworthy face.

"Tell me the truth," Susannah said, coming directly to the point and knowing she could rely on him. "Is my grandmother really sick?"

Joe shrugged and responded just as bluntly. "I can't tell. I've known her for a couple of years, but only as an acquaintance. I started doing some work on her house earlier this month, and Rose seemed pretty perky then. But now...well, I can't tell what's wrong, exactly. Maybe she's just feeling blue."

Susannah shook her head, concerned anew. "Not before Christmas. It's her favorite season. My Granny

Rose loves getting ready for parties and . . . well, everything."

"Don't jump to conclusions before you've seen her," Joe cautioned, his voice low and quieting. He put one hand on Susannah's shoulder to steady her and said with a grin, "Maybe you'll take one look at your grandmother and decide to belt me for dragging you to Tyler on a wild-goose chase."

Susannah appreciated his kindness. She didn't feel like belting him at all.

Joe looked down at Susannah Atkins and couldn't imagine her belting anyone. She was so small, for starters. On television, she looked average in size, but in person she was quite dainty. Her body was concealed by a flowing, camel-hair coat, belted casually around a slim waist and long enough to show slim ankles encased in trim black boots. But Joe was familiar enough with "Oh, Susannah!," the popular television show that came on after the noon news every day to know that Miss Susannah Atkins had a body worthy of great admiration.

And while she was pretty on the small screen, Joe hadn't been prepared for how exquisitely beautiful she was in real life. She had a delicate face with a sharp chin, pointed nose and thickly lashed blue eyes that were deep-set and luminous. Her shoulder-length blond hair was smooth and glossy, pulled back into a raspberry-colored beret that exactly matched the shade of her lipstick. With her quirky little mouth and those expressive blue eyes, she looked darling—just ready for someone to come along and muss her up a little.

With a lilting laugh, she said, "I don't believe in belting people, Mr. Santori. I leave that to my grandmother. Has she ever told you the story of when she chased off a burglar with a frying pan?"

She was charming, Joe decided. "There are burglars in Tyler?"

"No, it was just a teenage boy trying to sell encyclopedias, but Granny Rose didn't like the way he seemed to be casing the joint and she decided he was a burglar. Rather than call the police, she chased him for a block, waving a frying pan." Susannah turned and led the way up the sidewalk to her grandmother's house, saying, "As it turned out, he *was* a fraud. Granny Rose investigated the company he worked for and found it was a very shady outfit. Single-handed, she chased them out of the state."

Joe suspected Susannah was every bit as stubborn as her grandmother. He said, "Rose is independent, all right. I'm glad I don't have to tangle with her anymore. Maybe you can handle her."

"She doesn't need to be 'handled,' I'm sure," Susannah replied.

"Taken care of, then," Joe corrected.

"No," she said, mounting the porch steps. "Not that, either. The Atkins women don't abide people trying to control them. We like our freedom."

Joe stopped on the top step. "There's a difference between freedom and plain foolishness. Your grandmother needs supervision, Miss Atkins."

Susannah paused and turned to face him, lifting one narrow eyebrow as she studied Joe again. "Are you one of those macho fellows who wants to be in charge of everyone, Mr. Santori?"

"Hell, no, but—"

She smiled. "I bet you're the sole breadwinner in your family, and your word is law at home. Am I right?"

"Yes, but—"

"Then you're not used to women like my grandmother. She was the child of an immigrant farmer who built their house with his own two hands, and she worked hard all her life, Mr. Santori. Her husband died when she was still young, and she's outlasted her children, too, earning a meager livelihood but living a very full life. Don't think you can come in and start bossing her around now."

"Listen, Miss Atkins—"

"And you can't boss me around, either."

Joe's comeback was cut off by the sudden opening of the front door, and in another instant, they were joined on the porch by Rose Atkins herself, a feisty old woman in blue jeans and sneakers. She was just as diminutive as her granddaughter, and must have been every bit as beautiful in her day.

"What's going on out here?" Rose demanded, her blue eyes sparking. "Are you two talking about me?"

"Yes," Susannah replied at once, kissing her grandmother before saying smoothly, "Mr. Santori tells me you're furious with him, Granny Rose."

"I am," Rose snapped, glowering at Joe and folding her arms over her sweatshirt, which was imprinted with a *Far Side* cartoon concerning Holstein cows. "He's poking his nose in things he has no business poking into, and if he's ruined your vacation, Suzie, I'll never speak to him again."

"You have to speak to me," Joe replied calmly. "I'm not finished fixing up your back porch, and you can't stop yourself from checking up on me every five minutes."

"I want the job done right!"

"So you hired the best man to do it!"

"I hired you because you're the most entertaining carpenter I know, but I didn't plan on paying you money to butt into my personal affairs."

"I won't bill you for butting in."

Susannah began to laugh. "You two sound like a couple of toddlers who need naps. Granny Rose, I brought you some chutney I made in the fall. Invite Joe inside for a snack and we'll settle this once and for all."

Rose looked sulky. "He can come in, I suppose. But we're not going to talk about me."

"Well, it's a start."

Rose sent Susannah a glance that was suddenly glimmering with purpose. "Maybe we should talk about you."

"Me?"

"Joe, what do you think of a woman who is so busy being glamorous that she hasn't time to find a husband and start a family?"

"Granny Rose—!"

"It's a crying shame," Joe said, laughing.

"I have spent a lot of time trying to find the right man for my granddaughter, but she's very fussy, not to mention more disorganized than..." Rose snapped her fingers. "Good heavens! I don't know why it didn't occur to me before."

"What are you talking about, Granny Rose?"

"You and Joe, of course. Despite some rather obvious superficial differences, I suspect you'd make a perfect couple."

"A perfect—? *Granny Rose!*"

"Why, of course! Joe is so bossy and you're such a fool with keeping track of things that . . . why, you're ideal for each other!"

Joe began to laugh at Susannah's expression—a pink-cheeked, blue-eyed combination of mortification and profound fury. The glamorous television star in her stylish beret looked appalled at the thought of being half a couple with a blue-collar carpenter. She swung on Joe with fire in her eyes, as if blaming him for the sudden turn of events.

Joe was still laughing. "It looks like your grandmother's not the only one who resents interference, Miss Suzie."

"I never—I didn't—"

"Come inside, Joe," Rose commanded. "I want you to get to know my granddaughter."

It was a command Joe couldn't resist. He stepped inside the house on the heels of Susannah Atkins, the most beautiful little hothead he'd ever laid eyes on.

CHAPTER TWO

"I DID NOT COME to Tyler to meet men, Granny Rose." Susannah stepped inside the house and said vehemently, "I came to see you."

"Well, you've seen me, and I'm fine, so you might as well get to know Joe." Rose took Susannah's coat and hung it in the closet.

Susannah suppressed a smile and kept her patience. Rose Atkins had always been a stubborn lady, and old age hadn't changed that. "I know Joe as much as I care to know him—no insult intended, Mr. Santori—but I'm very concerned about you, Granny Rose."

Rose kicked off her sneakers, turned on the heel of her woolly white sock and padded back through the downstairs hallway, calling over her shoulder, "No need to be concerned. I'm in tip-top shape. Joe, you can take that bag upstairs—that should keep you out of trouble for a few minutes. The first bedroom on your right. Then meet us in the kitchen for cocoa. Consider it a peace offering. Come along, Suzie."

Amused and exasperated at the same time, Susannah looked at Joe, who was closing the front door. Tartly, she said to him, "This is starting to look very much like a wild-goose chase. My grandmother seems fine."

Joe grinned. "Ornery as ever, huh?"

"She's not ornery, she's . . ." Susannah stopped herself. "Come to think of it, Granny Rose *isn't* usually ornery."

Joe jerked his head to indicate the kitchen. "Go talk to her. I'll hang around upstairs and give you a few minutes together."

"Thanks," Susannah said, meaning it. "And, listen, about what my grandmother said—"

"About you and me?" With a laugh, Joe teased, "It's an intriguing idea, isn't it, Suzie?"

He had latched onto her nickname rather quickly, Susannah noted, feeling an absurd blush start. Hastily, she said, "Look, I'm not planning to get involved with anyone right now. I'm very busy, you see. I've got a lot of irons in the fire."

"And no time for love? That's a pretty sad commentary on your life, isn't it?"

Susannah opened her mouth to protest. Joe sent her another of his dazzling smiles and proceeded up the curved staircase with her suitcase in hand. Susannah swallowed an infuriated growl and stomped after her grandmother.

In the kitchen, Rose was already puttering at the stove with a carton of milk, a wooden spoon and a box of powdered cocoa. She hummed while she worked. "He's one of the most sought-after men in Tyler, you know."

Susannah threw her beret on the kitchen table. "Granny Rose, you're as maddening as ever!"

Laughing, Rose said, "Because I'm in the mood for cocoa? Or because I'd like to fix you up with Joe?"

"You're always trying to fix me up with somebody or other. Why him, of all people?"

"Why not him?" Rose cried. "Joe is available, good-looking and well respected, plus he's fun to be around. And he's a real man—not one of those overgrown boys you see in the city. What more could a woman ask for?"

"A little culture, maybe? I like men who *read* books, not just use them to fix a wobbly table now and then."

"Don't be such a snob."

"I'm not a snob," Susannah replied defensively. "I simply know my own taste, that's all. I like bright men with a certain amount of... of polish, I suppose."

"Joe has polish."

"I meant sophistication," Susannah shot back. "Not something you rub into fine furniture."

"*That* was the remark of a snob."

Susannah slid limply into one of the kitchen chairs. "You're right. I apologize." She rubbed her forehead. "You caught me off guard, that's all. This whole day has caught me off guard, as a matter of fact. I've been working very hard lately. I'm supposed to be going on my vacation tomorrow, but I'm more disorganized than ever. I guess I really do need some time off."

Rose turned and leaned against the stove to look at Susannah, as if ready for one of their patented heart-to-heart talks. For a moment, Susannah felt as if it were twenty years ago, and that she was still a teenager confiding in her grandmother in the privacy of their cozy kitchen. The room was filled with the fragrance of fresh baking, and rows of cookies filled sheets of waxed paper on the counter. The shelves were lined with jars of fruits and jellies that Rose had painstakingly preserved the previous summer. Sheaves of dried herbs and flowers hung from the beams overhead, reminding Susannah that everything she had become—

the cooking, decorating, entertaining expert of Milwaukee television—she owed to her grandmother, who long ago had taught Susannah gracious living and the value of hearth and home.

"It feels good to be home," Susannah said at last.

Rose relaxed and smiled. "It's good to see you home, dear."

She padded to Susannah and gave her granddaughter a warm hug and a kiss on the top of the head. "I wish you were home to stay, not running off to some hot beach tomorrow. I'm going to miss you this Christmas."

With a guilty pang, Susannah held her grandmother's hand a little longer. "I'll be back on Christmas Day, Granny Rose. I just won't be here for all the parties beforehand."

"Not even for your birthday?"

Susannah's birthday fell just a week before Christmas and had been the family excuse for a large pre-Christmas gathering ever since Susannah was born. The famous Atkins party was one of the social events of the season for the whole town of Tyler.

"I can't celebrate with you this year, I'm sorry." Hearing the wistful note in Rose's voice caused Susannah's heart to ache, but she said, "Roger bought the tickets, you see, without remembering my usual plans to be in Tyler for the week before Christmas. I hated to disappoint him, Granny Rose."

"Why? He disappoints you all the time." Rose released Susannah's hand and returned to the stove.

"He doesn't mean to disappoint me. He's just forgetful. He's a busy man."

"Too busy to be kind?" Rose sent her a short-tempered frown.

"I won't defend Roger today," Susannah said patiently, having endured Rose's low opinion of Roger Selby for a long time. "Roger and I understand each other, and that's what matters. Subject closed. I'd rather hear about you."

"I'm fine," Rose said at once, spooning cocoa into a saucepan full of milk.

"Joe says—"

"Oh, what does Joe know? I had a little episode, that's all."

"An episode?" Susannah echoed. "That sounds like a euphemism for something very bad."

"It wasn't." Rose shook a dash of cinnamon into the warming milk and reached for the bottle of vanilla from the open shelf over her head. "I just... I didn't feel well for a couple of hours. Maybe it was the flu."

"What happened, exactly?"

"I felt light-headed. Then, I... well, all right, I admit I blacked out."

"Good heavens! That's more than the flu!"

"Joe was here," Rose said hastily. "So I wasn't alone. It hasn't happened again. I'm fine now."

Her concern heightened, Susannah asked, "But what caused it? Have you been taking your blood-pressure medicine?"

Rose flipped her hand. "Off and on. When I need it."

"Granny Rose!" Truly angry, Susannah rapped the table with her knuckles. "You're supposed to take that medication regularly! It's not something you pop into your system now and then—"

"I've been feeling well without it."

"When was the last time you saw your doctor?"

"I have an appointment scheduled in January."

"That's not answering my question. When was the *last* time?"

Rose didn't respond, pretending to concentrate on the seemingly intricate task of stirring hot cocoa with the long-handled spoon. Frustrated, Susannah leaned forward on her elbows, trying to think of a way to force her grandmother to take care of herself. It seemed very odd, though, for Rose had been Susannah's parent for most of her life. To reverse roles and become her grandmother's caretaker felt . . . well, presumptuous. Until now, Rose had been perfectly capable of taking care of herself. What right did Susannah have to march in and take over?

"Look," Susannah said, endeavoring to keep her voice steady, "it's not my place to order you around. You're a grown woman with common sense, and you know you should take your medicine and see your doctor regularly. But for some reason you're not taking care of yourself, Granny Rose. That upsets me."

Impatiently, Rose said, "I promise to see Dr. Phelps after Christmas."

"Why not immediately? I'm sure he'd squeeze you into his schedule right this minute if—"

"I don't need to see him now."

"But if—"

"I'm fine, and that's final! Go on your vacation and have a wonderful time, Susannah. After Christmas, you can come see Dr. Phelps with me, if you're still upset. But I'm not going to budge until then, do you hear me? I'm fine!"

Susannah glared at her grandmother's turned back. "Granny Rose, are you afraid you'll spoil my silly vacation if you're sick?"

Rose was saved from answering that question. A thump sounded on the stairs, and a lofty baritone voice carried to the women in the kitchen, singing, "'Angels we have heard on high, sweetly singing o'er the plain....'"

Then Joe appeared, filling the kitchen doorway with his tall frame and broad shoulders. His gaze traveled swiftly to Susannah, and he lifted his brows as if to ask how everything was going. Susannah frowned and shook her head.

Rose turned from the stove. "You don't look much like an angel, Joe, but you can sing like one. Want a cookie?"

"As many as you can spare," he said cheerfully.

"Sit down, then. This cocoa is almost ready."

"Smells great."

Joe eased his body into the wooden chair opposite Susannah's, and he continued to watch her face while Rose's back was turned. "So," he said, "you two get everything worked out?"

"Yes," said Rose.

"No," said Susannah dourly.

"That's what I like to hear," Joe responded, reaching a long arm to snatch a cookie off the nearby countertop. "Détente, right?"

"The matter is closed," Rose said with authority. "Now we're free to talk about you two."

"There's nothing to talk about, Granny Rose." Susannah glowered at Joe, who grinned back at her before taking a sizable chomp out of his cookie. "Nothing whatever."

"There certainly is, dear. Given a chance, you and Joe might really hit it off."

To Joe, Susannah said, "She's just doing this so we'll leave her alone about her health. I don't know why she feels she needs to matchmake for me. I'm very busy in Milwaukee."

"Not the right kind of busy," Rose said. "Have you ever seen her show, Joe? It's really wonderful. Last week, Suzie showed how to make Christmas wreaths out of corn husks, how to roast a goose with sage leaves stuffed under the skin and how to make cranberry preserves in crystal glasses to give to your friends. Trouble is, Suzie's apartment has a front door hardly big enough to hang a wreath, she'd never roast a goose for herself alone, and I'll bet her friends in the city would rather eat caviar than cranberry preserves."

"There's no man in your life?" Joe asked bluntly, polishing off the first cookie and reaching for another.

"No. Yes." Exasperated, Susannah said, "I have a gentleman friend whom I see regularly."

"You 'see' him?" Joe inquired. "What does that mean exactly?"

"He's her boss," Rose supplied. "The station manager. It's not exactly a hot love affair."

"It's comfortable," Susannah retorted. "Roger and I don't have time to develop a serious relationship with anyone, so we...well, we're happy associating with each other. Dinner now and then—that sort of thing. Now could we please get back to the subject at hand—"

"They're going on vacation together," Rose added for Joe's benefit, disregarding Susannah's attempt to terminate the discussion. "But they're going to plan the next six months' worth of 'Oh, Susannah!' shows together. Can you imagine going to the beach to work?"

"No," Joe said promptly. "But then, I hate the beach. I'd much rather go hiking in the snow. What do you want to go to the beach for? You'll just get sunburned and sweaty."

"I like the ocean."

"It's too hot."

"It's beautiful!"

"It's boring."

"How could anyone be bored at the beach?" Susannah demanded. "It's so overwhelming and awe-inspiring—"

"I don't go on vacations to be overwhelmed."

"No," Susannah said, studying him cryptically. "I don't suppose a guy like you is ever overwhelmed."

From the stove, Rose interrupted. "I hope you like marshmallows, Joe. I don't trust a man who won't eat marshmallows."

"I love 'em," Keeping his lazy-eyed grin trained on Susannah, he said, "I have a terrible sweet tooth."

"But that's your only weakness, right?" Susannah asked softly. She felt uncomfortably warm under Joe's penetrating gaze.

He laughed. "How'd you guess?"

"Just a shot in the dark."

"You think I'm a legend in my own mind?"

"If the shoe fits..."

Joe leaned forward, bracing his elbows on the table and staring straight into Susannah's eyes. "And you," he said distinctly, "are so caught up in your big-city career that you wouldn't recognize a real man if you ran into one in a dark alley."

"I avoid dark alleys," she replied primly.

"Scared?"

"No, just smart."

"Sometimes even smart people have to take risks. Otherwise, life passes you by, Miss Suzie."

"Children, children," Rose cautioned, looking absurdly pleased as she carried two china cups of steaming cocoa to the table. Both cups were crowded with marshmallows. "You're making assumptions about each other before giving this whole thing a chance."

Susannah blinked in astonishment at her grandmother. "Five minutes ago you were threatening you'd never speak to this man again! Now you're practically angling for a marriage proposal! What's happened?"

Rose set the cups in front of her guests and said smugly, "I was blinded by a brilliant idea. I've never known two people who were more ideal for each other."

"Ideal?" Susannah objected, laughing. "You're always digging up men with whom I have nothing in common!"

"Hey!" Joe sat upright, feigning offense. "How bad do you think I am?"

"I don't think you're bad," Susannah said quickly, making an effort to be polite despite her frustration. "It's just that I'm perfectly happy the way I am, and I don't need a husband to make my life complete."

"Who said anything about becoming a husband?"

Susannah threw up her hands. "Oh, heavens, how did this conversation get started? Granny Rose, *you* never seemed to need a man in your life."

"The right one came along at the right time," Rose said peaceably, pouring herself a cup of cocoa from the saucepan and adding a generous pile of marshmallows on the top, "but he didn't last, that's all. When he passed away, I didn't feel the need to go looking all over again. I had my happiness. But you haven't had your chance yet, Suzie."

"I *am* happy!"

Rose sniffed. "Drink your cocoa."

"It's delicious cocoa," Joe said to Rose, cradling the cup in one rough hand and slurping marshmallows. "Unique, but classic."

"Thank you, Joe." Rose joined them at the table and sipped from her own cup approvingly. "I always add a dash of cinnamon and vanilla along with a pinch of sugar to sweeten the milk. I believe in going the extra step to make everything special...even with little things like cinnamon in cocoa. And I've taught Susannah to do the same. Why, you should taste her Christmas eggnog! It's—"

"You don't have to sell my wifely skills to Mr. Santori, Granny Rose," Susannah interrupted dryly. "I am not a prize heifer on the auction block."

"Don't be rude, dear, while Joe and I are having an innocent conversation."

"Must you be so obvious?"

"Obvious about what, dear?"

Susannah began to smile. It was impossible to stay angry with her grandmother, especially in such a ridiculous circumstance. In fact, it was almost a pleasure to be sitting comfortably around the old kitchen table, sharing a snack and laughing with old friends. And that was exactly how she felt about Joe Santori. For some reason, he fit right into the familiar scenery. He was relaxed and funny—surprisingly easy to be with. He bore Rose's needling in the spirit it was intended. His laughter rang off the ceiling beams and rattled the delicate china cups on their hooks over the sink. His grin was friendly...and ever so slightly wicked. Susannah couldn't help smiling back at him from across the table.

In a rough, manly kind of way, Joe Santori was very sexy. So sexy that Susannah found herself wondering if she hadn't missed something in life, after all.

To Rose, Joe said, "So you're not mad at me after all, Mrs. A.?"

"I'm annoyed, but not mad. I hired you to fix my back porch, not run my life."

"Well, the porch is almost done, but there are a few other things this house could stand to have fixed, you know."

"Like what?" Rose asked, drinking her cocoa.

"In layman's terms, this old place is falling apart."

Susannah said, "Surely you exaggerate."

"Not at all." Quite seriously, Joe addressed himself directly to Rose. "I took the liberty of looking around upstairs a little just now. I notice the roof leaks, for starters."

"Oh, it's nothing a few pots and pans can't take care of when it rains," Rose answered with a twinkle in her eye.

Susannah frowned. "I had no idea you were having problems with the house, Granny Rose. Why didn't you tell me?"

Rose shrugged. "Why should I spend my time worrying about an old pile of wood? It just has to last as long as I do. The only reason I had Joe work on the porch was that the posts were rotting."

Joe said, "You're going to live a good, long time, Mrs. A., so I think we should make sure your house doesn't fall down around your ears in the meantime."

"Oh, Joe, you're too busy to bother with an old woman like me."

Despite her objection, Rose looked suspiciously delighted to be the center of an attractive man's attention, Susannah noted. She said, "Maybe you ought to get some estimates from other carpenters, Granny Rose."

"Oh, I don't want anybody but Joe working on my house. If he's got the time, that is."

"I've got time," Joe said.

"Aren't you working on the old lodge for the Ingalls family?"

"It's coming along fine." Joe leaned comfortably back in his chair and reached for yet another cookie. "In fact, I think the Ingalls family is trying to decide if they're going to sell the old place or not. My crew is moving right along on the major renovations while they think about it. The improvements we've made should certainly help them get a better price."

Susannah's curiosity was piqued by that bit of Tyler gossip. "The old lodge is for sale? I thought it was condemned years ago."

"Not condemned, just closed up. It was in pretty bad shape," Joe said, "but Liza has been fixing it up again. Do you know Liza?"

"The youngest Baron girl? Yes, she was several years behind me in school—her brother, Jeff, was closer to my age—but I remember her. She was... well, a little wild, as I recall."

Joe grinned. "She hasn't changed. She's a pistol, but I like her. Liza's got a real artist's eye where old buildings are concerned."

"And," Rose added with a smile, "she got married recently. I think she's finally on the right track. Her grandfather is very proud of her."

The Ingallses were one of the town's most prominent families, and whatever they did was grist for the gossip mill in Tyler. Old Judson Ingalls had long been a community leader, and his daughter, Alyssa, was respected as one of Tyler's most gracious and generous ladies. Her good works were well known, and a great many people asked her advice on matters.

Alyssa's apparently fairy-tale marriage to Ronald Baron had come to a tragic end when her husband took his own life after a financial setback, but Alyssa and her three children seemed to have weathered the tragedy as well as could be hoped. Daughter Amanda was a successful lawyer, if Susannah remembered correctly, and Jeffrey had become a doctor. Only Liza, known for her wild ways, had failed so far to make her mark in the world in a big way. Susannah had always liked the feisty youngest child of Alyssa Baron, and she was glad to hear Liza was finally coming into her own.

She said, "Liza was always very talented."

"I hope she's also a good detective," Joe remarked.

"Why?"

Joe exchanged a glance with Rose. "Well, the Ingalls family has a mystery to solve."

"A mystery?" Susannah repeated.

Rose's expression brightened with excitement. "Yes, the whole town's been buzzing for months. Joe and his men found a dead body buried up at the lodge."

Susannah stared at Joe. "Whose body?"

He shrugged and appeared unaffected by the gruesome event. "Nobody knows. Whoever she was had been buried for a very long time—more than twenty years, I'm sure."

"She? How did she get there?"

"That's the mystery. We don't know anything, except that it was a woman—the police just figured that out, apparently—and she died under suspicious circumstances." Joe added, "In fact, I think she was probably murdered."

Rose set her cup down and said firmly, "I'll bet you a dozen doughnuts it's Margaret Ingalls."

"Judson's wife?" Susannah asked, astonished by Rose's revelation. "I thought she disappeared a long time ago. Her disappearance caused a big scandal years back, didn't it?"

Nodding, Rose said, "Everyone assumed Margaret left Judson and ran off with one of her boyfriends—she had a bunch of them. What a naughty flirt she was! I know where Liza got her spunk. Margaret ran away, but we never really learned what happened to her. The murder story makes sense, don't you think? Instead of abandoning her husband and never contacting her friends again, she was killed!"

Susannah couldn't help grinning as she noted Rose's fascination with the mystery. "That's what this town needs. A juicy murder mystery to help pass the cold winter nights."

"It's been the talk of the town," Joe agreed.

With even more fervor, Rose declared, "I always knew Margaret Ingalls would come to a bad end."

"Wasn't that wishful thinking, Granny Rose? You had a soft spot for Judson, if I remember correctly."

Rose blushed and got up suddenly from the table. "Oh, that was a long time ago. I never meant for Margaret to get hurt. Judson and I were friends, that's all, especially after my Henry died. That's the way things work in a small town. Everybody's known everybody else since the day they were born, and we look out for one another. Except Joe, of course. He's not from Tyler, are you, Joe?''

Susannah saw that Rose didn't want to talk about the details of her romantic past, and Joe must have seen the same thing. He played along, saying, ''Tyler is my home now, and my daughter likes it here.''

''Joe has a daughter,'' Rose said to Susannah, clearly relieved that the topic had been changed. ''She's a lovely girl. Perhaps you'll get to meet her.''

Amused, Joe heard the hopeful note in Rose's voice and knew exactly what the old girl was up to. Practically every woman in Tyler had tried to help Joe's love life along by introducing him to their daughters, their sisters, their maiden cousins from Chicago—any female who didn't have one foot in the grave.

And it wasn't just the women who tried to hook him up with marriageable ladies. A great many fathers, brothers, uncles and even a grandfather or two had made overtures on behalf of their female relatives. A widower like Joe was a prime target in a small town. In fact, Joe figured he'd met every eligible woman within a hundred miles of Tyler.

He liked meeting eligible women, of course. But Joe wasn't looking for one particular woman in his life. He was having enough trouble with his daughter. Another female around would surely spell disaster.

However, something about Susannah Atkins intrigued Joe, unlike all the other women he'd met since coming to Tyler nearly a decade earlier. He couldn't help noticing that Susannah Atkins was different.

As she sat at the cluttered kitchen table, her delicate hands cupping her hot cocoa, she looked beautiful, stylish and smart—not the kind of woman Joe was usually introduced to. But he liked the sound of Susannah's laughter, and he could hardly keep his eyes off her. His insides were churned up, too, with unmistakable physical attraction. And for some reason, he was fighting the urge to reach across the table and toy with her hand. She was that kind of lady.

He tried to figure out exactly why the bells and whistles were going off in his head. It wasn't just her beauty that drew his gaze, although her fine blond hair had started to come loose, and framed her face in silky, touchable wisps. Her features were more precise than the television camera portrayed. Her eyes were bluer.

But there was something more appealing than good looks about Miss Suzie Atkins. With a start, Joe realized he also liked the fact that she wasn't making bedroom eyes at him. In fact, she appeared to be downright determined not to start anything personal with him or anyone else.

Susannah was one woman who wasn't going to chase him, Joe decided.

She's a challenge, he said to himself.

For once, here was a woman who wasn't going to bake him cookies he didn't need or invite him to parties he didn't want to attend or fuss over him until he paid a compliment. She was cool and lovely and sophisticated, a woman who knew her own mind and could laugh when the moment warranted.

She laughed at Rose's suggestion of meeting Joe's daughter and shook her head. "I'm afraid I don't get along very well with children. Forgive me if I beg off, Mr. Santori."

"You don't have kids?"

She blinked, looking prettily surprised. "Me? Heavens, no. I never had the time."

"Not to mention a husband," Rose grumbled from the other side of the kitchen. "Don't you think it's a shame, Joe? A nice-looking girl like Susannah ought to have a big house with lots of children. A woman her age—"

Susannah pretended to be pained by her grandmother's not-so-subtle campaign. "Let's not discuss my age, Granny Rose, if you please. Mr. Santori doesn't need to learn all my secrets."

"Whatever your age," Joe heard himself saying, "it suits you very well."

Susannah laughed and Rose applauded. "Bravo!"

"Don't try turning my head with pretty talk," Susannah cautioned with a wag of her forefinger. "You're just trying to get me on your side, so you can spend the winter working on my grandmother's house."

"Can't blame a guy for trying." Joe grinned. Although he told himself he wasn't looking for any female companionship, he found himself saying, "How about if I take you on a guided tour of this house tomorrow, Miss Suzie? You can help your grandmother decide if any repairs should be made."

"I'm leaving for the Caribbean tomorrow."

"What time?"

"I'm not...I don't know." For the first time, her confidence appeared to waver. "I'll have to check with my secretary. I think the flight's in the afternoon."

"I'll come in the morning."

Rose said, "Come for breakfast. You two can have a nice chat together."

Susannah covered her face with one hand and groaned. "Granny Rose, must you be so obvious?"

"It's a date?" Joe asked with a grin.

"Yes, yes, all right. But please come early. I really do have a plane to catch."

"It's a deal." Joe slapped the table and stood. "Now I've got to get home before my daughter burns down the kitchen. She's just learning to cook."

Rose piped up, "Oh, Susannah could teach her everything about cooking—"

"Granny Rose!" Susannah warned. She stood also and moved to escort Joe to the front door. "You'd better get out of here before my grandmother calls the nearest minister and marries us."

"There are worse fates," Joe murmured under his breath, bending to give Rose a quick kiss on her cheek. She gave him a bright look and winked, which caused Joe to laugh before he followed Susannah from the room.

He found her waiting at the front door, with one hand resting on the handle. She wore a soft suede skirt that clung to her hips and flared with feminine grace around her legs. When she was sure Rose hadn't followed him, she said in a conspiratorial whisper, "Thank you very much, Mr. Santori."

Joe grabbed his parka from the small chair where he'd left it. "For what?"

"You know. Calling me about my grandmother. I appreciate your kindness."

"I hope it didn't screw up your day."

"On the contrary," she said, watching as Joe shrugged into his coat, "this trip has actually made my day."

Joe collected his tool belt. "You think she's going to be okay?"

"I'm not sure. But I'll spend this evening with her, and tomorrow morning, before I decide." Susannah met his gaze. "I must say, it's a comfort knowing that people like you are still here in Tyler, looking after one another."

He wrapped his tool belt around his hand, lingering. He wasn't quite ready to leave yet, and Susannah hadn't opened the door, either, he noted. He said, "I like your grandmother."

"And she likes you." With a hint of a blush starting, Susannah added, "I hope you don't think she's serious when she suggests...well, when she talks about you and me."

"I think she's dead serious."

"But... of course it's impossible—"

"She's determined," Joe said plainly, "to get you married and pregnant as soon as possible, Miss Suzie. And frankly, I agree with her theory."

Her eyes flashed. "I will put up with my grandmother's opinions, Mr. Santori, because I love her. But you—"

Joe chucked her playfully under the chin, unable to resist teasing her. "You ought to have a family and a home of your own, Miss Suzie, instead of spending your life showing everybody else how to do it."

"I'm perfectly content with my life the way it is," she said, turning cool. "I'm very busy."

"So you keep saying. Personally, I think a woman who's too busy to enjoy life is missing a hell of a lot."

He'd gone too far, Joe saw as soon as the words left his mouth. Susannah stared at him for a long, silent moment, then opened the front door. She didn't say goodbye. Joe considered apologizing, but decided the truth was the truth. He brushed past her, hunched up the collar of his parka and started down the steps.

But on the sidewalk, he paused and turned. Glancing back, he met her gaze and grinned. "See you in the morning, Miss Suzie."

CHAPTER THREE

SUSANNAH CLOSED the front door, then kicked it, fuming.

"Where does he get off telling me how to live my life? He's a *carpenter,* for crying out loud!"

What did a small-town, blue-collar, power-tool collector know about life in the fast lane? Susannah angrily glared out the beveled glass panes of the door and watched while Joe climbed into a battered pickup truck and drove away.

Hold on, her inner voice said. *You're being too touchy, my girl.*

Which was true. What was the sense in getting hot under the collar at the remarks of a man she'd never see again after tomorrow? Besides, in less than twenty-four hours, Susannah planned to be sitting on an airplane with Roger, heading for sun and sand and more than a week of relaxation. She closed her eyes and tried to visualize a wonderful vacation.

Too bad Roger doesn't look like Joe Santori, said that pesky inner voice again, breaking into her mental picture of softly waving palm trees. *I'll bet he's got a body built for a bathing suit.*

Susannah blushed at the thought and abruptly pulled herself together. She marched toward the kitchen, determined to have a shoot-out with her grandmother.

"Granny Rose, I can't believe you'd embarrass me in front of a perfect stranger," she lectured, once again entering the kitchen. "What in the world possessed you to think I'd have any interest whatsoever in a man like— Oh, God! Granny Rose!"

Susannah gasped and rushed to her grandmother, who was slumped over the sink, weakly grasping at the counter to stay on her feet. Just as Susannah reached her side, the elderly woman lost consciousness and slid limply into Susannah's arms. Lowering her grandmother to the floor, Susannah cried, "Oh, Granny Rose!"

She cradled Rose's head in her lap and fanned her grandmother's ashen face with a dish towel, her own heart thumping madly in her chest.

"Please, please, let her be all right," Susannah prayed. "Granny Rose? Can you hear me?"

A full minute passed—it felt like a week, at least—before Rose's eyes flickered. A hint of color began to bloom in her cheeks, and she opened her eyes. "Suzie?"

"Thank heavens!"

Gradually Rose's eyes focused, and she blinked. "What happened?"

"You fainted, I think. I was only gone for a minute or two, and when I came back, you—"

"I remember now. I blacked out. I was reaching for a casserole dish in that cupboard, and I—I—" Consternation filled Rose's expression, and she clutched weakly at Susannah's hand.

"Don't talk," Susannah commanded, holding tight. "Just rest quietly for a moment. Then I'll call the paramedics."

"Is Joe still here?"

"No, he just left. I'm here now."

Rose frowned weakly. "You should go on your trip, Suzie."

"Nonsense," Susannah said. "The Caribbean will always be there."

"But Roger—"

"Roger won't mind. He knows how important you are to me, Granny Rose. He'll want me to stay here as long as I'm needed. I want to be sure you're going to be okay."

"But you're too busy—"

"Hush." Susannah hugged her grandmother. "I'm never too busy to take care of you, Granny Rose."

JOE POINTED his rattletrap truck down the street and headed for his own home, just a couple of blocks away. Snow swirled across his windshield, but he knew his way around Tyler as well as a native, so the trip wasn't treacherous.

Joe Santori liked Tyler, Wisconsin. After growing up in Chicago and attending trade school and, later, engineering courses there, he'd been lured from the city by a job offer from the Ingalls Farm and Machinery Company at a time when he'd needed a change.

He'd never thought of himself as a small-town kind of guy. Despite years of hounding by his wife, Marie, who had wanted to raise their family somewhere other than the streets of a big city, Joe had resisted leaving the Windy City. But when Marie died of ovarian cancer, Joe decided to make the change she had always wanted.

He'd applied for the position with Ingalls Farm and Machinery before he was even sure he wanted to leave Chicago behind. But things had worked out well indeed, and Joe was glad he'd brought Gina to the rolling hills of Wisconsin.

For Joe, the culture shock had been tremendous at first. Wisconsin people didn't lock their back doors, and they sometimes left their cars running while they dashed into the pharmacy to get a prescription filled. It had taken him a while to relax and get over his big-city paranoia.

But his daughter blended into the small-town milieu very easily. Perhaps because she was a motherless child, Gina had been an instant hit in the neighborhood, a darling of families up and down the street. At the age of six, she had learned to run out to the sidewalk after breakfast to find playmates to ride tricycles with until noon. Now nearly fifteen, Gina led the busy life of a teenager, complete with track-team practice, Ski Club, pickup games of street hockey and baseball—and her dreaded piano lessons, the only concession to femininity Gina would allow.

Joe's only regret had to do with his wife, Marie. She would have loved the town, and he often wished he'd brought her to Tyler before her illness. He took consolation in the idea that she was watching from above and approved his choice of towns in which to raise Gina.

Joe pulled his truck into the driveway alongside the tall Victorian house on Church Street, just four blocks from the town square. He noticed the kitchen light was on, so he walked across the snow-dusted driveway and let himself in the back door, stomping slush from his boots and shaking the snow from his parka.

"No way, Gramps," Gina was saying into the telephone. "You couldn't *pay* me to be a cheerleader! It's so stupid cheering for a bunch of stupid boys when I could be playing ball myself. Besides, I hate to wear skirts."

Fourteen-year-old Gina lay flat on her back on the kitchen linoleum, her sneakered feet propped on the counter above, looking just as tomboyish as ever in her torn jeans and rumpled baseball shirt. She'd pinned the phone to her ear with her shoulder, leaving both hands free to braid her ponytail into a tight plait while she talked. When Gina spotted her father entering the house, she waggled her foot at him without breaking off her phone conversation.

"Forget it, Gramps," she said into the receiver. "You can't convince me it would be fun. I don't care if Mom was the captain of the squad in her school. It's demeaning to women. My piano teacher said so."

Joe opened the refrigerator and took out a quart of chocolate milk. For some reason, he wanted to enjoy the taste of Rose Atkins's hot cocoa all over again—and cold chocolate milk would have to do. He poured the last three inches into a jelly glass decorated with cartoon characters and listened to Gina's conversation with her grandfather in Brooklyn.

He was glad Marie's parents kept in touch with their granddaughter, despite the miles that separated them. Every summer, Gina traveled east to be with her grandparents, and Joe tried to invite Marie's family as well as his own mother to visit as often as possible. Gina needed an extended family to keep her grounded, he felt.

Gina sighed dramatically. "Yeah, okay, Gramps. I love you, too. I gotta go, all right? Give my love to Nana. Bye."

Without moving from the floor, she tossed the receiver to Joe, who hung it up. "Holy smoke," she groaned, covering her face with her hands as if holding back tremendous suffering. "When are they going to realize I'm not going to be just like Mom was? Now it's cheerleading!"

Joe grinned, leaning against the counter to drink his milk. "Your mom looked good in that short skirt. It didn't demean her as far as I could see."

"What do you know?" Gina asked witheringly. "You're a guy. A little old, maybe, but still a guy."

"Thanks, I think."

"Oh, Dad, you know what I mean."

"Sure. What's for dinner?"

Gina blinked up at him from the floor. Sometimes she showed signs of her mother's innate ability to play dumb when the situation warranted. She said, "I thought it was your night to cook. Weren't you going to bring home a pizza?"

Joe blanched. "I hate pizza."

"I never knew an Italian guy who hated normal Italian food the way you do," she groused. "Can't you like anything that's *easy* to make?"

"You were going to fix omelets tonight," Joe shot back. "Those are easy."

"We're out of eggs."

"Open a can of soup, then."

Gina sat up, objecting. "Dad, I need a high-carbohydrate meal tonight! We're playing a big scrimmage game tomorrow against Bonneville!"

The basketball team, Joe remembered. He had trouble keeping up with Gina's athletic endeavors sometimes. "Okay, okay, I'll make the ultimate sacrifice tonight. How about macaroni and cheese?"

"Great," she said with satisfaction, climbing to her feet and clearly believing she had manipulated her father into preparing their dinner. Joe knew his daughter hated cooking, but he was determined to see that she was competent in the kitchen at the very least. She said, "I'll keep you company while you make it. Where have you been, anyway? I expected you home half an hour ago."

Joe thought of Susannah Atkins at once. He turned around and put his empty glass in the sink, trying to keep his expression hidden from Gina in case it revealed his thoughts.

Keeping a casual tone, he said, "I met a celebrity today."

"Oh, yeah? Who?"

"Susannah Atkins. Of 'Oh, Susannah!'"

Joe felt Gina glance at him. She said, "Is she pretty?"

"Very pretty."

"Prettier than Mom was?"

"Different pretty," Joe admitted, walking a fine line, he knew. "She's very nice."

"How nice?"

"Just nice. You'd like her, I think."

"I doubt it," Gina said bluntly, hitching her behind onto one of the stools at the counter and dismissing the subject of Susannah Atkins. "But I like old Mrs. Atkins just fine." She splayed her elbows on a place mat and watched Joe wash his hands and dry them on the nearest towel.

"Me, too. I'm going to fix up her house a little."

"Why? So you can be close to the television lady?"

"No," Joe said shortly, "because her house needs fixing, that's all. The television lady is leaving Tyler tomorrow." Joe took a box of pasta from the pantry shelf and dug a block of cheddar cheese from the refrigerator. He said, "Maybe you'd come along and visit with Mrs. Atkins while I'm working there. She'd enjoy the company."

Gina shrugged. "Sure."

"Maybe," Joe ventured cautiously, "she could help you pick out a dress for the Christmas dance. Unless you already have a dress, that is."

Gina's dark brown eyes flew open in surprise, and the teenager sat up as if she'd been jabbed with a hot poker. For an instant, she could not find her voice, then she blurted out, "How do you know about the dance?"

"How could I *not* know about it? Every ninth grader in town is talking about the big Tinsel Ball. Your friend Marcy cornered me in the drugstore to ask what color your dress was."

"That nosy fink!"

"What color is it?"

"What?" Gina pretended complete bafflement.

"Your dress for the Tinsel Ball," Joe said patiently. "Marcy said you told her it was the . . . let's see, what word did she use, exactly? Slinky, that's it. The slinkiest dress in Madison. I didn't know you'd gone to Madison to buy a dress."

Hastily, Gina said, "You must have misunderstood, Dad. You know how fast Marcy talks. She must have said *her* dress was slinky—"

Joe set his ingredients on the counter and glowered at his daughter, ready to confront her with the truth. "Don't try to snow me, Gina. I know what Marcy said. Have you been lying again?"

Gina thrust out her lower lip and looked sulky, her automatic reaction to any accusation. She refused to meet her father's gaze, but said bravely, "I don't know what you're talking about."

Joe considered his options. There was no denying that Gina's biggest problem was stretching the truth. She could tell a whopper without blinking an eye and had been caught so often that Joe sometimes wondered how many times she'd actually gotten away with lying. The possibilities boggled his mind sometimes. Her teachers complained every year, but the problem had finally become such a daily event that lately they'd started pushing Joe to seek help from professionals.

The school psychologist had suggested that Gina was lying because she missed her mother. Joe had a hard time making the connection, because Marie had never told a fib in her life, but Gina seemed to do it just because it was more fun than telling the truth. If her lying was a bid to get more attention, it seemed to him that there were easier ways of doing that. He felt unable to understand or stop the situation. The psychologist hadn't been a hell of a lot of help and had encouraged Joe to find a therapist for family counseling.

Family counseling sounded like a lot of hogwash to him. He could handle the problem himself.

But he hated confrontations with his daughter and was experimenting with ways of handling the various troubles of adolescence without resorting to yelling at Gina. She only yelled back, and she was a heck of a lot louder than he was!

So he set about calmly cooking the macaroni and said, "Let's start this conversation all over again, shall we? Your friend Marcy thinks you're going to the Christmas dance next week and that you'll be wearing a great dress. The way I look at it, you need to get a dress so she won't think you're—"

"Yeah, okay," said Gina, jumping at the chance to get out of trouble. "I was going to ask you for some money, Dad, but you've been so busy lately—"

"I'm never too busy to help you buy some clothes, Gina. Trouble is," Joe said wryly, "I'm not going to be much help picking out a party dress. That's when I thought of Mrs. Atkins. I bet she'd love the chance to help you find something nice."

"Well..."

Joe heard a new note in Gina's voice and looked at her sharply. "You *are* going to the dance, aren't you?"

"Oh, sure," Gina said quickly. "Of course. I wouldn't miss it."

Joe suspected she wasn't quite telling the truth again, so he shot a suspicious look at his daughter. Why in the world did she act this way? Wasn't he giving her enough attention? Or maybe it was just the wrong kind of attention? Perhaps it was a case, as the school expert suggested, of Gina worrying that she was going to lose *both* parents. Not through death, necessarily; she might also fear losing him to another woman, to his work, to any number of possibilities. So she lied just to keep him hopping. And maybe she was lying again.

Gina wiped the guilty expression from her face at once. "Naturally, I'm going to the Tinsel Ball. I just... I haven't had the time—"

"What's the problem?"

"It's not a problem," she said immediately. "Not exactly. I just haven't found a date yet."

"You haven't—? How can you go to the dance if a boy hasn't asked you yet?"

Gina looked scornful. "Oh, Dad! This isn't the Dark Ages anymore! I'm going to ask a boy myself. I'm not going to wait around for some nerd to ask me when I could ask whoever I want in the first place. My piano teacher says it's demeaning to women to—"

"Yeah, I heard that line before." Joe growled, "Pretty soon Nora is going to start charging me for more than piano lessons. So if you're going to ask somebody, why haven't you done it yet?"

"I haven't gotten around to it, that's all!" Gina's voice rose petulantly. "You're not the only one who's busy around here, y'know!"

"Okay, okay," said Joe, placating his hot-tempered child before she really blew up. "I'll leave that part up to you. But if you need money for a dress or anything else in that department, I'll be happy to give you whatever you need—within reason."

"What's within reason?"

Joe hadn't the faintest idea how much a dress was going to cost—fifty dollars, maybe? But somehow he knew it would be a tactical error to admit such a failing. He said, "I'll think about it and get back to you. In the meantime, you can concentrate on finding a date."

"I can manage that, I think."

"Can you manage to fix us a salad, too?"

"Okay," said Gina, hopping off her stool to help. She hugged Joe from behind first and said, "I love you, Daddy. You're so understanding. You're the best father in the whole world!"

Joe grinned. He was wrapped around his daughter's little finger, and he knew it. He'd give Gina a hundred dollars for a dress. She deserved the best, after all.

She loosened her hug and said softly, "You know, if you wanted to see the television lady again, I guess I wouldn't blame you."

Joe laughed and turned around, cradling Gina in his arms. "What brought that on?"

She didn't meet his gaze. "I dunno. You're not a monk, I guess."

"A monk? Who have you been talking to?" Joe demanded, amused. "Your piano teacher again?"

Gina shrugged. "Maybe. She says you're an attractive man. She did, honest," Gina repeated when Joe laughed in disbelief. "She says I can't keep you all to myself much longer."

"Gina..." Joe began, massaging her arms and wondering what in the hell he was supposed to say.

But Gina stepped away from him, shaking her head rapidly. "I know it's true. You hate me sometimes—when I lie—and you want to have somebody nice around...."

"I never hate you, Gina."

"But..." Gina stopped, her voice suddenly clogged with tears. "You need a woman around."

Joe's heart melted. But he couldn't find the right words to ease his daughter's pain. Clearly, she was threatened by the idea of another woman entering his life, but he couldn't figure out how to explain that his feelings for Gina would never change. She was his *daughter,* for crying out loud! Nobody could ever change that bond.

"Listen," he said, attempting to josh her out of her mood, "let me decide what I need around here, okay? Nobody knows better than I do, got that?"

She tried to smile. "Okay."

"And the first thing I need is food," Joe declared. "I'm starving. Let's get dinner on the table, partner. Then we'll talk more about this dress business, okay?"

Gina's smile flickered at last. "Okay, Dad."

He released her and went back to fixing dinner. He'd find a way to get Susannah Atkins out of his mind eventually. The last thing he wanted was to alienate Gina. If giving up women for the rest of his life was required, then so be it.

But, damn, Miss Suzie was going to be hard to forget.

CHAPTER FOUR

THE PARAMEDICS GAVE Rose a thorough examination. "We could take you to the emergency room, Mrs. Atkins, but I'm not picking up anything really terrible," said the young woman with the stethoscope. "Your blood pressure's a little high."

"I don't need to go to the hospital," Rose insisted. "I was just a little dizzy. I feel fine now."

"Well, you should see your doctor tomorrow," the paramedic counseled. "Perhaps your granddaughter will take you."

"Oh, no. Susannah's going on vacation. I'll ask a friend to go with me."

"We'll see," Susannah said, then showed the kind paramedics to the door. When she returned to the parlor where Rose was reclining on the sofa, she said, "I think I'll call your doctor immediately, Granny Rose. Are you still seeing Dr. Phelps?"

"Heavens, don't bother him tonight." Rose sat up briskly. "He'll just tell me to come in in the morning."

"All right, I'll take you to see him first thing."

"I won't hear of you changing your plans for me, Suzie. I'm not feeble, you know!"

"But—"

"I don't need a nursemaid. You should take your vacation. You need it."

The argument went on for several minutes, and Susannah had never felt more helpless. How could she force a perfectly sane adult woman to see a doctor when she didn't want to? Her attentions only upset Rose.

"Granny Rose, I wish you'd be sensible."

"I'm perfectly sensible," Rose snapped, putting an end to the discussion by getting up and preparing a delicious supper of homemade soup and whole wheat rolls that she popped out of the freezer and into her warming oven. The rolls were perfect with Susannah's peach chutney, and Rose chattered at length about the soup recipe, one she felt Susannah could use in her TV program. Susannah was aware that her grandmother was trying to divert their attention from the problem at hand, but she allowed Rose to talk aimlessly about unimportant matters during the meal. Afterward, in the parlor, they enjoyed tea laced with brandy in front of a roaring fire. Talking local gossip, Susannah watched her grandmother's every move and syllable for signs of illness, but Rose seemed healthy and happy.

Rose always went to bed before ten o'clock. Since Susannah could hear her grandmother cheerily humming Christmas carols in her room, she tiptoed downstairs to telephone Roger.

She got through to his answering machine.

"Roger," she said to the recording, "I've run into a problem with my grandmother. I may have to postpone my flight. I'll call you in the morning when I know what's going on. I—I'm sorry about this." She wished she could say more, but it was difficult speaking to a machine. She ended by saying softly, "I'll be in touch. Good night."

She hung up, wishing she could have talked with Roger personally. Although he wasn't much of a listener where personal problems were concerned, he was a logical, unemotional thinker, which might be helpful. He could at least act as a sounding board for Susannah's worries about Rose. She needed someone to share her feelings—someone who could help her decide how to help her grandmother without compromising Rose's self-esteem and independence.

"How do I help Granny Rose without making her feel like she's incapable of taking care of herself?"

A good answer didn't occur to Susannah, so she went upstairs quietly and changed into her flannel nightgown. She left her bedroom door ajar in case her grandmother should cry out in the middle of the night, and climbed into bed. It was the same canopied princess bed where she'd slept during her childhood. The same gauzy white curtains festooned the frilly white bed that resembled—in Susannah's mind—the grand sleigh of a beautiful ice princess who drove a pair of milk-white ponies over the snowy land she lived in.

But the pleasant memories evoked by her bed didn't make Susannah feel any better. She lay awake for a long time, wondering what she could do. So many of her friends had taken care of elderly parents, but Susannah had never imagined the day when Rose might be incapacitated in any way. Such a vital, fun-loving woman as Granny Rose didn't deserve a slow, undignified slide into dependency.

Yet there was no stopping old age, Susannah knew. Eventually, Rose would need a great deal of care and the responsibility would be Susannah's alone. Somehow, she had to find a way to help Rose without hurting her pride.

In a few hours, Susannah knew, she could be winging her way to a beautiful beach bathed by sea breezes. But only a completely selfish woman would abandon Rose when she was most in need. Susannah intended to telephone Roger in the morning to cancel their plans. She hoped he'd understand.

Perhaps she'd invite him to spend Christmas in Tyler. She had often contemplated a more serious relationship with her boss. Perhaps now was the time. Roger might enjoy the endless entertaining, the hours of puttering in the kitchen while neighbors popped in and out to sample Christmas cookies and lend a hand. Roger might actually have fun decorating the tree with the hundreds of antique ornaments Rose and Susannah had collected over the years. Gilded fruit, yards of shining ribbon, garlands of pine—Susannah loved draping the house in finery.

Perhaps Roger would, too.

But lying in bed, Susannah knew that Roger wouldn't care for a Tyler Christmas in the least. He'd hate the pointless chatter, the foolishness of decorations that would have to be stripped down in January. He'd have a terrible time making small talk with the old ladies who'd come for eggnog. He'd find the church service boring and the family traditions charming but foolish.

Not that Roger didn't have other good qualities, Susannah told herself hastily. He was a nice man, of course. He had a wonderful head for business and knew broadcasting inside out. He had been a big part of the team that made "Oh, Susannah!" a success.

But he couldn't sit in a kitchen drinking cocoa and gossiping about the Ingalls family the way Joe Santori had—not without yawning, checking his watch and dashing off to make important phone calls every half hour or so. Roger was very single-minded. His work was his life.

Susannah felt the same way. Her work was important—the reason she got up every day. She loved the pace and the stimulation. Although trips to Tyler were relaxing and precious to her, Susannah thrived on her career.

But oddly enough, she found herself dreaming about Joe Santori when she woke the next morning. She sat up abruptly and threw off the quilt, which had suddenly turned very hot. Just conjuring up Joe's face caused a warm sensation to curl through Susannah's body.

"Why in the world is *he* floating around in my head?" she groused, reaching for the bedside clock to check the time. "Heavens, it's after eight! I wonder how soon he'll get here?"

Susannah's question was answered not by a voice, but by a tremendous *thunk* that sounded from the porch below.

"What in the world?"

She climbed out of bed and grabbed the white satin robe she had left draped over the rocking chair by the door. Pushing her rumpled hair away from her face, she went out into the hallway in her nightie.

"Granny Rose? Did you hear that noise?"

Rose had just emerged from her own bedroom, already dressed for action in a pair of baggy trousers and a sky-blue sweater embroidered with snowflakes. She was pulling a knitted cap down over her hair and looked ready to go out of the house. She also looked cheery and pink-cheeked—the picture of health. "Oh, that was probably the paperboy, Lars Travis. Sometimes he throws the paper from the street to build up his arm. Good morning, dear. Lars wants to be a football player, you see."

"Surely he'd get better practice on the football field." Susannah sleepily put her arms through the sleeves of her lace-trimmed robe as she followed her grandmother down the hallway.

Rose charged along the carpet as though powered by a full-throttle steam engine. "Oh, Lars practices whenever he gets the chance!" She laughed. "Good thing, too. He's just terrible, you see. But he's very charming. He's the town gossip, to tell the truth. Almost as good as Tisha Olsen at the Hair Affair."

Susannah grinned. "He sounds like someone worth knowing. Granny Rose, where are you going, may I ask?"

"Oh, I have a date at Marge's Diner. I promised a friend I'd lend her my coffeepot."

"Hold it!" Susannah cried. "What about going to see Dr. Phelps?"

Rose waved her hand breezily. "The office won't open until nine, I'm sure. I have plenty of time to get down to Marge's and back."

"See here, Granny Rose! Give me a minute to dress and I'll drive you down. After last night, you shouldn't be wandering around the streets of Tyler—"

"Why not?" Rose demanded, spinning on Susannah and startling the younger woman with the fire in her gaze. "I've lived here all my life, and I've never once so much as tripped over a crack in the sidewalk between here and the diner! I can hotfoot my way down there and back in fifteen minutes."

"But—"

"You're not my baby-sitter, you know!"

"If you'd just slow down a little—"

"The day I slow down is the day I die!"

Susannah held her tongue, ashamed that she'd upset her grandmother. She felt her face grow hot.

Clearly chagrined, Rose leaned forward and gave Susannah a kiss on her cheek. Then she turned and led the way down the stairs, saying over her shoulder, "Help yourself to tea or coffee. I just put some muffins in the oven—banana and pecan, a new recipe. We'll try them when I get back from the diner. Listen for the timer, please?"

"Of course." Susannah followed, not bothering to tie the sash on her robe but tiptoeing barefoot down the stairs.

"After breakfast, I'll help you pack for your trip. You *are* leaving today, aren't you?"

"Not until I've heard what your doctor has to say."

"Oh, I'm fine this morning." As if sensing Susannah's disapproval, Rose added hastily, "But if it will make you happy, I'll call for an appointment as soon as I get back. He keeps Saturday hours and will fit me in, I'm sure. Then you can go off and have a wonderful vacation!"

Susannah didn't argue further. She said, "I wish you'd let me go along to the diner."

"That's silly. I'll be back in two shakes. Why don't you read the paper while I'm gone? It's on the porch, I'm sure." From the enormous walnut armoire in the hallway, Rose removed an ancient duffel coat and pulled it on. "Just save me the front page and the obituaries—the important stuff. I'll go out the back door."

"Surely you won't ride your bike!"

Rose Atkins had long ago forsaken the automobile as her primary mode of transportation. Instead, she pedaled a three-wheeled, adult-size tricycle all over town—to the grocery, the local diner and her various meetings with friends and clubs. Although Rose claimed she used the bike for ecological concerns, Susannah suspected her failing eyesight was the primary reason she'd decided not to drive her car anymore.

Rose buttoned her coat and trundled down the hall toward the kitchen. "I ride my bike when the roads are clear, but this morning there's a little too much wet snow. I'll walk through Donohoe's backyard instead—that should make you happy. It's only two blocks to Marge's from there."

"Granny Rose..."

"Don't fuss, dear. I'll be back in no time."

What's the sense of arguing? Susannah asked herself bitterly when Rose grabbed her large coffeepot box, called goodbye and slammed out the back door. No matter what she said to her grandmother, she was going to anger Rose and perhaps make her even sicker than she was.

Fuming, Susannah hurried for the stairs, hoping she could jump into her clothes and catch Rose before she got too far from home. But in passing the front door, she heard another noise outside and wondered if the paperboy was having some kind of trouble. It would only take thirty seconds to grab the paper and be on her way.

As she unlocked the front door, Susannah wondered if the *Tyler Citizen* was still the same small-town paper she remembered—short on world news but long on the important events of the town, like hospital admissions, birthdays, obituaries and who was selling beagle puppies or used washing machines.

Just as she unfastened the latch, another noisy bang sounded on the porch. She opened the door, but didn't find a teenage paperboy standing on the porch in front of her.

Instead, she found herself face-to-face with a very amused Joe Santori.

"Well, well, Miss Suzie," he said, sending a smiling glance down her satin-and-lace robe with the flowing fabric of her white flannel nightgown showing beneath. His voice was smooth and bone-tinglingly low. "Did I get you out of bed?"

Susannah snatched her robe closed, appalled to be caught in her nightie by anyone, let alone Joe Santori! Did a man have a right to look so handsome in a plaid shirt and jeans? Did his smile have to be so bold and knowing, his air so rakish?

Suddenly Susannah knew exactly why Rose had been in such a hurry to leave the house. "Damn her eyes, she's making sure I fall over you every time I turn around, isn't she?"

Joe blinked politely. "Beg your pardon?"

Susannah shook herself, mustered some composure and said, "Nothing. I'm just going to murder someone when she gets back. What's all the noise about?"

"I dropped my toolbox here and went back for some other junk I'll be needing." Joe indicated the carved wooden toolbox sitting at his feet on the porch, but his gaze remained on Susannah, absorbing all the emotion she tried too late to conceal. He said, "I woke you, didn't I?"

"Of course not." She edged behind the door as best she could without feeling like a fool. Seeing Joe's expression, she felt more exposed in her nightgown and robe than if she'd answered the door dressed in plastic wrap. "I just... I haven't had time to dress yet, that's all."

Joe tilted his head so he wouldn't lose sight of her as she tried to hide behind the door. "That costume looks like cotton candy. And you look delicious."

"It's not a costume, and I'm not... I'm—" Susannah found herself so tongue-tied that she started to blush like a lovestruck teenager. "Oh, blast!"

His smile widened. He had the face of a lady-killer, she decided in that moment—not handsome, but very charming, with a dark glimmer at the back of his eyes.

In a languid drawl, he said, "Do I fluster you, Miss Suzie?"

"Yes, but I haven't the faintest idea why!"

"Maybe we ought to talk about that," Joe replied, his grin growing wider. "As soon as I take a look around the house, that is."

"A look around the house?" Susannah repeated stupidly. "Oh, you're here about the repairs, aren't you? I forgot."

Standing at the door with the cold morning air whispering around her bare toes and Joe Santori smiling down at her, Susannah felt very vulnerable. She was completely dressed, of course—swathed in layers of material, in fact. But something in Joe Santori's gaze made her feel as if she was wearing much less.

He said softly, "Would you like me to wait outside while you dress?"

"That's not necessary. It's freezing cold and you shouldn't... I mean, it's foolish to—"

"The neighbors will wonder if I step inside, though. You're the famous Susannah Atkins, and greeting a man at your door is risky business, wouldn't you say?"

"I'm sure there aren't any nosy reporters lurking in the bushes."

"But with everyone owning a video camera these days, who knows what might happen? 'Oh, Susannah!' could end up being exposed on national television. That's a very nice ensemble, if you ask me, but in the hands of one of those sleazy talk-show guys—"

"I'm sure the neighbors aren't watching."

Joe laughed. "You're positive? You must forget what it's like living in Tyler. If you make one mistake, Miss Suzie, the whole population will know by sundown."

As if to prove his point, another human figure appeared at that moment. A teenage boy ambled from around the mailbox on the corner. He was very tall and lanky, carrying a slouchy sack of newspapers over one sloping shoulder, and he walked like a camel—with a shuffling, long-legged gait. But his gaze was not that of a sleepy camel. Rather, he seemed to be scoping the neighborhood for any signs of life.

"Oh, heavens," moaned Susannah. "That must be Lars."

"Sure is," Joe said cheerfully. "And he's going to wonder what you're doing talking to me in your nightgown. 'Morning, Lars! What's new?"

The boy spotted Joe on the porch and Susannah in the doorway in her white satin, flannel and lace, and his eyes, already slightly protuberant, popped wide with excitement at having seen something interesting at last.

The boy's voice cracked as he called, "Nothin', Mr. Santori. Nothin's new. Except I heard Mrs. Atkins's granddaughter is back in town. You know—the famous TV personality!"

"No kidding?" Joe was grinning broadly.

"Yessir, have you seen her?"

"As a matter of fact, Lars, I have."

"That wouldn't be her, would it?" Lars asked, smiling shyly as he mounted the porch steps. He had obviously recognized Susannah from a block away, but he said, "Boy, you're even prettier in person!"

"You've got good taste in women, Lars," said Joe. He turned to Susannah. "Think it's worth losing your reputation?"

Lars wrestled a rolled-up newspaper out of his sack. "Could I have your autograph?"

"Certainly." Susannah didn't feel much like greeting another fan at that moment, but she forced herself to be pleasant. "Do you have a pen?"

Joe took a stubby pencil from behind his ear and offered it. "Will this do?"

"Sign my bag," Lars said, holding out the canvas sack. "In real big letters."

Susannah complied, then said shortly, "There you go. Now, if you'll forgive me, I'd like to get in out of the cold."

"Oh, sure. I didn't mean to keep you out here." Lars smiled and backed off the porch, still holding his bag and admiring Susannah's signature as if it were the Holy Grail. "Thanks, Miss Atkins. I'll never forget this. I've never been so close to a celebrity before. Uh...sorry to have bothered you."

Susannah glanced up and found Joe watching her.

He smiled curiously down at her, making no bones about admiring the way the sunlight cast its golden glow across her face. His own appearance was nothing short of breathtaking—that curly black hair, those deep brown eyes, that oh, so sexy mouth curled in a smile that spoke more than words could say. But there was more in his expression, Susannah saw. Questions.

Susannah released a pent-up breath in a great, dizzying whoosh.

He said, "You're pretty nice to your fans."

"It pays off."

"But there's something..." Joe caught himself, brow twitching, and said, "You seem a little upset."

Susannah hugged herself and stepped back into the house. "I'm not upset. Of course I like my fans. But this morning...I just—" Susannah realized she needed to share her dilemma with someone, and Joe seemed like a sympathetic ear. She turned and put one hand on the door handle, trying to decide if she could dump the whole story on him. He'd been relatively understanding yesterday.

"What is it?" he asked.

With a rush of relief, Susannah blurted out, "My grandmother was ill last night."

Joe's face changed, his concern appearing at once, and he stepped over the threshold to cup Susannah's arm instinctively. "Is she all right? Did you take her to the hospital?"

"No, although I certainly tried to talk her into going."

He closed the door. "What happened, exactly?"

"After you left, she fainted—just blacked out in the kitchen. I don't know why. I called the emergency number—"

"Paramedics?"

"Right. But they checked her and didn't find anything terribly wrong. They urged her to see her own doctor today, that's all."

"Where is she now?" Joe asked in a take-charge tone. "Upstairs resting?"

"Are you kidding?" Exasperation finally getting the best of her, Susannah burst out, "She ran off to Marge's Diner—on foot! I couldn't stop her."

Joe looked grim. "Good Lord."

"And she's carrying a coffeepot, too."

"Look," Joe said, opening the door again with a jerk—he was clearly a man of action who didn't waste words. "I'll go now and pick her up in the truck. Don't worry. I'll be right back."

"But she—"

"She shouldn't be walking around in the cold if she fainted last night."

Relieved, Susannah said, "Thank you. I really..."

But Joe was already out the door and halfway down the steps. Over his shoulder, he said, "Don't mention it."

He left, and Susannah gratefully hurried upstairs to dress. Her overnight bag didn't carry much, but Josie had insisted Susannah carry a few essentials at all times, including a pair of jeans and a sweater. Susannah only had enough time to climb into the clothes, brush her teeth and begin to pull on a pair of sneakers before she heard Joe's pickup truck drive up to the curb in front of the house.

She peeked out the window and saw that Joe had returned alone. He was storming up the sidewalk by himself. Frightened all over again, Susannah rushed downstairs with only one shoe on and the laces flapping.

She yanked open the door, breathless. "Where is she?"

Joe's face looked stormy. "At Marge's," he growled. "She's drinking coffee and having a wonderful time."

Susannah stepped aside and allowed Joe into the house. "You couldn't get her to come home with you?"

"No," he said shortly. "Are you as mule-headed as she is, or is Rose a throwback to some prehistoric female of the species?"

Susannah laughed weakly and pushed her hair back from her face. "We're both pretty stubborn. She's okay, though?"

"Just ornery," Joe said, grouchy and annoyed. "Mostly, she wanted me to get back over here and look around the house with you."

"I see," said Susannah, feeling herself color once again.

"In fact, she ordered me out of Marge's at knife-point!"

"Knife-point?"

"She grabbed a knife out of Judson Ingalls's hand just as he was cutting into his bacon. She looked like a terrorist. In another town, somebody would have called the police."

Susannah laughed at the picture he described. "Look, I'm really sorry, Mr. Santori, but I think my grandmother has decided we'd be good for each other."

He smiled ruefully. "That's obvious."

"And she can be relentless, in case you haven't guessed."

"Believe me, I guessed. She said she'd come back in half an hour, and Judson volunteered to bring her home."

Susannah relaxed. "That's kind of him."

Joe lifted his head. "What's that noise?"

It was the oven buzzer. "Muffins," Susannah said. "No doubt my grandmother made them so you and I could have a romantic breakfast together. Let me go shut off the oven and we can take that tour—"

"No, let me take care of the muffins." Joe put a restraining hand on Susannah's arm. "You go get your other shoe."

He wasn't just take-charge, he was helpful, too. "Thanks," she said, once again glad to have someone like Joe around when she needed it.

Susannah dashed upstairs and found her shoe under the bed, where she'd thrown it when she'd heard Joe's truck. She pulled it onto her foot and began lacing it.

But she stopped, laces frozen in her hands. From downstairs in the kitchen, she heard Joe start to hum. And in a few moments, as she brushed her hair and began winding it onto the top of her head, she heard him start to sing.

And, boy, could he sing! Not just the pop-tunes-in-the-shower repertoire, but real singing, like great opera baritones Susannah had heard on the radio. Joe's voice rose from the kitchen and rumbled in the rafters. Susannah stopped fidgeting with her hair and stood very still, listening, transfixed.

How could a man's voice sound so poignant? So emotional? So wonderful?

"Stop thinking like a star-struck teenager," Susannah lectured herself. "He may be helpful, and he may sing like Placido Domingo, but he's not your type at all."

No, Susannah Atkins only dated intellectuals. Or hard-driven executives. Or a combination of both. Most of the time, she dated Roger Selby, and he was a far cry from Joe Santori. Roger was very attractive—he kept fit on the racquetball court and was notoriously vigilant about his diet—but as Susannah fixed her hair, she found herself thinking that Roger was...well, kind of effete compared to Joe. Roger was witty and intelligent and a good conversationalist. But Joe seemed like a man's man, capable of talking sports or sweeping a woman off her feet if he wanted to.

He's not going to sweep me, *of course,* she said silently to her reflection.

Susannah was not the sweepable sort. She was a very levelheaded woman who knew what she wanted out of life. And the likes of Joe Santori did not fit into her plans at all.

With that thought held firmly in her mind, Susannah calmly descended the stairs, fully dressed, combed and in control.

She followed the heavenly scent of muffins to the kitchen. Rose Atkins's kitchen was mostly pink and as frilly as a Victorian lady's boudoir. Lace curtains were tied back from the windows by lengths of pink velvet ribbon. The round table was adorned by a pink tatted tablecloth, and a pot of poinsettias stood cheerily in the center. Small framed watercolors of assorted pink flowers hung on the walls, and the labels on the Mason jars that lined the shelves on one wall were pink and inscribed with Rose Atkins's name and the preserving date.

Big, rawboned Joe Santori looked very out of place.

"I couldn't resist," said Joe when Susannah arrived in the kitchen. "The best thing to drink with fresh muffins is the famous Santori Sizzler, guaranteed to make you bright-eyed and bushy-tailed. I'm just whipping up a couple now."

He had taken off his parka and was moving around the kitchen in his flannel shirt and jeans, making himself completely at home with the refrigerator and the blender. He had pulled the muffin tray from the oven and prepared a basket with a fresh white napkin, now brimming with gently steaming muffins. Bemused by his efficiency, Susannah replied, "My tail is fine the way it is."

"I quite agree," he retorted, making a show of pouring a frothy pink drink from the blender into two tall glasses. "But this will put a little more shine in your eyes, Miss Suzie. Here. Try it."

He thrust the icy glass into Susannah's hand and lifted his own drink for a toast. "What shall we drink to?"

"Mr. Santori—"

"How about drinking to strong-willed women?"

"What?"

"Your grandmother, to be specific. She's a lady I'm learning to respect. I was honestly afraid she might use that knife on me!"

He was harmless and completely charming, a big man feigning fear of an elderly woman. Susannah felt a smile tugging at the corner of her mouth. She lifted her glass, and Joe smoothly wound his arm through hers so their elbows were linked and they faced each other with glasses raised. His liquid brown eyes melted into Susannah's, and his voice was low and mellow. "To your grandmother. May all her wishes come true."

"Not *all,*" Susannah corrected with a laugh, lifting the glass to her lips as her small arm entwined with his larger, muscled one.

The Santori Sizzler was a sweet, tangy breakfast drink upon first swallow, but the kick came a few seconds later as the alcohol let its presence be known.

"Wow," Susannah gasped, her eyes watering. "What's in this thing?"

He patted her back. "A little orange juice. A little soda. A few things I probably shouldn't divulge—and Campari. Do you like it?"

"Well, it's not what I usually have for breakfast."

"Try it with a muffin."

With a bite of one of her grandmother's banana-and-pecan muffins, the drink was quite delicious.

"Do you like it or not?"

It was impossible to resist his grin. "Yes," Susannah admitted, helping herself to another sip. "It's very good."

His gaze was full of pleasure as he absorbed her smile. "Great. Shall we take the drinks with us while we look around the house?"

"All right," Susannah said gamely. "If my grandmother comes home and finds we haven't accomplished anything, she'll assume the worst."

"Or the best," he said, laughing as he led the way out of the kitchen with his glass in one hand and a muffin in the other. "Shall we start in the attic or the basement?"

"Attic."

"The attic it is." Joe got right down to business by asking a string of questions, fired so rapidly at Susannah that she had no time to think about anything else.

"Has your grandmother told you anything about leaking ceilings?"

"No, nothing."

"How about squirrels or bats living on the third floor? Termites? Cracked plaster?"

Susannah answered his questions as honestly and succinctly as she could. Joe pulled a tattered little notebook from his hip pocket, and after passing his empty glass to Susannah, began to make notes about the house.

She had to admit, he seemed to know his business. And his inspection of the old Atkins house was very thorough. He climbed over assorted junk in the attic to peer into the eaves and under the insulation. He tapped beams and looked for signs of carpenter ants between floor joists with his flashlight. In the bedrooms, he poked at the ceilings and lit matches around all the windows to check for air leaks. Every visible inch of the old plumbing came under his scrutiny, and he even jumped up and down in the hallway to check for squeaky floorboards.

And Susannah found herself fascinated. She responded to his questions and listened to him ramble—all for the simple pleasure of hearing Joe's mellifluent baritone voice. The timbre gave her a surprisingly warm, trembly feeling inside. The tone was both vibrant and mellow.

"We'll skip the fireplace for now," Joe told her when they returned to the first floor. "Judging by how bad the bricks look from outside, I think it'll need some attention that's more expert than mine. I have a friend I'll send over in a few days. He'll be able to tell us what needs to be done."

"All right," said Susannah, amazed that she was allowing Joe to make decisions. *What's happening to me?* Usually she made the tough decisions for the people around her, then Josie put them into motion. Here was Joe taking charge completely.

"Now, the basement," he said. "You want to leave these glasses in the kitchen before we go down there?"

Susannah stared at the empty glasses in her hands and couldn't remember drinking the rest of her Sizzler. But her glass was empty, and she felt a pleasant little buzz in her head. "Yes, I do."

He grinned a little. "Maybe you'd like another drink?"

"Not so early in the morning," Susannah protested. "I'm already feeling tipsy."

"Oh," said Joe, smiling into her eyes. "Good."

Susannah showed him the basement door without further delay. He escorted her into the darkness, and while following him down the steps, Susannah found herself admiring the breadth of his shoulders and wondering how it might feel to run her palms across the muscled contour—thoughts highly inappropriate for a woman who normally had little time for noticing attractive men.

Behave yourself, she thought.

The basement was cool and dry, and Joe's haunting voice echoed in the far reaches of the dark rooms. He shone his flashlight into the old coal bin, and Susannah watched the play of indirect light on his rugged face while he talked. It was not the face of a playboy, she thought. More like a slightly past-his-prime Roman god.

Stop it, she ordered herself. *You've got more important things on your mind.*

"So that's about it," Joe said, scribbling a few final notes in his little book. He was left-handed, Susannah realized, and he curled his hand around the pencil in a way that sent her imagination into action again. What else might that hand curl around so provocatively?

This is ridiculous, she told herself, closing her eyes.

"You okay?" Joe asked, pausing on the steps.

Susannah's eyes flew open. "Yes, I'm fine."

"You looked a little—"

"I just realized I need to make a phone call, that's all. My trip, you see. I should get in touch with some people."

"Oh." He leaned against the crooked hand railing. "You're going to the beach after all, hmm?"

"I haven't decided yet. But I need to alert my traveling companion about the uncertainty of my plans."

"Traveling companion," Joe repeated thoughtfully. "Last night your grandmother called him your boss. I guess he's more than just the guy who signs your paycheck."

"He's a friend," Susannah corrected carefully. "We're equals in the workplace, you could say."

"How about outside the workplace?"

"Mr. Santori—"

"You'd better call me Joe. I feel like a schoolteacher when you call me Mr. Santori."

"Joe, then. My relationship with my boss isn't important right now—"

"That's too bad."

"That's not what I meant!" Susannah protested, hearing the implication in Joe's voice. "Roger and I are... we... Sometimes we take trips together."

"To talk about work," Joe recalled. "You're going to the beach to plan your program."

"Yes."

"That doesn't sound like a relaxing vacation."

"For me, it's very relaxing."

"You must love your work."

"I do," she said truthfully. "It's exciting and challenging and . . . well, I'm devoted to it."

"I like my work, too, but I'd never say I'm devoted to it."

"Look," Susannah said patiently, "I know what you're trying not to say. You think I'm obsessed with my job."

Joe smiled a little. "Are you?"

"Maybe," Susannah said steadily. "But I like it that way."

"And your grandmother?"

"What about her?" Susannah asked, instantly on guard.

"Everybody gets old," Joe said, leaning back against the railing. "Someday, she's going to need you."

"I'm not sure that's true."

"How can you deny it?" Joe asked incredulously. "She's more than eighty years old, right? You think she's going to live forever?"

"Of course not," Susannah snapped. "But I can't step in and take over her life, can I?"

"Why not?"

"Why *not?*" Susannah cried. "Because she's a living, breathing human being who has lived a very full life and knows exactly how she wants to keep on living it. I can't march in here and boss her around!"

"So you're going off on a vacation—"

"Look, Mr. Santori—Joe, if that's what you'd like me to call you—maybe you're used to bullying your loved ones, but I can't do that. I respect my grandmother too much to interfere."

"And what happens if she freezes to death some night while you're enjoying the weather down south?"

"Then I have to assume that's the way she wants things."

"Are you kidding?" Joe looked amazed. "I can't believe you'd run off and leave her—"

"She wants me to go! What am I supposed to do? Stay here and spoon-feed her baby food? She's a vibrant woman! Where do I get off ordering her around?"

"To save her life, you have the right to do a lot of things."

"I don't feel that way," Susannah said staunchly, wondering how she could have imagined Joe Santori was an attractive man. Five minutes ago, she'd been admiring his shoulders, but suddenly she saw a gigantic bully standing in front of her. "My grandmother's life is hers to live, not mine."

"I suppose we should be grateful for small favors," Joe muttered.

"Exactly what do you mean by that?"

"Nothing," he retorted. "Except that your grandmother is obviously living a very full and happy life, while you're only worried about the subject for your next program. It beats me how you ended up in the same family!"

"It beats me," she snapped, "how you ended up in the human race. You're obviously a superior being—in your own mind, at least!"

She stormed up the stairs.

CHAPTER FIVE

"ROGER," SUSANNAH SAID on the phone later that morning, "I'm truly sorry about this."

"Not to worry," Roger soothed. "I'll call my friend at the airline and change our tickets. I find my own schedule has heated up overnight, and I shouldn't dash off today, either."

Susannah sighed. "Well, that's a relief."

She plugged her other ear so she could hear Roger's voice. She hadn't been able to reach him by telephone earlier. When she'd finally hiked over to Marge's Diner to find her grandmother, who was still there visiting, she tried again from the pay phone on the wall near the kitchen. The small restaurant was hopping with local townsfolk, all talking at the tops of their voices, it seemed.

Roger said, "Just let me know what your plans are once you've taken your aunt to the doctor."

"She's my grandmother, Roger."

"Right, right." Roger laughed. "I'm an idiot sometimes. Give me a call, okay? Thanks, Susannah. Bye."

"Bye," Susannah said to the dial tone.

"Well?" Rose asked when Susannah returned to their table. "How's Roger?"

"Fine." Susannah distractedly slid into their booth. "He sends you his love."

Rose snorted. "I'll bet. Did anything happen at the house after I left?"

Susannah sat back in the cushioned seat and folded her arms across her chest. "You know very well what happened, Granny Rose. Your charming friend Joe showed up."

Rose did a bad imitation of a much-surprised woman. "Oh, I forgot all about that! How did he look?"

"It doesn't matter how he looked, Granny Rose. I'm not going to fall in love with him."

"Why not?"

"Because he's an opinionated, pushy..."

"But he's very handsome, don't you think? And wait until you hear him sing! He's got a magnificent voice! The Methodist choir director swears she's going to kidnap him someday soon."

"Let's not talk about Joe, all right, Granny Rose? It's clear we have different opinions about the man."

"Whatever you say, dear. Here, let me warm up your coffee. Marge left us a pot, and there's still some left."

Rose poured more coffee into Susannah's mug and wondered if something had happened between her granddaughter and Joe while they had been alone at the house. She felt sure nothing bad had happened. Joe was a gentleman, of course. But Susannah had her prickly side, and Joe had a few rough edges, too.

Perhaps, Rose thought, they'd had words.

"Did Joe give you an estimate on the repair work?"

She heard Susannah sigh. Then the younger woman said, "No, he had to go home and write up a few things. I believe he said he'd drop off some paperwork later today."

Rose nodded. "He's very efficient, don't you think?"

"Oh, I have no doubts about his efficiency."

"Then what's bothering you, Suzie? Don't you like Joe?"

Susannah put down her mug and thought the question over. The noise of Marge's Diner swirled around them. The small restaurant was tucked on a side street just off the main square of Tyler, and for many years it had been one of the town's busiest spots. A hotbed of gossip and local news, the diner was packed with patrons on that bright winter morning. Christmas carols were playing on the radio, the smell of hot coffee filled the air, and Marge and the waitress both sported little sprigs of holly on their blouses.

Most of Marge's customers seemed very happy to be in the warm restaurant on such a cold morning. Hopping back and forth between tables or waving across the crowded room, everyone seemed to be spending as much attention on their neighbors as on breakfast. There was a lot of laughter and loud talk.

And a great many Tyler citizens came over to the table by the window to greet Susannah.

"It's wonderful to have someone famous in Tyler," Marge said, once everyone was finally allowing the Atkins ladies to enjoy their coffee in peace. Marge poured more coffee into their mugs and added, "Will you be filming your program from Tyler now and then, Susannah?"

"No," Susannah replied. "I doubt it. It's much more convenient to work in the city."

"But you're missing life in Tyler, you know. We may not have the same amusements you find in Milwaukee," Marge said with a grin, "but there's a lot of wonderful stuff here, right under your nose."

"But my work is in Milwaukee."

"Oh, work!" Marge scoffed. "There're more important things in life than work!"

Susannah smiled and said nothing, but afterward she looked squarely at Rose and said, "I had the same conversation with Joe a few minutes ago."

"Oh?" Rose asked.

"He intimated that I wasn't living a very full life, either." Susannah leaned forward. "How about you, Granny Rose? Do you think I'm wasting my life?" At her grandmother's searching look, she went on, "I just don't know sometimes. I love my work, I really do, but...well, you've been very happy here in Tyler, haven't you?"

"Yes, but I raised a family—two, in fact, if you consider I raised your father first, then you after your parents died. And I kept myself busy, but I certainly never had what you'd call a big career. It's a question of choices, I suppose. And my choices were different than yours."

"Better?"

"No, just different."

But Rose's words, spoken to ease whatever turmoil was in Susannah's mind, didn't smooth the expression of anxiety from her granddaughter's face. Instead, Susannah seemed to withdraw even further.

Rose leaned across the table and touched Susannah's hand. "Suzie, what's wrong? Did Joe say something to hurt your feelings?"

"No, he just...well, he's made me question the way I do things, I guess. He was pretty pushy about it, in fact."

"You mustn't hold his pushiness against him," Rose said with a laugh. "Remember, he *is* from the city—Chicago, to be exact."

"And he was married? He chased his wife away, I suppose."

"No, not at all. Joe's a widower," Rose explained, watching Susannah's expression change from frustration to interest. "His wife died of cancer, I believe, after a long, hard struggle. He doesn't seem to be bitter about it, but I'm sure his wife's death was very difficult."

Susannah swallowed hard. "I see. I think I'm starting to understand why he said some of the things he did to me."

"Suzie, are you all right? Did he really upset you? Is there something I can do?"

Susannah smiled uncertainly. "Of course not, Granny Rose. I'm just... Oh, maybe I've been working too hard lately. I'm a little touchy and burned-out. Maybe I was too sensitive."

"And now I'm causing you to miss your vacation."

"Don't say that!" Susannah squeezed Rose's hand back. "I'm not going to miss it. I'm just postponing it for a while. I want to hear what Dr. Phelps has to say about you."

"Oh, don't worry about me! I'm a tough old bird!"

"I have a right to be concerned, though. I love you, Granny Rose. I don't want to see you get run down—especially not before Christmas. I know how much you enjoy the holidays."

"I'm fine!"

"But you work so hard at this time of year. It worries me to think you'll soon be slaving to get ready for your annual party."

The week before Christmas, Rose always baked cookies, decorated her house for the holidays and opened her doors for an evening of singing and socializing. At one time, she used to bring out a birthday cake at eight o'clock—since the party was always held on Susannah's birthday. But as a teenager Susannah had refused to celebrate her birthday that way, so the party became a Christmas affair.

"I won't knock myself out," Rose promised.

"Will you let me help? I can do a lot before I leave for my trip."

"Why, that would be very nice, dear. We could decorate and do some baking."

"My favorite things." Susannah smiled. "So that's settled. Now, have you phoned Dr. Phelps yet?"

"Yes," said Rose, surprising her granddaughter with the truth. "I called just before you got here. I have an appointment at ten." Rose checked her watch. "In fifteen minutes."

"Wonderful! I'm glad he's going to see you so promptly. I'll take you."

"Don't be silly, dear. His office is a few blocks away. I can walk."

"Well, then, I'll come along."

Rose took a deep breath and said, "I'd rather see my doctor in private, Susannah. Do you mind?"

By the expression of surprise on Susannah's face, Rose could see that her granddaughter did mind. Obviously, she wanted to hear a prognosis from the horse's mouth. But she covered her dismay and said, "No, I don't mind. I understand completely. But surely there's something I can do. I'd like to be useful."

"Well," Rose said firmly, "there is one errand you could run for me."

Susannah smiled. "Name it."

"Go over to Joe Santori's house and tell him I'd like the other repairs on my house to begin immediately."

Susannah's blue eyes popped wide. But...but shouldn't you wait for an estimate from another contractor?"

"No need for that! I know Joe and his work, and he's the man for the job. My mind is made up."

Susannah was definitely flustered as she said, "But what if he can't squeeze you into his schedule? Maybe he's too busy for—"

"Oh, he'll find the time for me, I'm sure. He said so last night. Will you go see him?"

"Well..."

"Ask him if he could start on the kitchen first and save the boring things for later—the roof or whatever. I wonder if it's possible to have some of the kitchen work finished before my party? I'd really like to have a new counter and sink before then."

"It's starting to sound expensive."

"What's money for? That sink should have been replaced years ago. And wouldn't you like to see the kitchen looking new for my party?"

"Yes, of course," Susannah said faintly.

"And you can help, Suzie. I might as well choose some new wallpaper and such. You're such a whiz at that! Between you and Joe, I'm sure my kitchen will look wonderful in no time! Tell him I'd like him to start right away."

Susannah looked stricken for an instant, but she recovered. "No matter how good Joe is, he won't get all that done before your Christmas do. But all right. I'll go see him, Granny Rose."

"Fine."

Rose hopped up and grabbed her coat before Susannah could think of an excuse to avoid speaking to Joe again. She gave Susannah Joe's correct address and made certain that her granddaughter knew exactly how to get there. Then, with cheery goodbyes for everyone in the diner, Rose went off to her doctor's appointment.

With Rose gone, Susannah sat for several minutes, ostensibly to finish her coffee. Actually, she was working up the courage to go looking for Joe Santori. She finally paid Marge for their breakfasts on her way out the door. A chorus of goodbyes rang out as Susannah left the diner, making her feel as if she'd been warmly welcomed back to Tyler. She waved to everyone and set off down the street.

Determined to settle things with the exasperatingly attractive and annoyingly bossy Mr. Santori as quickly as possible, she walked briskly to Joe's house, a mere three blocks from the diner. The sun sparkled brightly on the snow-covered lawns of Tyler, looking very pretty. The whole town was just as delightful as it always was. She had to dart out of the way of a gigantic snowplow when she crossed Main Street, but the driver of the plow tooted his horn and waved to her in a friendly way. Susannah waved back.

When she arrived at the Santori residence, Susannah realized she knew the house. It had been the home of her second-grade teacher, Miss Sternburg, who'd unfortunately let the place go to rack and ruin in her later years. Susannah was glad to see that Joe had rescued the structure. It was a charming Victorian house—not nearly as large as Susannah's grandmother's, but every bit as picturesque, with gingerbread trim, a pretty side porch with a rose trellis, a picket fence draped with Christmas lights and a separate garage attached to the house by a covered walkway overgrown with grapevines. The house was yellow with white trim, and the mailbox at the front gate had been built to match the shape and configuration of the garage. Over the garage door was a sign that read simply, Santori Construction.

Looking at that quaint yellow house—so obviously a labor of love—gave Susannah pause. It was the house of a man who cared about little things. He cared about his house, his neighbors, his grape arbor, his roses. Obviously, he even cared about little old ladies who lived a few blocks away.

Susannah's courage almost failed her. Maybe Joe *was* right. Maybe she needed to butt in where her grandmother's health was concerned and damn the consequences. Perhaps Joe's experience with his wife's illness had led him to the conclusion that not interfering was far worse than hurting someone's feelings.

Torn, Susannah almost turned around and walked away. But as she hesitated on the sidewalk, who should come around the corner at that moment but Lars, the newspaper boy.

He spotted Susannah and gave her a big, loopy grin. "Hi, Miss Atkins!"

"Good morning again, Lars."

"What are you doing here? Looking for Mr. Santori?"

"Well, yes."

"Have you seen Gina yet?"

"Gina? Oh, his daughter. No, I haven't."

Lars looked disappointed. "Oh. I was hoping she'd be around this morning. Sometimes she's having breakfast when I bring the paper. I like to wave at her through the window. That's their breakfast room right there. Through that big window." Lars pointed a long, bony finger toward the large picture window at the front of the Victorian turret. "Once Gina opened the window and gave me an English muffin. It was a little burned around the edges, but I didn't mind."

"She's a friend of yours?" Susannah asked, amused by Lars's loquaciousness with a celebrity.

Lars sighed. "I wish she was. But most of the time Gina doesn't know I exist."

I should be so lucky with another member of the Santori family, Susannah thought. "Well, I'm sure that will change eventually."

Shaking his head, Lars said, "I don't know. Gina can be real tough sometimes. She's the star of the girls' basketball team, you know. Last game, she broke another girl's nose. It was an accident, of course—I guess basketball can get kinda rough under the hoops—but that nose was broken in two places. She's something."

Susannah had walked with Lars up the sidewalk and the porch steps. As they reached the front door, it was suddenly yanked open from within. A slim, dark-haired girl stood inside, looking belligerent.

"It's about time you got here," she said to Lars. "Where's the paper? I want to check the hockey scores."

"The paper's r-right here, Gina," said Lars, eagerly digging one out of his bag. "There's a sale at Gates Department Store, and a Kevin Costner movie is playing at the theater in Belton."

With sarcasm, Gina said, "Great. Too bad I hate shopping almost as much as I hate Kevin Costner." She snatched the newspaper out of the boy's hand.

"Yeah," Lars said faintly. "Too bad."

He shuffled off the porch, head drooping, and soon disappeared around the corner.

Susannah turned back to Gina. "Lars seems like a nice boy."

Gina shrugged. "I'm not into boys. Can I help you?"

Susannah maintained her smile in the face of the girl's blunt behavior. "My name is Susannah Atkins. I was wondering if your father is—"

Gina snapped her fingers. "The lady on television!" Her eyes widened as she recognized a celebrity standing on her front porch. *"Oh, Susannah!"*

Susannah smiled politely. "Yes, I'm Susannah Atkins, all right."

"I hate that show," Gina said with only the slightest trace of apology—a characteristic Susannah recognized she shared with her opinionated father. The girl leaned her shoulder against the open door and folded her arms over her chest, saying, "It's all girl junk. I think it's demeaning to women."

"It's a household-hints program," Susannah shot back at once. "I don't decide who actually performs the things I discuss on my show, do I?"

"I—I guess not."

"So it's only demeaning to women if you assume cooking and cleaning and making a home is solely women's work. *I'm* not the one who decides which member of the family ought to do the car repairs and who ought to do the laundry. That's up to my viewers."

"I see," said Gina, blinking and standing up straight.

"Now," said Susannah. "Is your father at home?"

"He's not, I'm sorry," Gina replied, remembering her manners at last and suddenly behaving like a girl who was accustomed to helping run her father's business. "Sometimes he works on Saturday mornings. After he got back from Mrs. Atkins's house, he went over to an auction in Bonneville to buy some salvage stuff—some old porch railings, I think. Are you the one he's buying them for?"

"No, I'm not. I have some other business to discuss with him."

"I'll take a message," Gina said. "Will you come inside while I write everything down?"

The girl stood aside, giving Susannah a glimpse of the cozy interior—a living room with overstuffed furniture and a jumble of books and magazines on the coffee table. Susannah quailed at the thought of setting foot in Joe's house. Already, she felt like an intruder in his life. And besides, there were some things best said in person.

"No," she said to Gina, backing down the first porch step. "I'll catch up with him later."

"I'll be glad to tell him anything," Gina offered.

"Thanks. I'm sure you do a good job for your father. But I'd rather talk to him face-to-face."

Gina shrugged, looking at Susannah curiously. "Have it your way."

Susannah went down the porch steps, feeling both relieved and frustrated. She'd been almost happy to avoid a confrontation with him, but a part of her wished she could have another chance with Joe. After all, his heart was in the right place. Once she'd screwed up her courage to confront him, she hated leaving without speaking to the man. But she had no choice.

Queerly churned up inside, Susannah walked back to the square and decided to do a little shopping to calm her nerves while waiting for Rose to finish with her doctor's appointment.

Shopping was better than tranquilizers.

Gates Department Store had always been *the* place to shop in Tyler. When Susannah was growing up, the establishment had been a child's adventure, with its three floors of merchandise, a quiet luncheonette in the basement and two brass elevators to whisk customers throughout the store. The display windows brought gawkers from far and wide with their beautiful and sometimes extravagant tableaux of merchandise. Ellie Gates, the founder and owner, had been an eccentric single woman with a flair for the dramatic and artistic. In her youth, Susannah had greatly admired the indomitable woman.

The lunch specialty on Saturdays had included a scoop of chocolate ice cream with colored sprinkles, a detail that was still surprisingly vivid in Susannah's memory. At Gates, Tyler citizens could buy a spool of thread, a pair of shoes, a toaster or even a parakeet, and the loyalty of the shoppers had prevented the development of a giant shopping mall that would have spoiled the surrounding countryside.

Susannah tried on a pair of pearl earrings, admired the selection of handbags and bought one for Rose for Christmas. Eventually she also bought herself a red sweater she didn't need—particularly if she intended to leave Tyler shortly for the Caribbean. The friendly clerk chatted as she wrapped the sweater and processed Susannah's credit card by running the papers through the store's old-fashioned pneumatic tubes.

Deciding to forgo the chocolate ice cream with sprinkles because the last thing she needed was a sugar-induced depression, Susannah walked back to Dr. Phelps's office.

"Oh, hi, Susannah. Your grandmother left about fifteen minutes ago," the receptionist, Anna Kelsey, told her.

"Where did she go? Is she all right?"

"She seemed fine to me. I think she was heading home."

Susannah thanked the woman and walked back to her grandmother's house along the snow-dusted sidewalks.

She froze on the corner when she noticed Joe Santori's truck parked at the curb in front of her grandmother's house.

"Now what?" she mumbled to herself, startled to find herself trembling all over.

She mounted the porch steps and let herself into the large house. "Granny Rose?"

No answer. With exasperation, Susannah wondered if her grandmother had intentionally left her alone to deal with Joe.

Susannah softly closed the door behind her and kicked off her boots. She cleared her throat and called unsteadily, "Anybody here?"

"I'd rather not be," rumbled Joe's voice from the kitchen.

Susannah followed the sound and entered the kitchen with trepidation.

She found Joe—or the lower half of him, anyway—lying on the kitchen floor wedged under the sink, while a pool of water puddled around his body. His long legs lay diagonally across the wet linoleum, with one boot braced against a kitchen chair. Water dripped from his jeans.

"What in the world are you doing?"

"Working on the sink," Joe replied from deep inside the cabinet. "What does it look like I'm doing?"

"Swimming," Susannah replied.

"There's always a comedian in every crowd," Joe grumbled, dropping a wrench onto the floor with a splash. "Is that you, Miss Suzie?"

Folding her coat over another kitchen chair and placing her Gates bag on the table, Susannah said, "It is. And I've been looking all over town for you."

"How flattering," said Joe from beneath the sink. "You missed me, huh?"

Susannah was glad he couldn't see her blush. "No." She leaned down and tried to peer into the darkness of the cabinet. "I was supposed to tell you that my grandmother wants you to fix up her kitchen before the party next week, but I see you got the message."

"Mrs. A. flagged me down on the street."

"Where is she now?"

Joe began to ease his way out from under the sink. His voice was a little breathless as he inched backward. "I dropped her at the drugstore, and then she was going to pick up some fabric for a quilt. She said she'd be home soon."

"Should she be walking?"

"Maybe not," Joe said. "But I had no luck convincing her that I could be her taxi."

A moment later, Joe emerged gingerly from underneath the sink, shaking his grease-stained hands to shed some of the water he'd collected. His hair looked curlier than ever, and possibly because it was Saturday, he hadn't shaved. The resulting growth of beard, even more noticeable now than earlier, gave Joe a tough, piratelike air. And Susannah had always had a soft spot for pirates.

Hastily, she banished that thought from her mind. "I was supposed to hire you for this job," she said primly. "What are you doing, exactly?"

Joe gestured with his thumb. "This old sink leaks. I figure I better check the pipes before I put in a new one or start replacing the counter."

"How is it going?"

"Miserably," he admitted, looking at his dirty hands.

"Perhaps you ought to call a plumber before you get in over your head."

"Oh, I don't mind getting in over my head once in a while." He glanced up shrewdly. "Do you?"

Susannah felt her face color, and she couldn't think of a good comeback. As a result, a short, uncomfortable silence stretched between them, during which Joe watched Susannah with a wary gaze. Apparently, he wasn't ready to forgive her for the scene on the basement stairs earlier that morning.

Susannah summoned her composure and said, "As a matter of fact, I'm no stranger to plumbing problems. Shall I have a look?"

He looked startled. "Are you kidding? This is dirty work. Plus I'm sitting in a puddle, in case you haven't noticed."

She'd noticed, all right. The water made Joe's jeans look like a second skin, and his shirt clung damply to his chest, too. But Susannah avoided looking at his chest. "Do you mind if I examine the situation?"

"Be my guest. But your clothes..."

"It will only take a moment to mop up this mess. Here. This is what I use."

From a nearby drawer, Susannah pulled a pair of rubber gloves—the surgical kind she recommended to all her television viewers. They were available in packages of a dozen or more, and Susannah found them highly useful for all sorts of household projects. She held them up, and Joe looked at them dubiously. When he had wiped his dirty hands on the cloth she gave him, she passed him a sponge mop from the broom closet. Joe set about willingly cleaning up the water, and Susannah donned the gloves and a wraparound apron that completely covered her clothing from neck to knee. Thus protected, she knelt on the floor.

She's a formidable woman, Joe thought as he edged out of her way, dabbing at his shirt with the cloth. He watched as the indomitable Miss Susannah Atkins peered under the sink with the air of a determined archaeologist entering a forgotten tomb for the first time. An attractive frown creased her forehead, and her blue eyes were narrowed into an intrepid squint.

"See anything?" Joe asked, hoping his voice sounded normal.

Lordy, she was attractive. More attractive than she knew, which made her even *more* attractive where Joe was concerned.

When she leaned into the cabinet, Joe closed his eyes and decided he wasn't going to be swayed by her appearance anymore. She might look like the best thing to hit Tyler in years, but she was pretty heartless.

Joe couldn't stop himself from taking a little peek, however. On her hands and knees, she was inadvertently giving him the full benefit of a view he hadn't enjoyed before. Her backside was nicely rounded, filling out her jeans and tapering down to her slim legs. She wore a pair of white socks and no shoes again. Her feet were small and narrow, Joe noticed. He could see through the transparent gloves that her hands, bracing her weight on the kitchen floor, were perfectly manicured with short, utilitarian nails, and Joe found himself wondering how they'd feel if she touched him.

He suppressed a groan of longing.

"Can you hear me?" she asked.

"What?" Embarrassed, Joe realized she had been talking and he hadn't heard a word.

"I said I can see the problem," she repeated from under the sink. "You were trying to force the pipe, but actually you need a new gasket."

"Oh, is that it?" Joe grinned wryly. He had known exactly what the problem was, but he was surprisingly pleased to hear Susannah come up with the same diagnosis he had. She was a woman of many talents.

"I don't carry gaskets in my truck," he said, leaning against the kitchen table. "I'll have to drive over to Murphy's Hardware to get one. I'll check out the stainless steel sinks, too. Rose said she wanted a double one."

Susannah climbed out of the cabinet, and if she guessed Joe had been taking in the scenery she displayed, she gave no hint. She caught his eye, though, and they both looked away and suddenly got busy. Joe finished mopping up, while Susannah stripped off the rubber gloves and began to tug at the strings on her apron.

But she got them tangled and gave up with an impatient sigh. "Listen," she said, exasperated. "This is ridiculous. We're two grown adults, but we're acting like a couple of kids caught shoplifting or something.

I'm embarrassed and you're... well, I won't presume to guess what you're feeling."

Straight out, she said, "I'm very sorry about what happened this morning. I was pretty short with you, and I recognize you were just trying to help."

"What brought this on?"

"What?"

"You had your mind made up this morning. What changed?"

"I... nothing." She was quite unhinged, Joe could see. Her hands were trembling, and at that moment, Susannah looked a far cry from the cool television personality she was most of the time. Sitting on the floor with grease smearing one cheek and her hair escaping the smooth style held in place by pearl combs, she looked vulnerable, embarrassed and genuinely sorry for what had transpired earlier in the day.

She also looked sweet enough to nibble.

She said, "I'm sorry for the way I reacted and for the things I said."

"All right," said Joe, sounding a little hoarse even to his own ears. "Apology accepted."

She smiled slightly. "Thank you."

"You know," he went on, hardly believing he was about to suggest such an idea, "just to show there's no hard feelings, I wonder if we should start all over again."

"How's that?"

"Well, how about having dinner with me tonight?"

Her expression relaxed. "Dinner?"

"And a movie or something. That is, unless you're going to run off with your boss tonight."

"No," Susannah said. "We're not leaving tonight. We've postponed our plans. But I can't leave my grandmother. She's just been to the doctor and I'd rather—"

"Let's take her with us."

Susannah laughed. "Now, that's the suggestion of a brave man! Can you imagine the three of us—"

"Tell you what," Joe said. "Don't say yes or no—not until you've talked to your grandmother. Maybe she'd like a night out, and you and I could mend our fences."

"Really, I... you and I could hardly have much to talk about."

"How will we know unless we try?"

"Well..."

But she didn't say more. She was stumped.

With the damp cloth, Joe leaned forward and touched her face. Gently he wiped away the grease on her cheek, meanwhile finding her cautious, doelike gaze irresistible. Her mouth parted—ever so slightly—and she released a long, pent-up breath. Joe thought about kissing that mouth, but caught himself. He could see the same idea had occurred to Susannah—it showed plainly in her eyes.

Well, well, Joe thought. *What have we here?*

CHAPTER SIX

JOE LEFT within the hour, promising to return, and Susannah had only five minutes to pull herself together before her grandmother showed up with flushed cheeks and sparkling eyes.

"Well?" she demanded of Susannah. "How did it go?"

"*You're* the one who had the doctor's appointment," Susannah cried, hoping her grandmother wasn't going to cross-examine her about Joe. She wasn't exactly sure *what* had happened, but she certainly knew she didn't want to discuss it.

Rose was not to be deflected, however. She said, "But *you* saw Joe again, didn't you?"

"Only because you orchestrated a meeting that was so obvious, Granny Rose.... Oh, honestly, why are you trying so hard to force us together? We have nothing in common."

"Nothing in—! Suzie, he finds you very attractive. And you think he's adorable, don't you?"

"I do not!" Susannah said hotly. "He's simply a man you've hired to fix your house! He's nothing to me! He's— How do you know he finds me attractive?"

Rose laughed heartily. "Because he said so, of course. He told me so this morning. Shall we make some cookies this afternoon? I have those extra pecans. I thought we'd whip up some tassies and put them in the freezer. What do you say?''

''I say you're driving me crazy.''

''Good. You could use some stirring up, I think. Let's have a quick sandwich, then get to work on the cookies.''

''Will you tell me what Dr. Phelps had to say while we work?''

''It wasn't much,'' Rose said vaguely, opening cupboards and organizing her ingredients.

But Susannah wasn't going to be put off any longer. ''Could the doctor explain why you fainted last night?''

''Oh, you know Dr. Phelps—he's so easygoing. He joked that I'd probably had too much sherry.''

''He was making jokes? Granny Rose, when I came in here last night and saw you falling . . . well, it was no joking matter.''

''I know, dear. It's just his way. Don't get huffy.''

''Granny Rose—''

''All right, all right!'' Rose gave up being evasive and faced Susannah squarely. ''He said I should be faithful about taking my blood pressure medicine. He was quite adamant about that, in fact.''

''Good.'' Susannah folded her arms to listen further. ''What else?''

''Well . . .''

''Come on, you're on a roll. Tell me everything.''

Rose sighed. When she spoke again, it was with reluctance. ''Dr. Phelps thinks my condition has changed somewhat. He'd like to do some tests.''

''What kind of tests?''

"Heart tests. I don't remember the different kinds. They all have initials instead of names—EKG, that kind of thing."

"What does he suspect?"

"Oh, he hates to speculate until he has some concrete evidence. Doctors are so hard to pin down these days. And he didn't want me to worry needlessly."

"All right, when do you start the tests? Can he fit you in quickly?"

Rose turned away and began to search the cupboard shelves. "Relatively quickly. Where did I put that can of tuna? I'm in the mood for a tuna sandwich. I told him I'd like to wait until after the holidays to start taking a bunch of tests. And he agreed. It's only a little more than a week or two, really."

"But a lot can happen in a week or two, Granny Rose." Susannah tried not to sound argumentative. "Especially around Christmas when you're so busy and excited. Are you sure you should put this off?"

"I'd be miserable if I had to give up my Christmas plans—you know that, Suzie. I'll do it in January—the day after New Year's, I promise."

The second of January was the best Susannah could hope for, she supposed. "And until then?" she asked. "You're going to take care of yourself?"

"Of course, dear! I'll pamper myself shamelessly. Now, how about some celery for a tuna salad? Will you get it out of the refrigerator, please?"

Susannah helped her grandmother in the kitchen and watched her like a hawk for signs of fatigue or lightheadedness. She wondered what the doctor had found when he examined Rose. He'd detected a change in her condition, but what kind of change? There was no use questioning Rose further, however. Susannah knew her grandmother wouldn't say more. She was too stubborn, and too determined to enjoy her Christmas plans.

They fixed quick tuna-salad-and-lettuce sandwiches, which they ate with cups of tea. Afterward, they buckled down to the task of making cookies for Rose's upcoming party. Susannah made sure that her grandmother got the least strenuous jobs, so Rose sat at the table and rolled the dough into balls, then pressed them into the tassie tins. Susannah bustled around the kitchen and attempted to clean up the mess as they went along.

About midafternoon, Joe Santori telephoned. Susannah picked up the receiver herself.

"How's your grandmother?" Joe asked without preamble. He didn't need to identify himself. What other man on the planet had such a mellifluous voice?

"Not bad," Susannah said, amazed by the way her pulse jumped at the sound of Joe's voice at the other end of the line. "She's going to have some tests after the holidays."

"Do you think it's wise to wait?"

"I'm not the one making the decision," Susannah said, noting that Rose was watching with an avid look in her eye.

"I see," Joe said. "And you can't make her see reason?"

"That's not our style," Susannah replied. "Have you prepared an estimate for the work you're going to do on the house?"

"Your grandmother said she didn't need one," Joe retorted, then laughed. "But I'm writing up one anyway. Don't worry, Miss Suzie. I'm not in the business of ripping off helpless little old ladies."

"She's not exactly helpless."

"Amen. What does she say about dinner tonight? Would she like to come along with us?"

"I don't think that's a very good idea," Susannah said, painfully aware that her grandmother was listening to every word of the conversation. "A quiet evening at home is what she needs, I think."

"But what about you?" Joe pressed. "My guess is that you've had far too many quiet evenings at home, Miss Suzie."

"Really, I can't go out to dinner tonight. I'm here to see my grandmother, not—"

"Go!" Rose cried. "Don't worry about me!"

"Granny Rose—"

"Is that Joe? And he wants you to have dinner with him tonight? Heavens, dear, don't be an idiot! Go!"

In her ear, Joe was laughing. "See?" he asked. "She's on my side!"

"Granny Rose, I can't possibly leave you alone tonight. I'm here to visit with you, not, well—"

"You can visit with me any old time," Rose shot back. "Besides, I don't want to miss 'EastEnders.' I get it on cable, and it's my favorite show. I was just going to go to bed after that. For heaven's sake, you'll be bored to death if you stay here!"

"But—"

"Don't argue, dear. Go have a good time."

"I can't—"

"Don't argue," said Joe, adding to Susannah's confusion. "We'll see a movie and have a late dinner—something quick so you won't be gone long."

"I don't have any clothes," Susannah objected, weakening fast as they ganged up on her. "Just my jeans and a sweater."

"Perfect. This isn't Milwaukee, you know. Just Tyler. People wear what's comfortable. See you at six-thirty?"

Susannah surrendered with a sigh. "All right. At six-thirty."

Rose gave a whoop of pleasure as Susannah hung up. "How delightful! Oh, you'll have fun. Isn't Joe a charmer?"

"He's a charmer, all right," Susannah grumbled, surprised by her own behavior. "I can't believe I agreed to go out with him. He's so... *different.*"

"You'll like him," Rose promised. "Now, let's get these cookies into the oven."

They finished baking cookies, although Susannah found she had a hard time concentrating on the work. Her mind wandered from Joe Santori to Rose's health and back again, so that she forgot to set the timer once and nearly burned a batch of pecan tassies.

Fortunately, they were only slightly overcooked. Rose cavalierly put them on a plate and offered the cookies to some neighbors who dropped in during the afternoon—Mrs. Connelly and her twin three-year-olds. The children were a couple of hooligans, in Susannah's opinion, but Rose didn't mind their noise a bit and invited them to make snowflakes by dipping bits of string into a hastily prepared starch mixture. The children were fascinated by the activity, and Susannah gradually found herself warming to them. She enjoyed herself, in fact. After she clipped the snowflakes to a string overhead to dry, she made a mental note to share the snowflake idea with her television viewers.

Late in the afternoon, when the neighbors were gone and the kitchen was cleaned up once and for all, Rose announced her plan to go into the parlor with a cup of tea and the newspaper.

"I'm just going to put up my feet and relax for a while," she said, toddling off toward the parlor. "Why don't you get ready for your date, Suzie? Isn't it getting late?"

"What time is it?"

"Nearly six."

"Good grief!" Susannah whipped off her borrowed apron and tossed it onto a chair. "I'm so terrible about times. If it weren't for my secretary, I'd be a walking disaster. Maybe I'd better cancel with Joe."

"You have plenty of time," said Rose, amused. "Remember, it was me who organized your life before you had the luxury of a secretary. Go take a bath and put on a pretty face for Joe. Don't cancel."

Cautiously, Susannah said, "I'd like to."

"Why? He's so sweet!"

"I don't know," she murmured uncertainly. "I just—I don't feel safe with him, somehow."

"Not safe? Suzie, he's the kindest man I know!"

"It's not that," Susannah said quickly. "It's... Oh, I'm not sure. I feel funny—not quite in control, I suppose."

"What are you afraid of?"

Myself, Susannah wanted to say. She didn't feel like herself with Joe. She didn't feel in charge. But she plastered a smile on her face and said, "Oh, nothing. I just have a case of first-time nerves, I guess."

"There's only one way to get over those," Rose said. "Plunge right in and get it over with. Now, go make yourself beautiful. Joe deserves it."

Susannah didn't know what Joe Santori deserved, but she found herself running a hot bath and pouring some of her grandmother's bath salts into the water before stepping into the tub. While soaking there, Susannah smeared a marvelous cream she'd recently discovered on her face and was glad to see her skin emerge pink and smooth twenty minutes later.

"Anything to fight off the wrinkles a little longer," she murmured to her reflection in the steamed bathroom mirror. "I'm certainly not doing this for his benefit!"

But she couldn't imagine why she applied her makeup with extra care. After all, there was nothing in the wind between herself and Joe Santori.

"We're very different," she told her reflection in the mirror. "Completely different. We have nothing in common. Besides, he's bossy, and I hate that."

After standing over her small suitcase and lamenting her lack of nice clothing, Susannah reached for her jeans again and put on the bright sweater she'd bought at Gates that morning. She tucked the sweater into her jeans and clasped one of Rose's narrow gold belts around her waist. A simple gold necklace made the outfit special. The effect was casual enough for a movie, she decided, but had a dash of panache, too—just the right impression to give Joe. Susannah wanted him to think she had a lot of sophistication—and no time for a relationship with a small-town carpenter.

She combed her hair, studied it for a moment, then pulled it smoothly back from her face and pinned it so that the curl brushed the back of her neck. Without thinking, she spritzed some perfume on her throat, then scolded herself. "For heaven's sake, don't do anything that might give him the wrong impression!"

But she couldn't resist adding just a glimmer of extra lipstick before snapping off the lights and leaving her bedroom. At the bottom of the steps, Susannah sat down to pull on her boots.

Rose emerged from the kitchen, drying her hands in a towel. "Joe called. He wondered if you'd mind walking over to his house. He's running late. Something about another job he's working on."

Susannah grinned. "That's the difference between Tyler and the city. If a man asked me out to dinner there and couldn't be bothered to pick me up, I'd be annoyed."

Rose nodded. "But here it's just a courtesy. Do you mind?"

"Nope. The walk sounds nice."

"I figure he'd like you to meet his daughter, Gina."

"I met her already."

Rose laughed. "Well, she improves as you get to know her."

"I don't intend to get to know her, Granny Rose."

"Why not? She's a nice kid. Just talk about sports with Gina, and she'll warm up. You'll see what I mean." Rose kissed Susannah's cheek. "Enjoy yourself, dear."

With her boots and coat on, Susannah felt her courage fail, and she turned to her grandmother anxiously. "Are you sure you don't want me to stay with you tonight? You've had a busy day, after all—"

"Don't be silly! I took it easy today!" Rose protested heartily. "Now, run along and leave me alone."

"But—"

"But nothing. I'm used to living by myself. Have a wonderful time, dear. Keep an open mind."

With mixed feelings, Susannah left her grandmother and headed for Joe's house. She walked the distance quickly, her gloved hands tucked into the pockets of her coat to stay warm. The air was cold and crystalline, and the light scent of wood smoke that hung over Tyler should have calmed her nerves. Most of the houses along Susannah's route were already lit up with Christmas lights. At the large brick house on the next corner, the family had gone overboard, with a life-size illuminated Santa, four electronic elves, and a lighted Rudolph. Chipmunk Christmas carols blared out of a loudspeaker in one of the trees.

Susannah turned up the walk to Joe's house and marched for the front door, determined that her courage should not fail her now. The knocker was a hand-carved woodpecker. She lifted it and rapped three times.

Gina answered the door, and the smell of pizza emanated from behind her. "Oh, hi," she said to Susannah. "It's you again. My dad's on the phone."

"I'll wait," Susannah said sedately. "May I come in?"

"Sure." Gina pulled the door wide. "But I warn you, he's got a date tonight."

"I know," Susannah replied, cringing inside at the word *date.* She stepped into the house. "It's with me."

"With *you?*" Gina's face froze. "I thought you came back for— I didn't think he meant *you* were the hot number that—"

"Hot number?"

"He said...he was just joking, and I...jeez, I didn't think you were *dating* him when you were here before."

"I wasn't. I'm not. We're getting together for...well, to talk about my grandmother."

"That's not what Dad said."

The accusation in Gina's voice was unmistakable, and Susannah knew she wasn't pleased that her father was seeing Susannah socially. And maybe she didn't like the idea of her father seeing *anyone*. The resentment in Gina's glare shook Susannah, but she decided not to let the girl upset her.

"Is that a stove timer I hear?" she inquired calmly.

The unmistakable bell of the microwave oven carried to them from the kitchen. Gina hesitated, then slammed the door and bounded for the kitchen, sending a look over her shoulder that was far from friendly.

Susannah stood uncomfortably in the hallway, wondering if she should follow the teenager or stay put. From up the stairs came the recorded strains of opera music—a soprano belting out a song Susannah didn't recognize. The hallway was cluttered with all manner of teenage goods—a book bag abandoned on the floor, several pairs of shoes hopelessly heaped near the throw rug, a set of headphones and a basketball balanced on the chair by the stairs.

There were signs of Joe, too. His scruffy parka had been left on the newel post, and just looking at it caused Susannah to speculate on how warm and soft it might feel.

On the small table by the door stood some picture frames. Susannah peeked at them and found several images of Gina—in younger years—grinning at her. The largest photo was that of a woman with a cloud of dark hair and solemn brown eyes, who looked very much like Gina.

With a start, Susannah realized she was probably looking at Gina's mother, Joe's wife. Hastily, she stepped back from the photo display.

Gina poked her head around the kitchen doorway. "If you're hungry," she snapped, "Dad made some hors d'oeuvres. I'm supposed to give you some."

Hors d'oeuvres. Intrigued, Susannah took off her coat and followed Gina into the kitchen to sample Joe's idea of an appetizer. She hoped his daughter hadn't had time to poison them yet.

The kitchen smelled spicy. She recognized the scent of basil and rosemary—very Italian smells, in her mind. Although Joe's was a modern kitchen, it was very cluttered, with a startling variety of pots and pans hanging overhead, a rack of fancy bottled vinegars and the largest selection of wines Susannah had ever seen outside a restaurant. Joe had converted an old side porch into a wine closet, and all the bottles were labeled and meticulously dusted.

Gina pulled a tray out from under the broiler and set it on the tile countertop. "Here," she said. "Dad said you'd like these. I think they're gross."

Despite that recommendation, Susannah gingerly approached the tray. "Mushrooms!"

"Yeah, they came from Italy two days ago." Gina dropped her hot mitts on the counter. "We have relatives who keep smuggling stuff like that to us. They've got some kind of cheese and fish inside. Go ahead and try one, if you dare."

Susannah did try one and found the combination of flavors delectable. The stuffed mushrooms practically melted on her tongue. "Marvelous!"

"You want a glass of wine? My dad picked out a bottle."

"Thank you. That would be nice."

Although Gina's manner was determinedly insolent, the girl did know her manners. Susannah was impressed that she knew how to entertain a guest while waiting for her father. From a distant counter, Gina removed a bottle of red wine that had been breathing there. She poured a stemmed glass half-full and passed it to Susannah, who carried it to one of the stools at the counter, where she could nibble on the mushrooms.

Gina began to cut up a microwave pizza. She licked her fingers when she was finished and caught Susannah watching her. Sensing disapproval, she said, "I make my own dinner when Dad goes out. He doesn't like this microwaved stuff, but I do. And he *hates* pizza. He says it perpetuates a stereotype. But it's easy to make."

"I'm sure he appreciates your self-sufficiency."

Gina looked suspicious, as if not believing Susannah's compliment. "Yeah," she said.

Susannah had never spent much time around children. Teenagers were even more mystifying, for their mood swings seemed completely unpredictable. Susannah found herself at a loss for conversation. Sipping her wine—a dry, flavorful red—she tried to come up with a subject.

The local newspaper had been left open on the counter, and someone had circled a notice with red marker. Susannah reached for the paper.

"Oh, the Tinsel Ball," she said, reading the notice. "I remember that dance. It was the biggest event of the year, after the homecoming weekend."

Gina threw a murderous look at the paper. "Yeah. It's next week."

"Oh! You're going, I suppose?"

Gina toyed with her pizza, as if suddenly not very hungry. "I'm thinking about it."

"Do they still decorate the gym and bring in a fountain for the evening?"

Gina nodded coldly. "And two hundred poinsettia plants this year. It's going to be real pretty."

"When I was in ninth grade, I bought my first strapless dress," Susannah said, recalling the dance as if it had only happened a few months ago. "And, of course, a strapless bra to go with it. But I didn't quite fill out the bra, if you know what I mean. So it kept slipping down all night. The dress stayed in place, but the bra ended up around my waist, and I couldn't do anything about it!"

A small smile appeared on the girl's face, but disappeared again quickly. Gina said, "I have a hard time imagining any embarrassing stuff happening to somebody like you."

"Believe me, I have my share of embarrassing moments." *With your father, for example.* "Fortunately, my date didn't have the faintest idea anything was wrong. Who is your date going to be?"

Gina froze in the act of biting into her pizza. "My date?"

"Yes. Or don't girls need dates to go to the Tinsel Ball anymore?"

"Oh, I could go alone if I wanted to," Gina said, suddenly concentrating on a speck of cheese on her pizza crust. "But I'll have a date. I just haven't gotten around to... well, I've been busy, see."

Susannah did see. Gina didn't have a date yet. Sipping from her wineglass, Susannah said casually, "Well, sometimes it's hard waiting for the right boy to ask."

Gina's eyes blazed. "Oh, I could ask a boy myself, if I just...if I wanted to. But like I said, I've been pretty busy."

Susannah began to catch on. Casually, she picked at her mushroom and asked, "Who did you have in mind?"

Gina shrugged. "I dunno. I'll get around to asking somebody sooner or later." She bit into her pizza and chewed, eyeing Susannah as she ate. It was obvious that she was deciding how to handle the situation. Finally, after swallowing, Gina asked, "Did you invite my dad out tonight, or did he invite you?"

"Ah, he did the inviting."

Gina nodded thoughtfully. "Do you like him?"

Caught off guard, Susannah said automatically, "Why, yes, I do."

"He's kinda weird sometimes."

Warily, Susannah said, "He seems very nice."

"Do you like him a lot?" Gina pressed.

Susannah cleared her throat. "I've only just met him."

She couldn't guess what was going on in the teenager's mind, for Gina's face did not readily reveal her thoughts. The girl chewed her pizza, staring at Susannah for another long, contemplative moment. Then she said, "You're pretty nice."

"Why, thank you."

"My dad knows lots of nice ladies, but you're nicer than most."

"That's nice of you to say."

"But you know," Gina went on, "that he already has a girlfriend."

Susannah nearly choked on the bit of stuffed mushroom that suddenly lodged in the back of her throat.

She took a slug of wine, but it didn't help. She coughed.

Joe had a girlfriend? *Of course, you ninny,* she lectured herself. *A man as pleasant and attractive as Joe would naturally have a steady female friend. It's just surprising he has only one, when you think about it.*

When she could breathe again, Susannah looked at Gina through watery eyes. "Oh, really?" she managed to ask.

Gina nodded, looking decidedly pleased with herself. "Yeah, they've been going together for years. She's really pretty."

"I see."

"They go back a long way," Gina added. "And I like her a lot, too. Her name's, uh, Angelica. Yeah, that's it. Angelica."

"That's quite an unusual name," Susannah said vaguely, still recovering from the surprise.

Gina's brow puckered. "You think so?'

"Unusual, but very pretty."

Gina grinned. "Yeah, I think so, too."

Susannah ate another mushroom and told herself she shouldn't be disappointed. On the contrary, she should be thankful! Joe wasn't looking for companionship at all. He already had a relationship. Since he was already attached, Susannah thought she should feel relieved.

But, oddly enough, she didn't feel relief.

The mushrooms suddenly weren't so delicious anymore. She took another long swallow of wine but a persistent lump remained in her throat.

A whistle and the thud of footsteps on the carpeted stairs heralded Joe's arrival in the kitchen. He appeared a moment later, looking quite different in a blue button-down work shirt with a red knit tie and a clean pair of jeans. His hair was combed, his face was shaved, and he was every bit as dashing as before—just cleaned up. He looked tall and handsome and full of extraordinary vitality. Susannah's heart was suddenly kerthumping in her chest.

His grin was sexy and familiar as he scanned her outfit and returned his gaze to her face. It was a glance that turned Susannah to butter inside. "Hello, Miss Suzie," he said, his voice caressingly mellow. *What a voice!* "I'm sorry I took so long."

Susannah slid off her stool, wondering why she had to feel like such a gawky girl when he appeared. She couldn't remember a man ever making her feel so nervous. "Hello. Gina and I were just...we had a chance to chat."

"Great. Learn anything I ought to know?"

"Oh, Dad."

Joe laughed and gave his daughter's neck a fatherly squeeze. Susannah couldn't speak. For her, the moment was suddenly fraught with what might have been. *He's already got a life,* she said to herself. *And it doesn't include you.* She was surprised to find herself feeling very disappointed.

"Did you like the mushrooms?" Joe asked, turning on Susannah again.

She summoned a smile. "Yes, they're delicious. You're an accomplished cook."

"Don't give me the credit. It's the mushrooms."

"Gina said they came from your family in Italy."

He scooped one of the appetizers off the tray and popped it into his mouth with gusto. "They did indeed. I'm sure my relatives are breaking half a dozen laws by sending these all the time, but what can I do?

We might as well enjoy them before we get arrested by the customs agents. Here, have another."

"Oh, I've had enough—"

"You'd better have another," Joe warned. "The movie I want to see starts at seven-thirty. There's no time to eat before the show. Do you mind? I've been waiting for this one to come to town for a long time. I don't want to miss it."

"Sounds intriguing."

"Great." Another heart-stopping grin. "Then we can have a quick dinner afterward."

After what? Susannah wondered what kind of movie Joe Santori anticipated with such relish. Something with football players and car crashes? Tough guys getting thrown through glass windows? She managed a weak smile.

"We'll talk then," Joe promised. "And get to know each other."

The look he gave Susannah—long lashes drooping over smoldery dark eyes—positively crackled with implications. Susannah almost laughed nervously. How did he think he could get away with making bedroom eyes at her while his pretty Angelica lurked in the wings?

Susannah set her wineglass on the counter. "Shall we go?"

"Sure."

Joe wolfed down one more mushroom and indicated the front door with his outstretched hand. Susannah started to leave, then turned back to face the teenager. "It was nice to talk with you, Gina."

The girl looked startled for a second, and Susannah realized she had caught her in an unguarded moment. For a second, Gina had been smiling with great delight at some inner joke. But she quickly collected herself and said, "Nice talking with you, too, Mrs. Atkins."

"Miss," Joe corrected. "Or is it Ms.?"

"I'd rather be Susannah."

Gina was blushing by that time. "Okay, Susannah. See you around."

"Thanks for the snacks and drink."

Momentarily puzzled by the girl, Susannah walked to the front door and picked up her coat from the chair where she'd left it. Smoothly, Joe took the coat from her hands and helped her into it. She turned around to face him while she fastened the buttons. "Your daughter is very nice."

Joe grinned and kept his voice low. "Sometimes. That kid will be the death of me yet."

"Oh?"

"I think I'm raising a pathological liar. Or a professional athlete." Joe stopped Susannah's hands, for she had begun to do up the buttons crookedly. As if they had known each other for years, he pushed her hands away and buttoned her coat himself, saying, "She plays every sport offered at her school—at the loss of her study time."

Susannah felt a little breathless when his gentle touch seemed to linger over her breasts. She said, "Gina seems very bright and—and attractive."

"The brightness came from her mother," said Joe, finishing the buttons. "But the attractive part is purely from my side of the family."

Susannah found herself smiling up at him in the shadowy hallway. "And the humble part?"

"None of us are humble," Joe replied.

They stood toe to toe for a long moment, and Susannah held her breath. With Joe's hands still on her coat, it was a simple matter for him to tug her even closer. She did not resist. Nor did she try to stop him when he slowly bent closer yet and pressed a warm kiss on her mouth. Susannah didn't pull away, although she'd been caught off guard. Her brain commanded her to step back, but she found she couldn't obey. His kiss was warm and gentle, and the sensations that suddenly bubbled up from inside her were pleasantly exciting. Before she knew it, she was standing on tiptoe and kissing him back, eyes closed and every nerve ending alight.

Then he released her gently, setting her back down on her heels.

"What was that for?" she whispered.

"I'm not sure. I thought you wanted it."

"I thought *you* wanted it."

"Well, no harm done, right?" He grinned and ran one fingertip down her cheek—a touch that was quick and light, but just as powerful as a punch. Susannah swayed and caught her breath.

Obviously aware of his effect on her, Joe flashed her another smile as he turned to the closet to find his own coat. It was a navy duffel coat, warm and serviceable. He slid into it while ushering Susannah out the front door.

"'Night, Gina!" he called back into the house.

"'Night, Daddy! Have fun!"

"We'll be back before eleven."

"I'll study till then."

Joe laughed under his breath and shook his head. "See what I mean?" he said to Susannah. "The kid lies like a rug."

"Maybe she really will study," said Susannah, relieved to have something to talk about.

"*Sports Illustrated*, no doubt. But it *is* Saturday night." Joe took her arm quite naturally as they started down the porch steps together. "I hope you don't mind riding in my pickup."

"I could have driven my car. . . ."

"I like to be behind the wheel."

"You like to be the boss," Susannah shot back lightly.

"My wife used to say I'd make a good president, except that I'd have to do everything myself."

Susannah appreciated the tight pressure of Joe's grip on her arm. It made her feel secure, even brave. "I saw a photo of your wife in the hallway. She was lovely."

"Yes, she was," Joe said promptly. "In lots of ways. I still miss her."

Susannah was surprised to hear him speak so bluntly and unselfconsciously, but it was a pleasant quality in a man. She let him guide her to his pickup truck, parked in the driveway by the garage. It looked battered and well-used, but when Susannah slid into the passenger seat she noticed the vehicle was clean and as carefully maintained as everything else in Joe's life. He closed the door and walked around the truck, humming.

The drive to the theater took twenty minutes, for it was located in the next town, Belton. Joe drove sedately and asked Susannah a few questions about her grandmother and the house repairs he was going to make. Those were safe subjects, and Susannah was glad to answer him—glad he wasn't making her uncomfortable by talking about the spontaneous kiss that had happened in his hallway. She wasn't quite sure what had happened, since she didn't usually allow such familiarities on a first date. But Joe was unusual. Definitely unusual.

During the ride, Susannah was glad Joe had to keep his eyes on the road—and off her. It gave her time to relax. While he drove, she stole glances at his profile, illuminated by the dashboard lights. In the half-light, she decided, he was even more attractive than ever. His dramatic profile and curly hair were those of an operatic hero.

And his voice in the small confines of the truck—! His laughter tingled in her ears, and his quiet murmurs sent shivers of some nameless emotion quivering into the deepest recesses of Susannah's body.

What does he have up his sleeve? she wondered. *If he's already got a lady friend, why is he taking the time to get to know me? Is he trying to reach the same kinds of conclusions about me that I'm trying to reach about him?*

The theater lay midway along the main street, and Joe found a parking space a block away.

"The movie's not going to attract a big crowd," he said, slipping the truck into the space.

"Oh?" With some apprehension, Susannah asked, "What movie are we seeing?"

"Didn't I tell you? It's *La Traviata.*"

"What?" Susannah asked, surprised that he'd mentioned the name of an opera. Surely some hotshot Hollywood filmmaker had given the same name to a karate movie. Susannah asked apprehensively, "What's it about?"

"It's an opera. Oh, don't worry. It's got subtitles," Joe assured her, surprising the heck out of Susannah. "It's had mixed reviews, but who cares about the production values and acting? It's the music I love." He sang a couple of bars, then looked at Susannah with brows raised. "You do like opera, don't you?"

She couldn't stop a smile. "I know very little about opera."

He blinked at her in amazement. "You're kidding. Not even *La Bohème? The Barber of Seville?*"

"I'm sorry." Susannah spread her hands helplessly. "When I think of opera, I think of huge women wearing braids and Viking helmets. I'm almost completely ignorant. But not," she said hastily, "unwilling to learn. It sounds like fun."

His gaze grew warm again. "Aha. At last, a willing pupil. Gina refuses to appreciate opera. But tonight, Miss Suzie, you will be transported."

And she was, in a limited way. The tiny theater—one of four that the old Belton cinema had been remodeled into—was completely empty except for one elderly man wearing a Siberian fur hat, which he didn't take off during the entire movie. Joe felt free, therefore, to whisper occasional asides to Susannah during the two-hour presentation.

The music was magnificent, she had to admit. And thanks to the subtitles, Susannah could follow the plot without too much difficulty. Joe explained the subtleties of the story and characters, and Susannah appreciated his soft murmurings in her ear when things became confusing.

"It was wonderful!" she declared when the credits had rolled and even the man in the Siberian hat had left the theater.

"You're not just saying that? I know opera can be an acquired taste."

"I enjoyed it very much," she said honestly as they climbed into their coats and drifted out the rear doors with the crowd coming out of a more popular movie. "How did you come to love opera so much?"

"My father was a tenor."

"A tenor? You mean a real opera singer?" Susannah was astonished.

"Yes, a real singer." Joe grinned at her expression. "He performed all over the world. Not in the largest concert halls in the most important roles, but he did have a respectable career. His favorite role was *Don Giovanni.* He sang in Venice twice—probably his career highlight."

"My goodness, how wonderful! And you followed in his footsteps?"

"Not exactly." Joe's smile grew nostalgic. "I didn't have what it took. And my father died when I was quite young. I never really knew him well, to tell the truth. But I listened to his recordings for hours and that's how I picked up most of what I know."

"I've heard you sing," Susannah said shyly. "You sound marvelous to me."

"Thank you, Miss Suzie, but I know my limitations. I'm afraid the only performances I'll ever give will be in the shower."

"You're better than that," Susannah said, but she did not press him further. As they got back into Joe's truck, she asked with genuine curiosity, "Will you tell me more about your family?"

He talked offhandedly during the ride back to Tyler, telling Susannah about his younger brothers and a sister who all lived in Chicago. His mother was also living, for she had married young. Her husband, Joe said, had been twenty years her senior, but she—a young girl in Palermo—had fallen madly in love with him and married the older Italian-American man despite her family's objections. He'd brought her to the States and fathered four children. When he died at the age of forty-seven, she raised their children singlehandedly, without benefit of any life insurance policies. Joe's father, it seemed, had gambled away most of his earnings as a small-time opera star.

"It was tough on her," Joe said, "but I don't think my mother would have it any other way. She likes to work. Even now, she helps out in soup kitchens, and at the church, teaching English to immigrants."

"She must be a remarkable woman."

"She is."

"And your brothers and sister? Do any of them sing?"

"No, we had all seen the underside of the glamorous life," Joe said without a trace of bitterness. "None of us wanted a career in music. My brothers all work with their hands—Carlo is a stonemason, Anthony owns an auto body shop that specializes in foreign cars and Frank is a sculptor. My sister Gina is a chef in a restaurant."

"You named your daughter after your sister."

"My wife did, actually. She and Gina were friends and grew up together. That's how I met Marie in the first place. She came home with Gina all the time when we were kids."

"So you married your childhood sweetheart?"

"I guess so," Joe replied, in a tone that indicated he had ventured as far as he wanted to go into that story for one night.

"So how did you end up in Tyler?" Susannah asked.

"Oh, that's not a very interesting tale. I had been a carpenter in Chicago, but I didn't like working for somebody else. I didn't like working for the crooked operations, and that's just about all there was at that time. I went to night school and became an engineer so I could get into another line of work. After Marie died, I needed a change of scenery, so I shopped around for another job and ended up applying at Ingalls Farm and Machinery. It was the best offer I had, so I came."

"But you didn't last at Ingalls, I notice."

He sent her a smile. "I didn't, did I? I guess I still hadn't gotten over that part about working for somebody else. I started moonlighting—doing fix-up jobs. Pretty soon I was swamped with calls from people who wanted me to build them something, so I started working for myself."

"And you've done pretty well, I understand."

He laughed. "Oh, I'm keeping one step ahead of the bankers. And I'm putting a little money away for Gina's education, so I feel pretty comfortable."

"Sounds like your life is in order."

"Well," said Joe, "I won't go that far."

Joe was surprised to find himself talking so freely to Susannah Atkins, of all people. He had expected to be attracted by her all evening—especially after that first glimpse of her standing in his kitchen in her fire-engine-red sweater and snug jeans. But he hadn't expected to find her such a good listener. She seemed truly intrigued by the things he talked about.

But good conversation went two ways, so he switched the subject. "How about you?" he asked. "How come you left Tyler?"

Susannah sighed and gazed out the truck window for a moment. Her pensive look had a melancholy quality all of a sudden, and Joe wondered if he'd inadvertently said something to upset her.

"I'm not even sure now why I left," she said musingly. "To look for something I couldn't find at home, I guess."

"Did you find it?"

"I wasn't sure what to look for. I'm still not."

"What is 'it,' exactly?"

"My life," she said wistfully. "Things you already have—work and family and your interest in opera, things that you value. But I . . . well, sometimes I think I've botched things along the way. Despite my success, I haven't really got what I want out of life."

CHAPTER SEVEN

HE HEARD HER LAUGH abruptly, as if uncomfortable with the intimacy of the moment. "Oh, that sounded pathetic, didn't it?"

"Not really." Still serious, Joe said, "Sounded like you'd like to make some changes."

Susannah was silent for a little longer, and Joe glanced at her. She looked thoughtful and said, "I would, but I'm not sure how."

"A woman with your kind of success ought to know how to unbotch her life."

She smiled sideways at him, shyly. "You'd think so, wouldn't you? But I can't help feeling sometimes that my... my success, as you call it, was just accidental."

Joe snorted. "Are you kidding?"

"Lots of people could do what I do. It's not that difficult to conduct my program."

"I couldn't do it. In fact, I don't know anybody who could. You've got the right combination of looks and brains and personality."

"You've seen my show?"

"Who hasn't? Oh, I admit I'm not a regular viewer, but I've caught bits and pieces over the years. It's neat."

"Well, thanks. I guess I'm feeling inadequate these days."

Joe mulled that over for half a mile and suddenly found himself driving into Tyler. "Hungry?"

Susannah smiled. "Yes."

"I meant to take you out to the Heidelberg, but it's getting late. How about a burger at Marge's?"

"It's exactly what I'm in the mood for."

Joe parked and they walked across the street to the diner. Though it was Saturday night, the small restaurant wasn't that crowded. A family of four sat at one table, empty dessert plates in front of them while they chatted, and there was the usual contingent of high school kids. Only one waitress was on duty, and between customers she was filling salt and pepper shakers by the counter.

Joe took Susannah's coat and hung it with his own on the rack by the door, then went to join her at the booth nearest the front window. From that vantage point, they'd be able to look out at the street and see the corner of Gates Department Store. As usual, the store windows were beautifully decorated for the season.

But the department store windows couldn't have rivaled the front window of Marge's Diner at that moment. In her red sweater and touches of gold, with her soft blond hair and gentle expression, Susannah Atkins could have been a young Mrs. Claus as she gazed out at the snowy street.

Her eyes looked so dreamy that when Joe approached the table, he couldn't help asking, "What are you thinking about, Miss Suzie?"

She turned to him and smiled guiltily. "Onion rings."

Joe laughed and slid into the seat opposite her. "I imagined you were dreaming about Christmas in your hometown."

"That, too," she said. "Food was a big part of the holidays when I was growing up. We made cookies by the truckload, not to mention a goose and all the trimmings. But just now I was thinking of my mother's onion rings. They were works of art."

"Then we'll have onion rings tonight," Joe declared, waving off the menus when the waitress approached. "The lady and I would like to have hamburgers, onion rings and—what else? A milkshake?"

"No, no, just coffee for me."

"Coffee for the lady, and I'll have a milkshake. Chocolate, please. And do you have any pie left tonight?"

The waitress smiled. "Pumpkin."

"Perfect. Save me a piece."

Snapping her notebook closed, the waitress sketched a salute. "Consider it saved. Your dinner will be just a couple of minutes, Mr. Santori."

When the young woman was gone, Joe leaned his elbows on the table to drink in Susannah's face. She smiled back at him, no longer tentatively, but with a genuine gleam of pleasure in her eyes. It almost took his breath away, until he remembered he should be cautious with her.

"So tell me about yourself," he said. "Tell me about growing up in Tyler."

It took some coaxing, but Susannah talked. She explained the circumstances of her youth—her mother's early widowhood, then her death from an illness Susannah did not divulge. Although clearly regretful of losing her mother and father, Susannah appeared to be devoted to her grandmother, who'd taken custody of Susannah when she was ten. As Joe listened, he began to wonder if Rose Atkins had perhaps shielded her sensitive granddaughter from many things during her youth. From the sounds of it, Susannah had led a very sheltered childhood.

Unlike many girls from small towns, she had not gone off to college and lost her head when confronted with so much freedom. On the contrary, she had devoted herself to studying and had graduated with a teaching degree.

"But jobs in home economics were hard to come by, so I took a part-time gofer's job at the television station."

Joe nearly choked on his hamburger. "A gopher's job?"

With a smile, she said, "Sure. I was the one they sent to 'go for' coffee or 'go for' paper clips or anything else they needed."

Joe nodded. "I get it. And someone discovered you sitting in the station commissary in a tight sweater and made you a star, right?"

Susannah laughed. She was eating her meal with gusto, but rather than munching on her hamburger like the average human being, she broke it into little pieces and nibbled them bit by bit. It was very dainty and highly erotic, Joe decided. He couldn't take his eyes off her fingertips, her lips, the small flashes of her even white teeth. She was mesmerizingly delicate.

"Nobody made me a star but myself," she said. "One day the woman who did the weather report on the noon news didn't show up. She had gotten a better offer from another station and left without telling anyone—she left a letter of resignation on the boss's desk, but of course it got lost. So I stood in for her at the last minute, because I was the only female working at the station and the weather forecast *had* to be done by a woman in those days."

"You must have been pretty good."

"Not bad," she said modestly. "After a few months, I suggested trying a household-hints segment on the noon news."

"Your idea? It must have taken some guts to propose it."

"You better believe it." She smiled, slightly flushed. "The station was run by very grouchy men, but I was too young to be afraid of failing. Anyway, the household-hint thing took off like a rocket. My popularity grew, and the grouchy men gave me my own show when a soap opera got canceled."

"And the rest is history. 'Oh, Susannah!' became a hit."

She nodded. "It took years to build the audience, but it was a modest success from the start."

"Thanks to your personality, I think."

Susannah laughed. "Are you kidding?"

"No, I'm not. You come across as very warm on television—genuine. You're a small-town girl who's made it big, but you haven't forgotten what it's like to share recipes with your neighbors or make do with homemade things instead of running off to the nearest store to buy something."

She cocked her head. "That's very perceptive of you. I try to think of my viewers as my friends and neighbors. It's the only way I can make it all work."

That was interesting. Joe asked, "What do you mean?"

She concentrated on her hamburger again, clearly thinking about what she had said. "I have never put it into words," she answered at last, "but the whole television milieu feels false. I have to be perky to a camera instead of a real person, and sometimes it's... well, I have trouble keeping my energy up. But when I think of all the people who are out there watching..." She smiled shyly. "Oh, it's silly."

"No, it's not."

"I remind myself that my viewers are my closest friends, that's all."

Joe considered what Susannah said, and his thoughts must have shown on his face, because she asked, "What's the matter?"

He shook his head. "Oh, I was just thinking how sad that sounds. As if you don't have many real friends."

"I do," she countered at once, but she didn't sound convincing. Darting a look at Joe she amended, "Well, I have few close friends, but I'm very busy, you see. My job keeps me extremely busy."

"So you said before."

"I'm fine, really," she insisted, having heard the dry edge in his voice. "My secretary, Josie, is an invaluable help, and I muddle along pretty well. I wouldn't have my life any other way."

"What you mean," Joe said slowly, "is that you can't figure out any other way to have it."

Susannah stared at him for a few seconds, and during that time, he began to believe he'd overstepped his rights. But she looked away and picked at her hamburger again. "Maybe you're right," she said softly. "I'm on a treadmill."

"And you can't get off?"

She shrugged. "I'm not completely sure I *should* get off. What if I stop working and my life doesn't get any better?"

"Maybe you should consider slowing down a little, instead of quitting."

"I can't," Susannah objected. "If I don't give one hundred percent, the show will fail. I can't let everybody down."

"You're responsible for everyone else?"

"Yes, in a way. A lot of people have jobs because of me. If I stop making the 'Oh, Susannah!' shows, they'll be out of work. I can't do that to the people I've come to think of as my family. Why, my cameraman would be fired if I quit, and Josie might never get her shot at the big time."

"Doesn't it seem strange for a woman like yourself to have a cameraman of her own instead of a child?"

Susannah's expression hardened. "I'd make a terrible mother."

"I doubt that."

"You do?" Sarcasm dripped from her words. "Well, I'm sure you're right, Mr. Santori. You know me so well, after all."

"I know you well enough," Joe replied, unruffled by her anger. "You're smart and caring and—"

"You know nothing about me!"

"I know—"

"You're getting bossy again," she said sharply. "You can ask me to come look after my grandmother and you can force her to fix up her house, perhaps, but you can't step into my life and know what's good for me."

"You're telling me to mind my own business?"

"Yes."

"All right," Joe said, without heat, "but before I shut up, I have one more comment, okay?"

"Just one?" she asked archly.

"Yep." He leaned forward, elbows on the table. "This is it—why don't you take a leave of absence for a while and try something else? College professors take sabbaticals, don't they? Hell, even carpenters take a little time off now and then. Just take a break for a bit and look around you. Look for something you'd rather do with your life."

"Are you always so full of advice?" she asked. "Or do I bring out that quality in you?"

Joe grinned, sure in his heart that she wasn't furious with him. "I'm always full of advice. But you seem to need it more than most people."

Susannah laughed abruptly. "Maybe you're right. I need a keeper most of the time."

"A keeper?"

"Somebody to keep me on track. Usually it's my secretary. Sometimes it's Granny Rose. Sometimes I long to be more independent, but I'd be a disaster on my own."

"I have a hard time working for somebody besides myself."

She smiled into his eyes. "Because you'd always have a better way of doing things, right?"

He laughed, too. "Exactly right!"

"I know what you mean. Once in a while I think I'd like to be my own person. On television, I have to conform to the station's standards and ideas in everything I do. I am constantly edited, and sometimes it really goes against my grain."

"I can understand that."

She eyed him thoughtfully. "I think you do. But I've also come to realize that I need more structure than most people. That's why I'd be a disaster as an author, for example."

"Would you like to be an author?"

"Sure, who wouldn't? And I've got some good ideas for books—books that would spring from my television show. Like Martha Stewart or Heloise. But I'd never cope with the deadlines."

"You never know until you try."

Nodding emphatically, she said, "Yes, I know my own work habits. They're atrocious. I can't keep a schedule. I get too caught up in the details and miss the big picture. That's why I need a producer and a secretary. But I have good ideas and I can implement them as long as I have the support staff. I'd like to expand my horizons, try new things, get a second chance at...well, at some things I've missed out on. But I'd need a lot of help."

"So hire some people. Write your book, if that's what you want."

Her eyes sparkled when she smiled. "If I thought I could make a living by writing, that would be ideal. Maybe I'd have time to look around a little, to enjoy life more."

"And you'd be great at selling books, too. I'm sure you'd be a hit on all the national talk shows."

"I can plug as well as anybody," she said with a hint of pride.

"You could do a series of books."

"Why not? Weddings and holidays, crafts to do at home, maybe a book on activities for children."

Joe enjoyed the animation in her face as Susannah let her imagination begin to roll. She looked prettier than ever, and full of optimism.

"My first book would have to be terrific, wouldn't it? To make a big enough splash."

"I'll bet you come up with something," he predicted, feeling absurdly glad that she had come to the conclusion that writing a book wasn't in the realm of total fantasy. Susannah looked happy as they sat at the table and finished their meal.

But then she glanced at her watch and reacted with surprise at the time. "Goodness, it's late!"

Joe checked his watch, too, and hastily agreed to depart. A pang of guilt caught him off guard. He hadn't planned to keep her lingering over the meal, but they had allowed the conversation to carry them along. Joe paid the dinner check at the cash register and took Susannah's arm to leave. It felt natural to touch her, he noted. It felt very good, in fact.

As Joe handed her into his truck again, Susannah found herself feeling strangely at ease with him.

This is a man I could really fall for, she said to herself, watching as he waved goodbye to the waitress through the window of Marge's Diner. *He's sweet and considerate and funny and—oh, damn, he's taken. I hope Angelica knows how good she's got it.*

Reminding herself of Joe's existing relationship, Susannah allowed herself to be drawn into only superficial conversation as he drove her back to her grandmother's house. He appeared not to notice her change of heart and again talked idly about the repairs he intended to make to the old house. He was back on a safe subject, Susannah noticed.

Maybe he felt the possibilities, too, she thought. Perhaps Joe had felt comfortable with her all evening and had enjoyed himself as much as she had enjoyed being with him. Also reminded of his commitment to Angelica, he had backed off.

Nice guy.

Susannah didn't wait for him to get out of the truck and open her door. When he appeared at her side of the vehicle, she was already standing on the pavement, shivering slightly.

"Thanks for a very nice evening," she said, holding her ground and determined not to allow him to see her to the door of the house. "I enjoyed myself very much."

He took her arm without ceremony and guided her up the sidewalk. "My pleasure. I always jump at the chance to introduce someone to the joys of opera."

"And the hamburgers were wonderful. I'd forgotten how good they are at Marge's."

He gave her a grin. "You're a woman of mixed tastes, Miss Suzie. I like that."

Their gazes met, and Susannah stumbled on the sidewalk. Joe steadied her instinctively, turning her body so that they stood face-to-face at the bottom of the porch steps. His hands were firm on her arms.

"You're shivering, Miss Suzie."

His voice would have warmed the bones of any woman alive, but Susannah couldn't seem to control the trembling of her limbs. "It's a cold night."

With one hand, he pulled the scarf from around his own neck and draped it loosely around Susannah's shoulders. His long fingers brushed through her hair for an instant.

"Better?"

"I should... I'll just go inside. I'll be warm in a few moments."

"I can think of a faster way."

Susannah wasn't sure how it happened. One minute she was a perfectly sensible woman standing at the bottom of her grandmother's porch steps, and the next minute she could hardly breathe for the tautness in her chest, the pounding pressure building in her throat, the dizzy sensation in her head as Joe bent closer.

"Joe..."

He brushed his lips along her hairline—so gently that Susannah went weak in the knees. "Yes, Miss Suzie?"

"Joe," she said again, then found she couldn't say anything more.

He murmured her name again and lowered his head until their lips were a scant inch apart. Susannah sensed his smile—a very sexy smile—and she couldn't resist. In another heartbeat, her fingers crept up his chest. That touch communicated her willingness, and Joe gave a low laugh. Susannah tilted her face up to his and found the velvety warmth of his gaze on hers. She let out a shaky sigh, then closed her eyes. An instant later, their mouths met in a soft, warm kiss.

Susannah's mind seemed to fill with a wonderful, sensual fog. She clung to his tall frame, taking pleasure in the strength of his arms and the powerful muscle that tightened beneath her caress. Joe's body felt alive and manly, and his kiss communicated a kind of hunger that was very exciting.

As if some other woman had suddenly come alive inside her, Susannah found herself kissing Joe back with all her heart. She reveled in the sensations evoked by the press of his belly against her own. The powerful hardness of his thighs radiated through their clothing, and Susannah savored their contour. Was there a sexier man on earth? She doubted it.

But what about Angelica?

Her inner voice interrupted with a mental shout that made Susannah jerk in Joe's embrace. The kiss ended abruptly, and Susannah's heart began to pound anew.

Yes, what about Angelica? She wanted to ask him then and there.

But she didn't. She pushed her way out of Joe's yielding embrace and tottered up the steps. Although afraid to look back, Susannah knew Joe was watching her.

"Sweet dreams, Miss Suzie."

That voice. So rich and vibrant. He could turn a woman's bones to butter with it. Hastily, Susannah let herself into the house, hoping she'd heard the last of that voice for one night.

But, of course, she'd probably dream about it all night long.

TUCKED IN HER BED upstairs, Rose heard the front door close quietly and quickly reached across her nightstand to snap off the light.

But Susannah appeared at her door a few minutes later and tapped lightly. She whispered, "I saw your light, Granny Rose. I know you're still awake."

Rose flipped on her light again and sat up in bed. "I wasn't waiting up for you, Suzie. Honestly, I wasn't."

Susannah stepped into the room, smiling. "How are you feeling?"

"Fine," Rose said at once. "I dozed for a while, but woke up again and decided I might as well sleep in my bed as on the parlor sofa. So I came up here and put on my nightgown, but suddenly I'm wide awake."

Susannah looked at her askance. "And you couldn't wait to hear how our evening went, could you?"

"Do you blame me? You two aren't exactly kindred spirits."

"Then why are you trying to get us together?" Susannah sat down on the edge of the bed, looking genuinely puzzled as well as amused. "I don't understand, Granny Rose. We're complete opposites."

"But do you like him?"

"Well, yes, he's very nice, I suppose—"

"And he likes you?"

"Yes, but that doesn't make up for everything else, you know." Susannah's pretty brow puckered in a frown. "He's...I'm...we're... Oh, I don't know how to say it without sounding like a snob. We're just different, that's all."

But meant for each other, Rose wanted to say. But she kept quiet. She couldn't explain her desire to see Susannah settled and happy. She couldn't describe the sudden urge within herself, as if someone had started a clock ticking and there wasn't much time left. Rose had always wanted everything for Susannah, and there seemed to be only one thing left for her talented granddaughter to achieve—a happy home and family to go along with the career and busy life.

Rose reached out for Susannah's hand, remembering the many nights during her granddaughter's teenage years that they had sat exactly this way—with Rose in bed and Susannah coming home from a date looking lovely and a little windblown. She asked, "Did you have a good time with Joe tonight?"

"Yes."

"Care to tell me about it?"

Susannah made a fuss of smoothing the bedclothes and didn't answer.

"Oh-ho," said Rose when the silence stretched. "It was that good, was it?"

Susannah blushed. "It was fine. It wasn't bad, I mean, but it... oh, I'm not sure how it was." She gave a flustered sigh. "We saw a wonderful movie—an opera—and he explained things as it went along. He's quite an expert—something I didn't expect, I guess. We had a hamburger at Marge's afterward, and we got along very well. He told me a lot about himself."

"And?"

Susannah turned her head to avoid meeting her grandmother's eyes. Her voice tightened. "What he didn't tell me about was his girlfriend. Gina told me about her."

That news struck Rose like a lightning bolt. For a moment, she was dazed. "What girlfriend?"

"A woman by the name of Angelica something. Gina said Joe has been seeing her for quite some time." Judging by the way Susannah suddenly leaned forward and began rearranging the clutter on the nightstand, Rose guessed she wasn't the least bit happy to have learned about Joe's love life.

Rose frowned, thinking. "Angelica? There's nobody in Tyler by that name."

"No? Well, she must be from Belton or Bonneville then."

"Could be." Rose frowned. "Well, that changes things, doesn't it?"

"Not really," Susannah said curtly. She got up and began to pace the small bedroom. "I don't really care. I don't care whether or not Joe Santori is married to Elizabeth Taylor or Betty Boop."

"Right. And the moon is made of green cheese."

"Granny Rose!"

"Well, I'm not blind," Rose protested. "Any fool can see the two of you are perfect for each other."

Susannah threw up her hands. "He's already got a steady friend—if Gina is to be believed, that is. Besides, I'm certainly in no position to start any kind of relationship."

"Oh, stop sounding like a guest on a talk show. Be honest. Joe's just what you need—steady and responsible, yet full of fun and very sexy, if you ask me. Don't laugh! I know what I'm talking about. And you're both consenting adults who've reached a certain level of maturity. . . ."

Susannah started to laugh. "Is that a polite way of saying we're both getting on?"

"You're only as old as you feel. It's a cliché that happens to be true. Do you feel old when you're with Joe?"

"No," she admitted. "But you can't go around matchmaking for him, Granny Rose, because he's not free. At least, that's the way it sounds."

Rose contemplated the situation and decided she needed more time to think. An unexpected wrinkle never stopped her for long, and Rose had come to the conclusion that she wanted to see her granddaughter spend more time with Joe Santori. A lot more time.

But she needed to think things through first.

"Well," she said briskly, "let's not settle this business tonight. You must be tired, and we've got a busy day ahead of us tomorrow."

"All right, I'll leave you alone." Susannah headed for the door again, then turned back. "You're truly feeling all right, Granny Rose? I felt very bad about leaving you alone tonight."

"Nonsense, dear. I'm accustomed to being on my own. Sleep well."

Susannah smiled, but Rose detected a hint of sadness in her eyes before she turned away and slipped out of the room. Perhaps, Rose guessed, Susannah had begun to recognize her need for a life outside the television studio. Joe Santori had given her a glimpse of what happiness could be.

Rose turned off her light again and nestled down in the bed, listening to the small sounds Susannah made as she prepared for the night.

Before I die, I want to be sure Susannah is happy, she thought just before she went to sleep.

In the morning, Rose woke up late and felt decidedly sluggish. She wanted to roll over and go back to sleep, but she heard noises in the kitchen and eventually worked up the energy to go downstairs. She found Susannah already preparing breakfast for the two of them. Her granddaughter had made tea in a big pot and fussed over Rose as she sat down at the table in her bathrobe. No mention was made of Joe Santori, and Susannah seemed content to bustle about the kitchen chatting.

"What about your vacation plans?" Rose asked as she sipped tea from the cup Susannah had poured for her. "Have you talked to Roger?"

"I'll call him later today," Susannah promised. "He likes to sleep in on Sundays. In the meantime, I'd like to help you get ready for the holidays. What can I do?"

Party preparations were one of Rose's favorite pastimes. She warmed to the subject eagerly. "Well, after church, I was hoping you'd come up to the attic with me and go through the Christmas decorations."

Susannah laughed. "That sounds like an all-day expedition. Of course, I'll do it. You shouldn't be climbing around up there."

"I do it all the time. And tomorrow, if you're still in town, how about getting me a Christmas tree? I can't start decorating the parlor until I have a proper tree. Would you take me shopping for one?"

"Of course!"

Susannah finished making breakfast, then sat down at the table. As they ate, they made more plans. When she'd washed the dishes and wiped off the countertops, they both went upstairs to dress for church.

The rest of the day passed peacefully enough, and Rose decided Susannah was enjoying getting back into the swing of life in Tyler. At the church service, she chatted with several of Rose's friends from the Quilting Circle and received warm welcomes back to town. After church, she drove her grandmother home for a light lunch of leftover tuna salad on toast.

The afternoon was spent rummaging in the attic for Christmas decorations. And once Susannah had carried the boxes downstairs, it was impossible not to open them and start spreading Christmas cheer all over the house. Rose loved seeing her home swathed in its Christmas finery.

The house was particularly suited to the Christmas season because of its large windows, handsome woodwork and long staircase. With pleasure, Rose helped Susannah place candles in all the windows and hang a red-wreathed hunting horn on the front door. Later she'd make a garland of evergreen bows, laden with fruit and nuts, to twine around the staircase railing.

Around three o'clock, the telephone rang, and Rose picked up the receiver to hear Joe Santori's voice on the other end of the line.

"Hi, Mrs. A.," he said cheerfully. "How are you feeling?"

"Why is my health suddenly so interesting to everyone?" she growled. "Was my picture on the front page of the newspaper this week or something?"

Joe laughed. "I must have missed that issue." He made conversation for a while and finally got around to asking about the house repairs. He listened to Rose's wishes and gave her some ballpark prices for certain items. Then he asked after Susannah.

"Is she still there?" he asked Rose.

"Why? Did you think you scared her out of town last night?"

He chuckled. "It would take more than me to chase Miss Suzie out of anywhere she wanted to be. She's quite a woman."

"I agree," Rose declared. "Would you like to talk to her?"

"Please."

Rose called Susannah to the phone and left the kitchen so her granddaughter could have some privacy. Judging by Susannah's bright eyes as she accepted the receiver, however, Rose guessed she didn't mind talking to Joe.

But Rose didn't get a chance to find out what transpired during their call. Mrs. Dahlstrom appeared at the front door with a plate of warm cookies, saying she'd been baking that day and wanted to share her new recipe. Rose ended up talking with her friend for nearly an hour, and Susannah joined them without commenting on her talk with Joe. Then they finished decorating, and ate a light supper sitting in front of the television, watching "60 Minutes."

By evening, Rose was pleasantly tired and had forgotten about Joe.

"So we'll get a tree tomorrow?" she asked over cups of hot cocoa before bedtime. She sipped from her cup while Susannah meticulously arranged the hand-carved figurines in the crèche.

"First thing in the morning, if that's what you want," Susannah promised.

"Early bird catches the worm—or the nicest Christmas trees."

"I wonder," Susannah said slowly and with studied nonchalance, "if you'd mind if we ran another errand while we're out?"

"I don't mind at all. What kind of errand?"

Rose noticed that Susannah kept her face turned away as she adjusted a few of the shepherds and said, "I accidentally came home with Joe's scarf on last night. I'd like to return it to him."

"Sounds like fun," Rose said after just a split second's hesitation. "I'd like to see how you two behave around each other."

Susannah sat up straight and looked mortified. "Granny Rose, don't you dare embarrass me in front of Joe!"

Rose laughed. "Would I do such a thing to you, Suzie?"

"If it suited your purposes, yes!"

Still chuckling, Rose carried their empty cups toward the kitchen. "If I didn't know you better, darling, I'd say you were a little nervous about seeing Joe again."

"Why would you say a thing like that?"

"Because you just put the donkey in the manger!"

CHAPTER EIGHT

In the car the next morning, Rose decided she couldn't put off breaking the news to Susannah any longer.

After they were both buckled into their seat belts and Susannah was reaching for the ignition, Rose said, "I took the liberty of butting into your life, darling, by calling the Santori house this morning."

Susannah dropped the car keys. "Granny Rose, you promised not to interfere!"

"I promised nothing of the kind," Rose said with a regal lift of her nose. "For that false accusation, I may not tell you what I learned."

"You're bursting to tell me, so get it out."

"All right—I talked to Gina. I didn't want you to drive us over to Joe's house only to discover he's off working somewhere, because you'd just leave the scarf with his daughter and let matters drop."

Susannah's gaze narrowed suspiciously. "What did you do, Granny Rose?"

"I asked Gina where her father would be working today, and she told me. We have to drive out to Timberlake, the Ingalls family lodge, if we want to see Joe in person, and I know you do."

"What if his friend Angelica wants to see him, too?"

"Why are you worried about another woman, Suzie? You're so beautiful and charming that Joe couldn't possibly choose anyone else—"

"I'm not in a competition, Granny Rose. If Joe has a good relationship with someone, I'm not going to go vamping around to break them up. It's wrong, not to mention embarrassing! If it's even true, that is."

"What? What do you mean?"

Susannah bent down and picked up the car keys. "Nothing. Just something that occurred to me last night after I went to bed."

"Oh? You didn't sleep well?"

Susannah gave an exasperated sigh. "I slept well enough, thank you very much. I just wasn't especially sleepy, that's all. I got to thinking about Gina Santori."

"What about her?"

"Don't get that gleam in your eye again, please. I won't have you plotting anything for my benefit, all right? I'm serious, Granny Rose. Stop the matchmaking."

"All right," said Rose, lying through her teeth.

"Promise?"

Rose looked out the car window as Susannah started her car and pulled out of the parking space. "It's a lovely day, isn't it? I love seeing sunlight glistening on the snow."

"You're changing the subject, Granny Rose."

"What subject?"

Susannah sighed again.

Rose smiled.

TIMBERLAKE LODGE, a fine old summer house up on the lake that needed extensive renovations, had provided Joe with a steady income for several months. But he had come to see the lodge as something more than money in his pocket. He really liked the old place. It was a beautiful, rambling building with a long veranda, from which the view of the lake was breathtaking.

Joe enjoyed working at the lodge.

And he didn't mind that it was haunted.

"There's no ghost," Liza Baron Forrester insisted. She was the granddaughter of Judson Ingalls, who owned the lodge, and Liza had moved into the place the previous summer. "That's just a silly story that got started around town. The lodge is not haunted."

"Whatever you say, Liza." Joe strapped on his tool belt and proceeded into the entrance hall where he was currently working. "Then the weird sound I hear when I'm pounding nails is just the wind, right?"

"Right."

Joe chuckled. "You're the boss. To tell the truth, I wouldn't mind the ghost if there really was one. She's a nice ghost."

"She?" Liza followed him into the entrance. "Why do you say it's a she?"

"I dunno. Just a feeling, I guess. Why?"

"Cliff says the same thing," she mumbled.

Liza was one of the most spectacular women Joe had ever met. She had style and flash. Her long blond hair could have done justice to a movie star, and her face, though not exactly beautiful, was very striking. She was also tall and lean, with a way of walking that reminded Joe of a languid leopard.

Prone to flashes of anger as well as artistic brilliance, she was perhaps the most temperamental woman Joe had ever known, too. Even the earrings she was wearing suggested that. From one ear dangled an angel, and in the other ear Liza wore a devil with a naughty grin on its face.

People around town predicted that her marriage to the reclusive Cliff Forrester would soon tame her down a little, but Joe doubted it. He suspected Liza would remain a fiery, exciting woman until her dying day.

"Well," said Joe, changing the subject, "my crew will get here as soon as they finish fixing up the studio in Nora's garage. What do you want us to work on this week?"

With a frown still lingering on her brow, she sat down on the rolled-up Oriental rug that lay in a corner, out of the path of the flying sawdust. She folded her legs and put her chin in the palm of one hand to gaze at the large room around them. It was a pose Joe had come to recognize as Liza's thinking position.

At last she said, "I think you'd better finish the trim work in here first. My granddad has all but finalized the sale of the lodge to Eddie Wocheck, so he doesn't have to show it again. But we're still going to have our big Christmas party here—I finally talked Mom and Granddad into it. It would be nice if this room, too, were finished."

"Okay. That'll take only a day or so. Then what?"

Liza sighed, toying with her angel earring. "You've done such a great job on all the main areas, Joe—I think everything's all set for the party.... My grandmother's bedroom is next, I guess. There's an old mirror I'd like to get rid of, but it seems to be bolted to the wall. I'm afraid to touch it, since I've been known to bring sections of the roof down around our ears when I get out my crowbar."

"I'll take a look." Joe began piling lengths of old trim board on the floor far from the beautiful rug. When Liza showed no signs of getting up, he commented, "You don't seem too excited about selling the lodge."

Liza gave him a lazy grin. "It's not mine to sell, so I don't have much input on the decision. My granddad is determined to get rid of it. There are too many bad memories for him here. And since we found out that my grandmother... that the body..."

"I heard about it, Liza, that it really was Margaret's body we found up here in the summer. I'm really sorry...."

Suddenly stricken, Liza shook her head. "She disappeared so long ago, and all my life I thought she might be out there somewhere.... Poor Mom! And poor Granddad! It really broke his heart!"

"Do you think so?"

Liza looked sharply at Joe. "What's that supposed to mean?"

He shifted a bit uncomfortably. "You know how people love to speculate."

Her gaze began to burn and she snapped, "What are they saying now?"

Joe shrugged. "They're wondering who killed Margaret Ingalls, and why."

"Do they think Granddad did it?"

That surprised Joe, and he dropped a long section of trim board with a clatter. "Judson? No, nobody's said that. At least, not to me."

With a twinge of bitterness, Liza said, "Well, that won't last."

Joe didn't want Liza to think he was pumping her for information, but he couldn't help being curious about the mystery that had consumed the whole town for months. "What do you think happened to your grandmother?"

"I don't know." Liza got to her feet and flung her long hair back over her shoulder. "But I'm trying to find out. I have a feeling whatever the answer is, it's not going to be good for my family."

"Have the police uncovered anything else?"

"Not much. Chief Schmidt was trying to track down my grandmother, but his leads went nowhere—and no wonder! She wasn't out leading a wild life somewhere, she was buried here at the lodge. The cops finally found her dental records and matched them with the body."

"The investigation's really picked up now the chief has retired, it looks like."

"Right. His replacement's a real go-getter. She came over with Brick Bauer when he told us about... about my grandmother."

"I heard the new chief was a woman. Too bad Brick didn't get the position—he would have done a good job."

Suddenly Liza's worried brow cleared, like sunshine after a rain. She smiled, and her expression matched the devilish face that swung from her left ear. "I wonder what Brick thinks of working for a woman?"

Joe found himself laughing, too. "Oh, a woman might do a lot of good where Brick is concerned."

With her hands cocked on her hips, Liza eyed Joe and said mockingly, "I wouldn't talk, if I were you, Mr. Eligible Single Santori. There are a lot of people who think a woman would do you a world of good, too."

"I've got my daughter to contend with," he shot back. "That's enough woman for one household. What about you? How's married life?"

If it were possible, her smile grew even more naughty. "It's wonderful, thanks. After the uproar of the wedding, things have settled into a very nice groove."

"And Cliff?" Joe genuinely liked the man who had lived at the lodge for years with very little human contact. A casualty of some horrifying experiences in Southeast Asia, Cliff had been a recluse until Liza burst into his life. Now, just a few months after meeting, they were happily married and living in the lodge boathouse, a small building that Liza had transformed into an idyllic love nest, perfect for a pair of newlyweds who didn't care to have a lot of contact with the rest of the world.

"Cliff's okay," Liza reported. "He still has his moments, but it's been a big relief to have his brother in town when things get tough. I don't expect miracles, though."

"I'll bet," Joe said, "Cliff considers you a miracle."

Surprisingly, Liza blushed and laughed. "Only in bed," she retorted, making Joe laugh, too.

They were interrupted by the crunch of car tires in the gravel of the driveway.

"Visitors?" Joe asked.

"I'm not expecting anybody. I'll go see who it is."

"Hang on a minute." Joe stopped her and began digging into the pocket of his flannel shirt. "I found something last week that I meant to give you. Here."

"What is it?"

Liza frowned at the slug of metal Joe dropped into her upturned palm.

"It's a bullet."

She jerked her head up to look at Joe, her gaze piercing his for the truth. "A *bullet?*"

Joe nodded, attempting to keep his expression bland. "I found it in a baseboard I was ripping up last week. I thought you might want to keep it."

"Why?"

Joe didn't answer. When he'd found the bullet, he'd realized the significance of his discovery. Someone had been shooting in the lodge many years ago, and one bullet had ended up embedded in the woodwork. How it had got there was none of Joe's business. But it might be Liza's.

Liza's expression changed, and she closed her hand around the bullet. "Thanks," she said. "I'll hang on to this."

Joe nodded, glad to have the bullet out of his possession. He could have turned it over to the police, but with the recent changes in the department, he wasn't sure who would do the right thing with such evidence. Besides, Joe felt a certain loyalty to Liza. She had helped him out by providing him with steady work for a long time. If she wanted the police to have the bullet, she'd take care of that herself.

He patted her shoulder rather than verbalize his feelings. "Shall we see who's outside?'

It was Susannah Atkins's station wagon parked in the driveway, and when Joe stepped out onto the veranda and saw the car, he felt his heart do a strange flip-flop in his chest.

"Hey," said Liza, sounding startled. "Isn't that 'Oh, Susannah!'?"

"Why, Liza, you're becoming positively domesticated. Why are *you* watching 'Oh, Susannah!'?"

"Doesn't everybody? Hi, Mrs. Atkins!"

Rose Atkins climbed out of the passenger seat and waved merrily at Liza. "Hello, Liza! Don't you look pretty today?"

Susannah got out of the car much more slowly, and for a few moments she had the look of a martyr on her way to the stake. But Joe caught her eye and held it while Rose and Liza chatted, and soon her face began to glow with fresh color. For a split second, Joe felt as if the whole world had narrowed to just the two of them.

She looked utterly charming with her bright-colored beret on her head and the collar of her camel coat turned up around her ears. Her face, adorned with less makeup than before, looked surprisingly younger to Joe.

"Hi," he said to her, having gone down the steps without thinking.

"Hi." Her voice was breathless, and her blue eyes shone with a variety of emotions.

"Liza," Rose was saying on the veranda, "if I didn't know better, I'd say you were putting on a little weight since you got back to Tyler."

"You think so, Mrs. Atkins?" Liza asked indulgently.

"Is Cliff cooking these days or are you?"

"Neither of us is exactly the Galloping Gourmet."

"You're looking very healthy," Rose said with a twinkle. "I wonder if you'll have some news for us someday soon, my dear?"

"How does anybody keep a secret in this town?" Liza demanded with a laugh. "There's no truth to the rumor that I'm trying to have a baby."

Rose whooped with joy. "A baby! Now, isn't that wonderful? You and Cliff must be very happy."

"I'm sure we will be," Liza admitted with a grin. "We've been talking about it, anyway. Sometimes Cliff likes the idea. The rest of the time we're both scared to death."

"That'll pass, darling—but not until your children are completely grown, and then the problems just change shape." Rose gave the tall girl a supportive hug.

Susannah came up the veranda steps and put her hand out briskly. "Hello, I'm Susannah Atkins. I remember you when you were a little girl."

Liza shook Susannah's hand. "Hi. I remember you, too. I've seen your show and enjoy it. Everyone in Tyler does."

For the first time, Joe got a glimpse of the professional "Oh, Susannah!", as Susannah smiled and chatted with Liza in a way that made the younger woman relax and behave as if she met famous television personalities all the time. Joe decided Susannah had the gift of making other people feel important. The questions she posed to Liza were easy to answer and showcased Liza's best qualities.

At the same time, Joe suspected Susannah was sizing up Liza and making some decisions about her—all positive. In a few moments she had charmed Liza and drawn her out effectively.

That ability would be invaluable in selling a product nationwide, Joe thought. If Susannah had the right thing to sell, she could turn it into a winner, he was sure. He wondered if she'd thought any more about the idea of writing a household-hints book.

"The lodge looks marvelous, Liza," she was saying when Joe began following their conversation again. "And I hear you've done all the design work yourself. Joe says you're very talented."

"Thanks. This is the chance of a lifetime, of course. I hope to put all my ideas into the finished product—even though we're selling the lodge before the renovation is complete."

"I'm sure the new owner will want Liza's talent as part of the package," Joe put in.

"May I have a tour?" Rose asked. "I used to come up here in my younger days and I'd love to see—"

"You did?" Liza asked quickly. "You visited the lodge in my grandmother's day?"

"Of course. We all came to Margaret's parties. Why, I remember them distinctly."

"And you knew my grandmother?"

"Certainly," said Rose, clearly not noticing how the information seized Liza's imagination. Blithely, she went on, "All the fashionable people from Chicago used to come in the summers, and Margaret used to invite some of us from town. It was not long after my husband died, and if the truth be known, I was rather popular with Margaret's friends. I guess they thought I'd be fast."

"I'll bet you were very fast," Joe said with a chuckle.

"I knew how to have a good time," Rose admitted, smiling. "Liza, how about if you give me a tour while these two take care of their business? Do you have time?"

"Sure." Liza linked her arm with the older woman and guided her into the house. "Maybe you can tell me about my grandmother, Mrs. Atkins."

"You sure I won't bore you with my memories?"

"I'm sure," Liza said firmly.

They disappeared into the house, leaving Joe and Susannah standing together in the sunlight on the porch.

"What was that all about?" Susannah asked, watching curiously as Liza drew her grandmother inside.

"You noticed, too?"

"I don't know her well, but Liza seemed . . ."

"I know," Joe murmured, also studying the way Liza bent her head close to Rose's to ask a stream of questions. "I think she's got a tough job ahead of her. She's trying to solve a mystery that happened forty years ago."

"Well, I'm trying to solve a mystery that's not nearly so old," Susannah said, turning to Joe and jauntily changing the subject. She pulled a knitted scarf from the deep pocket of her coat. "Can you identify this piece of evidence, sir?"

With a grin, Joe accepted his scarf. "Why, yes, I believe it's mine, Detective Atkins. Where did you find it?"

Archly, Susannah played out the role. "Around the neck of a woman, two nights ago."

"I hope she's still alive."

"Very much so. Would you care to make a statement?"

"Not without my lawyer present."

"You must have something to hide." She looked at him sideways, amused and playful.

"Nothing at all. Except I'd like to see that woman again sometime."

At that, Susannah gave up the game and turned away. She put her hands into her coat pockets and hunched her shoulders slightly. "I'm not sure that's wise."

Joe frowned. "Has something changed?"

She sent him a forced smile. "Not really. I just think it would be wiser if we... well, if things didn't get out of hand. Saturday night, I let myself get carried away."

Leaning against the porch railing and folding his arms over his chest, Joe said softly, "That's what you're afraid of, isn't it? Getting carried away."

Susannah regarded him steadily. "I like to stay in control."

"But when you're with me, you're a little on edge, aren't you?"

"Joe—"

"Look, Susannah, I'm not a boy, and you're not a little girl anymore. And neither of us is so old we don't know there's something going on between us." He took a breath. "I'd like to nurture it, whatever it is. I'd like to see what happens. Wouldn't you?"

"You've got other commitments," Susannah said solemnly. "I don't want to come between you and—"

"I'm an adult," Joe interrupted, brusque and impatient. "Don't worry about my commitments. I can take care of myself."

If she was worried about coming between Joe and his daughter, Susannah didn't know him at all. Gina was the most important element in his life right now, and nothing—not even the sexiest lady to come into Tyler in a long time—would ever break the family apart.

But instead of arguing with her, Joe said, "I think we need some time to get to know each other better."

"What about my vacation in the Caribbean?"

He grinned. "What about it?"

"I promised someone I'd go."

"Is he as good-looking as I am?"

Susannah smiled ruefully and shook her head. "I've got a life in Milwaukee, you know. I've got a job—one I don't intend to leave. If I stay in Tyler to get to know you better, what's going to happen? I can't help wondering where this is leading."

Joe waggled his eyebrows. "There's only one way to find out, isn't there?"

He tugged her hand out of the pocket of her coat and drew Susannah closer, until they were pressed warmly against each other. She didn't resist. Although still leaning against the porch, Joe remained taller than she by several inches. Susannah tilted her head and looked up at him through thick, black eyelashes. In her eyes, Joe could see a battle raging. She wanted to give in, but she couldn't allow herself to. Not yet.

He said, "How brave are you?"

She smiled. "What do you have in mind?"

"Dinner at my house, maybe? I'm a pretty good cook, you know."

"I'm not ready for that. It's too fast."

"Fast?"

"Too intimate, perhaps. Do you understand? In your house, with your daughter... I just can't do that yet."

"You have a better idea?"

She seemed relieved that he didn't push the matter. "Maybe I do. I promised my grandmother I'd take her shopping for a Christmas tree. Why don't you come along?"

"To *shop for* a tree?" Joe feigned shock and disapproval. "You mean you don't hike into the snowy woods with a saw and a flask of spirits to cut your own?"

"My grandmother is in her eighties," she reminded him. "She likes to go to the Kiwanis Club's sale down at the church parking lot."

"How about you and me, then?" Still holding her hand, Joe lifted her fingers to his mouth and kissed them seductively. "I said I'd find a tree for Worthington House, plus I need one for my own place."

"This is starting to sound like a venture into the lumber business."

"When can we go?"

With a smile, she lifted her shoulders. "I'm free anytime, but—"

"Afraid to go into the woods with me?"

Susannah shook her head, amused. "You don't look as much like the wolf as you used to."

Joe kissed her quickly for that—a soft brush of his lips against her cheek. He wanted more. But he knew better than to press his luck.

Just hold on a little longer, he told himself.

Susannah felt his kiss and closed her eyes briefly as if to sustain the moment. She wished it hadn't been over so quickly. The gentle kiss promised a lot more, and suddenly she felt that same urge that had swept over her the evening she'd found herself in Joe's arms. The longing inside nearly overwhelmed her.

For heaven's sake, she lectured herself. *Don't melt into a puddle of hormones!*

As if he'd heard the words, Joe began to laugh, so Susannah hastily composed her face. She managed to look completely innocent when her grandmother and Liza returned to the veranda. As they appeared, she pulled her hand from Joe's grasp.

"Did you remember the lodge as clearly as you expected, Granny Rose?"

"There have been a lot of changes," Rose admitted. "But the place is going to be grand."

"Mrs. Atkins was able to tell me about some of my grandmother's friends," Liza said. "What was that one man's name? The bounder, as you called him?"

"Roddy," said Rose promptly. "He was Margaret's special friend the summer she disappeared. I remember him distinctly—such a good dancer!"

"Would you recognize his picture, Mrs. Atkins?"

"Certainly. Do you have one?"

Liza shook her head. "I found a whole packet of old photographs in my grandmother's belongings. I gave them to my sister, though. I could pick them up and bring them to your house someday soon."

"That sounds like fun," Rose proclaimed. "Why don't you bring them Thursday night? Susannah and I are having our annual Christmas open house, and we'd be delighted if you'd come—and bring your husband, too."

"Oh, I'm not sure if Cliff's ready for all these crowds. Mom's having her traditional Christmas bash out here on the twenty-third—you're coming, I hope—all of you."

"I've never missed an Alyssa Ingalls Baron Christmas do," Rose answered. "And it'll be lovely out here at the lodge. But ask Cliff to *my* party, won't you?"

she suggested kindly. "He might surprise you. And, Joe, I want you to come, too. Bring Gina."

Joe looked surprised and pleased. "I've heard you throw a heck of a wingding, Mrs. A."

Rose laughed. "You're a pistol, Joe Santori. Will you come?"

"Yes," he said without hesitation. "But I'm not sure about Gina. She's got an important dance coming up the following night. You know how that can be."

"Yes, she told me on the phone this morning. But we'd like to get to know her better," Rose said, glancing at Susannah slyly.

"Yes," Susannah added bravely. "We'd all like to get to know her, Joe."

SUSANNAH WAS RELIEVED when her grandmother declared herself too tired to go tree hunting that afternoon. As she helped Rose into the car, she noticed that she was looking very pale. Susannah wondered if her illness wasn't more serious than the doctor believed.

"Feeling okay, Granny Rose?"

Rose had put her hand unconsciously to her chest and was sitting with her eyes closed. But at the sound of Susannah's voice, she opened them quickly. "I'm fine. My heart's pounding a little, that's all."

"Did you take your medicine this morning?"

"Oh, yes. I'll be fine. Don't worry, please. It's passing."

Susannah made an inner vow to keep an eye on Rose. Although she was accustomed to a lot of activity, the combination of the upcoming Christmas party and all the tensions of the holidays couldn't be doing her any good.

They were looking forward to a quiet lunch at the old Heidelberg Restaurant. It was one of Tyler's classier spots—an Old World-style establishment run by the third generation of a German family who had settled in Wisconsin a century ago. The surroundings were elegant and the menu more diverse than Marge's. Rose ordered a Welsh rarebit, and Susannah opted for a mixed salad with an assortment of Wisconsin cheeses grated on the top. The salad arrived at their table in a bowl made of delicious French bread. Feeling festive, Susannah ordered a carafe of white wine to split with her grandmother, in hopes that a small drink might help to calm Rose down.

"Are we celebrating something?" Rose asked, surprised when the wine was delivered to their table.

"Maybe," Susannah replied, though she declined to explain what. Her feelings hadn't changed toward Joe, but she felt as if they'd taken an exciting step.

"I'm going to go hunt for Christmas trees with Joe this afternoon," Susannah said. "He needs one for himself and one for Worthington House. Shall we look for one for you? Or would you rather pick it out yourself?"

Rose waved her fork. "I trust your judgment, Suzie."

"I'll be happy to take you tomorrow if you'd rather—"

"Nonsense, dear. I'd rather stay at home, I think. Besides, looking for three trees today will keep you out late. Why, maybe you'll even get stuck in a snowdrift with the man!"

"Whose side are you on?" Susannah demanded on a laugh.

"Yours, darling. Definitely yours."

So at four o'clock that afternoon, Susannah dug into a cedar closet and found an old pink parka for herself—obviously an end-of-the-season bargain she hadn't been able to pass up, for it was trimmed in white fake fur and sported a dancing penguin on one sleeve. In the same closet, she also found a pair of hiking boots she had left at her grandmother's house, since hiking in Milwaukee usually amounted to getting to the nearest bus stop. She tucked her hair into a tasseled ski cap.

"Are you sure you want me to go out?" she asked her grandmother as she laced the boots. "If you'd rather not be alone today..."

"I won't be alone. Mrs. Dahlstrom's coming back," Rose said. "She'll be here if I start feeling a little..."

Susannah looked up. "Are you all right?"

"Of course!" Rose said at once, wiping the guilty expression off her face. "Go have fun with Joe and let me finish making my telephone calls about the party."

"Granny Rose..."

"Don't worry about me, darling. Mrs. Dahlstrom will be here in half an hour. There's Joe's truck. Run along."

Susannah tried to resist, but her grandmother practically pushed her out the door. Susannah gave up protesting and went down the sidewalk to meet Joe as he pulled up against the curb.

He leaned across the seat and popped the door open without getting out. "Is that you, Miss Suzie? Or an elf escaped from the North Pole?"

A blast of warm air from his heater struck Susannah as she climbed in beside him and closed the door. "Be a good boy, Mr. Santori, or I'll see that Santa leaves you a stick and a lump of coal this Christmas."

"You'll know if I've been naughty or nice?"

"I'm sure I'll be the *first* to know, as a matter of fact."

He laughed in that wonderful musical voice of his. Then he put the truck in gear and drove off with her.

CHAPTER NINE

SUSANNAH'S EARLIEST memory of the Vaughn farm was from the Christmas before her father died, when her parents had taken her there for a sleigh ride.

"I must have been five or six," she told Joe. "The sleigh belonged to my great-grandparents, and we keep it at the Vaughn farm. They were friends of my parents, and they still let us use a horse once in a while."

The Vaughn family had suffered the same economic hardships as other farmers in the area, with the result that they'd sold their cattle and leased most of their land to a large farm cooperative. At Christmastime, though, they opened a shop in the old dairy store, and sold wreaths, garlands and homemade decorations and treats. Hot cider was bubbling on the potbellied stove, filling the shop with a crisp, tangy scent. The harness bells hanging on the door gave a cheery jingle when Joe and Susannah entered.

The Vaughns made a fuss over Susannah's return to Tyler, plying them with cups of cider, then gave Joe permission to go hunting for Christmas trees up in the grove.

"Take the sleigh," Mr. Vaughn insisted. "Bessie won't give you any trouble, Suzie. You're old friends."

Bessie was the same old pinto mare Susannah knew so well. Even in recent years, she and Granny Rose had kept up the family tradition of driving the old sleigh to church every Christmas morning. The mare dozed outside the shop's back door, harnessed to a gleaming old red sleigh that had been draped in holly and sported a plaid blanket on the front seat. Bessie cocked her spotted head to look through her blinkers and whickered softly when Joe and Susannah came out of the shop.

After patting the horse's neck, Susannah climbed into the sleigh without hesitation, telling Joe the story of driving the sleigh every Christmas. "It's been a family tradition since Granny Rose was a little girl."

"I'm from Chicago," Joe protested, upon being introduced to Bessie by the laughing proprietor. "The only horses I knew were painted ones on carousels."

"There's nothing to it," Susannah said with a laugh. "I'll drive, if you like. Or would you like me to teach you?"

"You drive." Joe laid his saw in the back seat and stepped warily into the sleigh.

He sat down and began to spread the blanket over their knees, while Susannah gathered up the reins and released the brake. Mrs. Vaughn rushed outside and pressed a thermos of hot cider into Joe's free hand. Then Joe settled back with the cider in one hand and his other arm flung over the seat behind Susannah, looking like the king of all he surveyed.

"I like this," he said, as Susannah clucked to Bessie and the sleigh started off with a jerk. With the wind in his face, he declared, "Over the river and through the wood, Miss Suzie! With luck, maybe we'll get lost together."

"Bessie will find her way back."

"She's a horse, not a homing pigeon!"

Susannah drove the horse cautiously over a little stone bridge past the barn. Bessie slowed down at the barn door, but when Susannah chirped, the mare picked up her feet obediently and kept going, kicking up snow as she trotted along the path beside the paddock fence.

The chill in the air nipped at Susannah's cheeks, and her lungs tingled with the cold. The steady thud of Bessie's hooves created a rhythm that soon had Joe humming "Jingle Bells."

Since Susannah had not been hunting for Christmas trees for many years, she deferred to Joe's opinion on where they'd find the best selection. He directed her through a pasture and up the slope to a grove of pines, then west into a deeper section of the forest.

"Where are we going?" Susannah asked suspiciously as they passed several likely-looking evergreens. "Are you trying to be alone with me?"

"That, too," he said with a grin. "But the best trees are up ahead. Here, turn into that clearing."

Bessie picked her way carefully through the snow and finally came to a stop of her own accord, in the middle of a quiet clearing.

"Wait," said Joe, putting a restraining hand on Susannah's arm to prevent her from driving onward. "Just listen a minute."

Around them, the tall trees whispered softly, and the air was filled with large, immaculate snowflakes that drifted down from the sky so slowly they seemed loath to touch the ground. The afternoon light had begun to wane, and for a moment the sun was caught between the bare branches of a majestic oak. The sheen of crystalline light on the snow-covered ground gleamed like a fairy landscape.

"Hear it?" Joe whispered.

Susannah listened acutely and finally heard distant church bells ringing in Tyler.

Until that moment, Susannah had been enjoying the brisk air, but suddenly she felt the comforting warmth of Joe's body next to hers. It drew her inexorably until she realized she had nestled her thigh snugly against his.

"Makes you glad to be alive, doesn't it?" Joe murmured.

"It's beautiful," Susannah breathed.

"Only one thing missing."

"What's that?"

He turned her face toward his by placing his forefinger beneath Susannah's chin, a light yet commanding touch that she dared not disobey. Joe's gaze was alive with warmth, and a single lock of his dark hair curled temptingly over his forehead. Susannah wanted to touch it with her fingertips, but in another heartbeat, Joe had leaned closer and kissed her. He tasted tangy and delicious, and he murmured something against her lips. But Susannah was too lost in the quick sensations that filled her to hear. A hot twist of excitement began deep inside, and the sudden acceleration of her pulse rendered her breathless. Joe's body heat was wonderful, and the strength in his arms gave her the feeling that they could recline there for days before he'd get tired. His mouth was firm and sensual, and it tantalized Susannah until her mind was completely blank.

With a gentle nudge, Joe parted her lips, and his tongue traced a slow swipe across her lower teeth. Then he gradually lessened the contact until their mouths were barely clinging, and Susannah shivered with pleasure.

When it was over, she found herself swimming in the dark, turbulent depths of his gaze. "You were right," she said when she could speak. "That was the only thing missing."

Then Bessie snorted and shook her head violently, filling the air with a protest of harness bells. With a laugh, Joe said, "Bessie says we've got miles to go before we sleep, Miss Suzie, so I guess we'd better get to work."

Reluctantly, Susannah slid out of his embrace.

Joe leaped lightly from the sleigh and pulled his saw from the back seat. With care, Susannah unlooped the long reins and tied them fast around a stout tree. Bessie put her nose down into the snow and blew gustily to uncover a few blades of dried grass. She nibbled them daintily and watched the humans from behind her blinkers.

Setting off together on foot through the snow, Susannah and Joe began to argue over the merits of the perfect Christmas tree. Joe wanted a round, sturdy tree to go into his front bay window, whereas Susannah preferred a tall, slim tree that would fit in the corner of her grandmother's parlor. Within half an hour, they each found the ideal tree for their own homes, and Joe was gracious about cutting both. They dragged the trees through the snow back to the sleigh, and Joe loaded them into the back seat one after the other.

"Now I need one for Worthington House," he said, dusting pine needles off his trousers. "I want to knock some of those old folks off their roller skates with the biggest, prettiest tree I can find. You have to help me."

"We'll never agree!" Susannah protested on a laugh. "It'll be dark soon, and we'll have to go home empty-handed."

He grabbed her arm and dragged her into the woods again, shouting, "Never say never, Miss Suzie! We'll find the perfect tree if it takes all night! Weeks from now, they may find our frozen bodies in the snow...."

"I'm not freezing to death over a Christmas tree! We'll come back tomorrow if we have to. I'm too old to be gallivanting—"

"You can't use your age as an excuse. There's magic in the air tonight, can't you feel it? Come on, Miss Suzie!"

She laughed and let him lead her into the snowy forest. As dusk gathered in the trees, they hiked farther and farther from the sleigh, but Susannah trusted Joe and was caught up in the excitement of the moment. They walked on and on, circling one tree after another, flushing birds from the underbrush and leaving a trail of footprints behind them.

Finally the woods ended, and they burst out onto a hilltop overlooking the lake. Susannah gasped. The panorama that spread out from their feet was breathtaking, a scene worthy of a picture postcard. The dark lake gleamed in the fading light as if lit from within. The snow-covered banks crept down to the water's edge and turned to a thin coating of ice.

On the opposite hillside Susannah could see the rooftop and gables of Timberlake, the lodge she had visited just that morning. Below it lay the boathouse. A wisp of smoke curled from the chimney of that building, and a warm light glowed in the windows. Susannah knew that Liza and her new husband were snug in their new home, building their life together and planning a family.

"It's beautiful here," she whispered.

Behind her, Joe said, "Magnificent."

He pulled her against his body, and they stood there for a long moment, drinking in the view and marveling at the beauty of the landscape. Susannah leaned against Joe, her head resting against his chest so that she almost imagined she could feel his heart beating against her hair. His arms were gentle around her, and his hands unconsciously caressed her arms to warm them.

"Come on," he said in her ear. "Let's go back."

"We haven't found your tree yet."

"You're shivering. You must be cold."

"I've never felt warmer."

But she turned away and reached for Joe's hand with her own. They had turned to walk back to the sleigh when suddenly they stopped in their tracks, simultaneously struck by the sight of a perfectly symmetrical pine tree standing amid the snowy drifts.

"That's it," said Susannah.

"I almost hate to cut it."

She tightened her grip on his hand and smiled up at Joe. "Then we won't. Next year it will still be here. We'll come and visit."

As soon as the words were out of her mouth, Susannah felt her heart give a jerk of surprise. How odd! She had actually spoken about the future—a future together with Joe. She blinked in astonishment, mouth open.

Joe didn't say a word, but he smiled at Susannah. He didn't make a joke or pretend not to understand, but accepted her words as the truth. He kissed her. His mouth was delightfully sure on hers, and his hands tightened on her body. She let herself be kissed, too surprised to respond in kind. Then Joe released her gently.

"You're right," he said. "That tree's too special to cut."

They walked silently back to the sleigh and happened upon a tall, straight tree near the clearing, one that Susannah, still shaken by the idea her subconscious had produced, declared ideal for Worthington House. Joe clambered through the snow and cut the tree down speedily. Each grabbing a lower branch, they dragged the huge tree to the sleigh, and Joe hoisted it on top of the others.

Bessie was happy to head for the barn, and Susannah had to be firm to keep the mare moving at a sedate pace. They reached the Vaughn farm just as night gathered its shadows. Mr. Vaughn helped Joe put the trees into the truck, while Susannah paid the bill and bought a jug of cider to take home to her grandmother. On a whim, she also purchased two pumpkin cookies and shared them with Joe in the truck on the way back to town.

The first stop was Worthington House, where Joe was greeted with great affection and Susannah was treated to the star treatment, Worthington House-style.

"You look prettier in person," snapped old Inger Hansen, an eternally cranky woman who had once conducted excruciating deportment classes for the young girls of Tyler. She glared into Susannah's face and demanded, "How come you don't look so nice on television?"

Other residents of Worthington House were much happier to see the visitors and crowded around as Joe dragged the Christmas tree into the old parlor. Their voices rose in excitement as he began fastening the tree securely in an antique iron stand. Someone pressed a cup of tea on Susannah, and several elderly people engaged her in conversation. But one of the well-meaning attendants began banging out Christmas carols on the piano in the corner, drowning out attempts to talk, and Susannah was content to watch Joe in action.

He was friendly and kind to the elderly residents of the institution, treating everyone with the same magnanimous good humor he did anyone he encountered on the streets of Tyler.

Watching him, Susannah began longing to be alone with him again. She wanted to bundle him into his coat and scarf once more and slip her arm through his to walk out to the truck. She ached to feel the warmth of his body against hers again, to listen to his whispered laughter in her ear and seek his kisses in privacy. Impatiently, she willed him to finish adjusting the damn tree.

I want you for myself, she thought. *Forgive me for being so selfish, but I want to hold you in my arms again.*

Getting out of Worthington House took forever. One woman insisted that Joe take a look at the Christmas quilt she had been working on with the other members of the Quilting Circle.

"You'd be interested in this, Susannah," said the woman as they crowded around the quilting frame. "Your grandmother helps us every Tuesday and Thursday. We're hoping to finish the quilt in time to raffle it to raise money for the children's wing of the hospital."

Susannah had to admit the quilt was a masterpiece. Made of green and red patches—all circles—combined with gold appliqués and a subtle gold thread that traced the figures of a madonna and child, the quilt was of museum quality. Perhaps Joe didn't fully appreciate the design and workmanship, but Susannah was most impressed. She told the members of the Quilting Circle so, and exchanged tips with the ladies. If she'd been looking for ideas to use in her "Oh, Susannah!" program, the Tyler Quilting Circle would have made an excellent feature.

"Sure is pretty," Joe announced to the crowd of beaming ladies. "I guess I'll have to buy a few chances."

Then he caught Susannah's arm and gave her a surreptitious tug—a silent signal she interpreted to mean he was anxious to leave, too. But the piano player begged him to sing for everyone and he was soon swept away, much to Susannah's frustration.

"Are you and Mr. Santori an item these days?" asked one gimlet-eyed woman.

"Just friends," Susannah said, but the woman's smile was knowing and called Susannah a liar.

"Excuse me," said another voice at Susannah's elbow. "Aren't you Oh, Susannah?"

She turned and found herself face-to-face with a handsome middle-aged man who had a strong, distinguished face and flecks of gray at his temples. "Why, yes, I am."

He shook her hand warmly. It was obvious to Susannah that he was not a resident of Worthington House, but was perhaps visiting an elderly relative there. A tall, vital man, he seemed to radiate wealth and power. His cable-knit sweater was of fine quality, and his tailored trousers looked expensive, too. Susannah got the impression that he had taken off the coat of his business suit and put on the sweater to pay a social call at Worthington House. The top of his tie showed at the neckline of the sweater.

Pleasantly, he said, "You probably don't remember me. I'm Edward Wocheck."

"Why, of course!" Susannah smiled, finally putting a name to his familiar face. Although Edward was several years older than she, he had spent his youth in Tyler and she remembered seeing him around town when she was a little girl. "How have you been?"

"Very well, thanks." He seemed pleased to be remembered. "I catch your program on television now and then, and I always say to myself, 'There's that pretty young Atkins girl from my old hometown!' I must say, you make all of us Tyler folks proud."

She laughed. "Thank you very much." She stepped back from the crowd and into an alcove with Edward, and they began to chat. Politely making conversation, she said, "What about you? Are you still living in Tyler?"

"No, my business takes me all over the country. I'm just back in town because I'm in the process of buying a piece of property—Timberlake, in fact, the Ingallses's lodge. Do you remember the place?"

"Oh, yes, I was just visiting the lodge today." *So it's Eddie Wocheck who's buying Timberlake,* she thought. "The building is still magnificent, isn't it?"

He grinned as if they were sharing a secret. "I think so. I'm hoping to turn the lodge into a resort. I may even put an addition onto the place to make more hotel rooms. To tell the truth, I can see a wonderful European-style hotel running up there on the lake."

"How exciting!"

He laughed. "It is for me. Tonight I'm visiting my father to learn more about the old place."

"He used to work for the Ingalls family at the lodge, didn't he?"

"Yes. And I've been trying to pump him for information—just to learn a few things about the past so I can build on it."

"I see. Your father is a resident of Worthington House?"

"For the time being. He retired as caretaker of the lodge when Judson Ingalls hired that Forrester fellow, and he's lived at Kelsey Boardinghouse ever since. But he fell and broke his hip recently, and can't really take care of himself. My father seems happy to be living here." Edward lifted his palms helplessly. "I wish I could be in Tyler to look after him more, but he seems to be in good hands. The staff here at Worthington House have really made him feel welcome."

"That's one nice thing about a small town. People stick together."

"Yes."

Susannah tried to mentally file away all the information she had learned from Edward Wocheck so she could relate the details to her grandmother. Like everyone else in Tyler, Rose would be very interested in learning who was planning to buy the lodge. Susannah almost asked Edward what he thought about the mystery that was consuming the Ingalls family, but she decided the question might be inappropriate to ask the new owner.

Looking over at the group of people gathered around the piano, Edward said, "That's Joe Santori, isn't it? The fellow singing over there, I mean. I met him at the lodge when I was touring the place. He's a contractor."

"Yes, he is."

"He certainly has a wonderful singing voice."

That's not all, Susannah almost said. At the mention of Joe's name, she gazed into the crowd to find him among the elderly residents. He looked happy as he sang a jaunty version of "I Saw Mommy Kissing Santa Claus" to the laughing group of women. When he finished singing, he could hardly edge his way out of the merry throng.

But at last he approached Susannah, smiling. "Ready to go?"

"Yes. You've met Edward Wocheck, haven't you, Joe?"

"Sure." Joe shook the older man's hand. "How's your deal with Judson Ingalls going?"

Edward gave him a rueful smile. "As well as can be expected, I suppose. Judson and I don't have a good history."

"Oh? I didn't notice any hard feelings when you two were at the lodge the other day."

"Well, our argument goes back a long way," Edward said, though he did not go into detail about the conflict. He added, "Maybe time has healed the wound a little. Anyway, I think we've just about made a deal. Judson's being reasonable."

"He's been having a rough time lately," Joe said.

"I'm sure everything will turn out fine," Edward said. "Well, I must get back to my father. It's been nice talking with you two. I hope you have a merry Christmas."

"Thank you," Susannah murmured as Edward walked off into the residents' wing of Worthington House. To Joe, she said softly, "I wonder what's going on around here."

"What do you mean?"

"I'm not sure," Susannah said slowly. "But there's something fishy, I think. The deal with the lodge... doesn't it seem odd that Judson has kept Timberlake all these years and now suddenly he's decided to sell it? Just after you discovered a body on the grounds? And why was Eddie so secretive about his 'argument' with Judson? I just wonder if we know the whole story yet."

"Maybe we can discuss that later. Right now there's only one story that's got me on the edge of my seat," Joe said, bending down to whisper in Susannah's ear. "What's going to happen between the two of us?"

The warmth of his breath along her hairline gave Susannah the sudden urge to close her eyes and sigh. But that rude inner voice interrupted again. *Don't you mean what's going to happen among the three of us?* she thought. *What about Angelica?*

If she existed. Susannah had a suspicion that something fishy was happening with Gina Santori, too, but she didn't mention her theory to Joe. If Gina had lied about the existence of another woman in Joe's life, that was an issue Susannah felt should be taken up with Gina, not her father.

But she didn't say that. Instead, she couldn't resist taking Joe's hand and pulling him toward the door. Joe grabbed up their coats from the hallway and they called their goodbyes to the gathered residents of Worthington House who were just starting to string colored lights on their Christmas tree.

Outside on the porch, Joe helped Susannah into her coat, but instead of zipping it up, he pulled her close and kissed her mouth abruptly. Despite the cold air, Susannah felt very warm indeed.

"What was that for?" she asked, smiling up at him when he pulled back.

"For being a good sport," he replied. "The most beautiful good sport I've ever known. I want to be alone with you, Miss Suzie."

"Take me home, then."

"Your grandmother's there."

"Your home?"

He shook his head. "My daughter's got a friend spending the night. They're probably destroying my kitchen at this very moment."

It was a long drive to Susannah's apartment in Milwaukee, but for one mad moment she thought of proposing such an expedition. She knew exactly what Joe meant by wanting to be alone with her. She wanted the same thing. In a private place, they could let their instincts take over. It was a scary thought, but Susannah felt as if a primitive side of herself was already in command.

"I guess your truck is the best we can do," she said with an unsteady sigh. "It's a good place to talk."

"Talk isn't what I had in mind," Joe said darkly, but he slipped his hand under Susannah's elbow just the same and guided her down the porch steps.

Joe felt his heartbeat start to race as soon as he deposited Susannah on the seat of the truck. A minute later he climbed in the driver's side, his breath clouding the air inside the truck. He knew he ought to be feeling cold, but he wasn't. Instead, his insides felt as if they were on fire.

Susannah was shivering, he could see. But Joe didn't reach for the ignition to get the heater going. He suspected Susannah wasn't shivering from the cold, either, but from something else.

He half turned in the seat to look at her in the light that slanted from Worthington House. "You're trembling, Miss Suzie."

Her blue eyes were wide, and she stared at him with the expression of a frightened doe mesmerized by headlights. "I'm not sure why. I had a nice time tonight. The tree looked lovely...."

"Forget about the tree. That's not why you're shaking like a leaf. Shall I take you home?"

"No..."

He felt his own grin start. "I'm not ready for the night to be over yet, either."

She remained on her side of the seat, observing Joe through eyes that looked positively smoldering in the shadowy light. Then Joe laughed and reached for her hand. "Miss Suzie, when you were a teenager, did you ever climb into the back seat of a car with a boy?"

"Heavens, no."

"Then it's time you tried it."

He pulled, drawing an unresisting Susannah across the seat toward him. Softly, he asked, "Shall we pretend we're a couple of kids again?"

She was in his arms then, willing, but charmingly awkward. "Necking in the cold?"

He laughed against her cheek, enjoying the fragrance of her soft skin and the warmth of her slender body. He couldn't help slipping one hand inside her jacket, finding the curve of her back and running a caress down her spine. "The idea turns me on, Miss Suzie. Does it do the same for you? Do you feel young again?"

"With you, yes."

She looped her arms around his neck, but she didn't press close. Her half-turned position invited his touch, and Joe found himself tentatively exploring the contours of her body. His hand on her clothing made a quiet, staticky sound, and Joe felt the tiny flickers of electricity at his fingertips. He slid down her back, then found her hip and memorized its shape. From there, he allowed his fingers to slowly travel up her side, to brush across her belly and reach the underside of her breast, where he hesitated. He could feel her breast, so deliciously full and tempting. As he caressed her gently, sensing the weight of her womanly curve, he watched Susannah's face. It was perfection—all smooth ovals and delicate skin lighted by those lovely blue eyes that suddenly looked languorous, and he paused before touching her intimately. She parted her lips ever so slightly to allow a small sigh of pleasure as his hand lingered beneath her breast.

He loved that expression—so sensual, yet with the light of intelligence, kindness and humor unmistakable in her eyes.

"I feel like a kid myself," Joe said huskily, brushing his fingers back and forth along the underside of that wonderful curve. "I'm afraid to touch you the way I really want to, Susannah."

"You won't hurt me."

"No, but...I want you in a very grown-up way, and I'm afraid to start something I won't be able to stop. I find you hard to resist, Miss Suzie."

Her hand traced a line from Joe's neck down his chest, to rest just above where his heart had begun to hammer. She whispered, "I'm having a hard time resisting you, too. I barely know you, Joe, but I can't help feeling the way I do."

"How do you feel?"

She smiled, but turned her head away shyly, so Joe touched her chin and brought her face up to look at his again, forcing her to answer him straight. Her gaze was dreamy. She said, "I feel like making love with you."

He melted inside and kissed her. Her mouth was sweet and pliant, her tongue met his joyously. She caressed him, too, finding the sensitive spots on his body with her trembling hands. She touched his thighs, his hips, his belly—and brushed one sensual caress across the throbbing ache that most threatened his composure. Joe felt a sweat break out on his brow.

"Suzie..." he said hoarsely.

"Touch me."

He took possession of her breasts then, rubbing his palms against her sweater until the hard nubs of her nipples came erect. He could feel her breath catch and heard her soft sound—half moan, half whisper—as he caressed her through her clothes. He wanted more. A lot more. And so did she, if he read the signs correctly. Before he could think straight, Joe found himself tugging at the hem of that damned woolly sweater and pulling the tail of her shirt out of the way. The bare flesh of her stomach felt like silk and she writhed at his touch.

All the maneuvers of typical teenage grappling came back to him then, and Joe found a way to get under her bra. He caressed her, teasing her nipples, stroking the smooth roundness of her until Susannah gasped with pleasure. He wanted to explore those pretty breasts with his mouth and tongue, and began to push her down across the seat to do just that.

Then he heard the snap of his own jeans, and a new fire leaped up inside his body. She wanted him, too. Susannah fumbled, but her breath came in determined gasps, and in another moment she was going to have her way with him right there in the front seat of his truck, in full view of Worthington House.

Joe caught her wrist, laughing against Susannah's lush mouth. "Wait..."

"You feel wonderful."

"And you make my head swim." He held her hard, almost pressing her down across the seat. But with all the strength he could muster, he held back. "Susannah, we can't—"

"Kiss me again," she whispered with a deliciously erotic lack of control.

Who could resist? He kissed her, and for a long moment they were both lost in their own world of temptation and passionate desire.

But a minute later, Joe became aware of giggling.

He lifted his head, and Susannah froze, too. Through the steamy windows of the truck, they could see a circle of curious elderly faces peering at them from the porch. A group of Worthington House residents had come outside, and some of them looked appalled at the sight that greeted their eyes. Joe could see old Inger Hansen glaring furiously at him.

But the rest of the crowd began to laugh at the sight of two grown adults necking in the front seat of a pickup truck.

"Goodness!" Susannah cried, sitting up hastily and straightening her hair. But she was laughing, too, Joe noticed with relief.

He also laughed—half to release his own pent-up tension and half because of the foolishness of his own actions. He jauntily saluted their audience before starting the truck and pulling away from Worthington House.

"Are you all right?" he asked when they stopped laughing.

"Just embarrassed."

"Don't be. We're two consenting adults."

"Adults don't act like... like—"

"Like sex-crazed teenagers? Don't bet on it, Miss Suzie. I don't know about you, but I enjoyed it very much."

She slanted a smile across at him and said, "So did I."

BACK AT HER grandmother's house, Susannah's euphoria must have been obvious.

"You had a good time," Rose observed from the chintz-covered chair where she sat reading the newspaper.

"A wonderful time," Susannah said, stripping off her jacket and hugging herself as if to hold in the butterflies in her stomach. "Joe and I got to know each other a little better. He's really very sweet."

"Yes, he's a good man," Rose said, setting aside the newspaper. "And his daughter's not bad, too, for a teenager."

Susannah laughed. "What does that mean?"

"Oh, I wish we could find her a date for the Tinsel Ball, that's all. She has her heart set on it."

Sometimes brilliant ideas arrive like bolts of lightning, and that was exactly how Susannah felt when she bent to pick up the newspaper: the perfect solution came down out of the heavens and hit her on top of the head.

"Good grief! Why didn't I think of it before?"

Rose looked startled. "What?"

"Not what—who! Lars! The paperboy!" Excited, Susannah cried, "We'll get Lars to take Gina to the dance."

"Do they even know each other?"

"Of course! And Lars has been mooning around after Gina for ages! He adores her!"

"What does Gina think of Lars?"

"I'm not sure," Susannah admitted. "She seems to be determined to dislike everyone—me included. But here's my chance to settle a couple of things...."

"What things?"

"Never mind. The point is, Lars and Gina would have a wonderful time at the Tinsel Ball."

"Now you're starting to sound like me! Matchmaking must run in our blood." Rose's pleasure shone in her face. "How do we get them together, partner?"

"I'll call Lars," Susannah said, already heading for the telephone. "If properly coached, I think he'll be delighted to invite Gina to the Tinsel Ball. Where's the phone book?"

Her grandmother followed, smiling. "In the drawer."

"What are you smiling about?"

"You." Rose patted Susannah's hand. "It's nice to see you so concerned about Joe's daughter."

"I just thought of a good solution, that's all. It's not as if I'm trying to win her affection."

"Of course not," Rose agreed, straight-faced. "But you're going to make a lot of people very happy."

"It's the Christmas spirit, that's all," Susannah said. But she knew she wasn't quite telling the truth. It was love that motivated her to telephone Lars that evening. Love that was growing every day for a man whose daughter needed a little help.

CHAPTER TEN

"THE PLAN'S IN MOTION," Susannah told Rose the next day. "I persuaded Lars to invite Gina to the dance."

"Was it hard?" she asked, delighted to see Susannah looking so pleased with herself.

"Lars didn't need encouragement, just tips on handling Gina. He called after school to report that everything went smoothly."

"Wonderful!"

Rose decided to put her own plan into action and telephoned Gina to invite the teenager on a shopping trip. There were some things a girl needed help with, and buying the right dress for a big occasion was one of them. Rose suspected Joe could handle most crises that arose from raising a rebellious daughter alone, but no father should have to endure a trip to the formalwear department of Gates Department Store.

Gina was surprisingly gracious about accepting Rose's offer, and they made arrangements to meet at Gates that afternoon.

Although styles had changed dramatically in the past twenty years, girls' attitudes weren't very different from when Rose had taken Susannah shopping for prom gowns. Girls still wanted to look pretty for a date to a dance.

But Gina was hard to please, for she didn't want to look "dopey," as she said to Rose. "I don't want a dress that makes me look like I'm going to a masquerade party."

The headstrong Gina finally selected a red dress with puffy sleeves and a sleek way of clinging to her athletic figure. She used every penny of the money her father had sent along, and chipped in thirty dollars of her own. When Rose saw the dejected look on the girl's face when they carried the dress past the shoe department, she encouraged her to choose a pair of shoes that matched her new dress. At first, Gina politely refused the offer, but Rose didn't have much trouble persuading the teenager to accept the gift. In return, Gina helped Rose choose a birthday gift for Susannah at the jewelry counter.

Afterward, they trooped down to the basement luncheonette to enjoy a predinner scoop of ice cream. Joe arrived at the curb outside the department store at the appointed hour, and drove Rose home.

"How did it go?" Susannah demanded when Rose let herself in the front door after the trip.

"We had a wonderful time," Rose replied, sinking gratefully into the nearest chair. "But I'd forgotten how tiring a shopping excursion can be. Gina's quite a handful!"

Susannah's face folded into a frown. "I'm worried about your color, Granny Rose. I think I'll call Dr. Phelps."

"No, no, I'm just a little worn-out. And I had a snack at the store." Rose touched her stomach. "It may not be agreeing with me. But I enjoyed myself thoroughly. Gina is a sweet kid under that hard-as-nails exterior she tries so hard to keep in place."

"You shouldn't have exhausted yourself for her, Granny Rose. I could have taken Gina shopping."

"Oh, stop fussing." Belatedly, Rose realized her tone sounded too sharp. She reached for Susannah's hand and squeezed it. "Don't mind me, dear. Did you call Roger? What are your plans?"

Susannah took a deep breath. "My plans are canceled."

"Canceled?" Rose stared up at her granddaughter. "What do you mean? What about your vacation?"

"I can go to the beach anytime." Susannah knelt by Rose's chair and turned up her face to her grandmother. "But a Christmas in Tyler comes only once a year, Granny Rose. I want to be here for your party."

"But...but what about all that money you've spent?"

Susannah shrugged. "Roger said he'd try to get a partial refund, but I'm not worried about that."

Rose felt a pang of guilt. "You're worried about me, aren't you?"

"A little," Susannah agreed carefully. "But I'm being selfish, too. I love spending the holidays in this old house with you."

"I wonder if anybody else contributed to your change of plans?" Rose inquired teasingly. "Anybody I know?"

"I haven't the faintest idea who you're talking about," Susannah replied cheerfully, getting to her feet. "So let's not even open that subject, shall we? Hang on to my arm and I'll help you into the parlor. Would you like a cup of herbal tea to settle your stomach?"

"That sounds wonderful, Suzie."

"Keep your ear tuned for the doorbell," she said over her shoulder. "My secretary is sending some of my clothes and things by courier."

"How nice! You won't have to wear those jeans to my party!"

"I might anyway," Susannah shot back with a laugh.

Although Rose felt bad about spoiling Susannah's vacation, she was also delighted to have her granddaughter at home for the holidays. Not only was Susannah good company, but she was a great help around the house.

For Rose, the week passed in a flurry of preparations. Joe Santori and his men appeared promptly at eight each morning to work on the kitchen, to get it ready in time for the party. Susannah managed to be on hand when Joe was in the house—to spare Rose the ordeal of supervising the job, she claimed. And she took Rose out of the house for various shopping excursions, too. Each evening after the men departed, Rose and Susannah hurriedly baked the goodies that would cover the buffet table at the party. Once Rose caught Susannah surreptitiously wrapping packages on the dining room table. They took a turn at delivering Meals on Wheels on Wednesday, and Susannah found time to polish the silver, too.

Relieved to have such expert help in the house, Rose allowed Susannah to do more than her fair share of the work. Together, they baked cookies and shopped for wines, draped the whole house in garlands of fragrant pine and took turns telephoning friends and neighbors to extend invitations. At the end of each day, Rose found herself very tired, and she was happy to allow

Susannah to tuck her into a comfortable chair for a nap before dinner.

But Rose did not allow her exhaustion to slow her down for long. She loved holiday entertaining.

The annual Atkins open house was a party that half the town of Tyler made it a point to attend. It was a highlight of the Christmas entertaining season, and Rose took absurd pride in the event.

"Maybe this year we should cut back a little," Susannah said the afternoon she discovered Rose nodding off at the dining room table, where she'd been tying green satin ribbons around the fruitcakes she gave to her closest friends. "You seem tuckered out, Granny Rose."

"Nonsense, my dear. I'm just saving up my energy for the party."

Susannah's face registered concern. "I'm sure your friends won't mind if you skip the fruitcakes this year. Eventually, you'll have to slow down a little."

"Who says?" Rose challenged her granddaughter, snipping ribbon with renewed vigor. "I'm going to do everything I please for as long as it pleases me—and if it shortens my life by a few months, what does it matter? Having this party makes me happy."

Susannah laughed. "All right, have it your way. But let me finish these fruitcakes, will you? I'll make you a cup of tea and you can relax for a little while."

Despite Susannah's constant fussing over her health, Rose enjoyed the days she spent preparing for the party. It was a long time since her granddaughter had been home for an extended visit, and they chatted together for hours.

Also, it was a joy for Rose to see Susannah blooming under the attention of Joe Santori. Although Susannah denied any feelings for the man, it was obvious that she was falling in love with him. Rose could see the glow in her granddaughter's eyes whenever Joe appeared at the door. And when he got into the habit of telephoning each evening on the excuse that he needed orders for the following day's work, Susannah seemed to take great pleasure in just listening to his voice.

It made Rose happy to see Susannah so taken with Joe. But her granddaughter steadfastly refused his further invitations for dinner or other nightly entertainments.

Wondering if Susannah was still worried about Joe's relationship with this Angelica woman Gina had told her about, Rose decided to discuss the situation with her friends in the Quilting Circle when they met at Worthington House to finish the Christmas quilt.

"We ought to do something to get Joe and Susannah together," said Martha Bauer as she slipped her needle in and out of the fabric.

"We can hardly break up Joe and his other girlfriend, this Angelica person."

"Angelica who?" demanded Inger Hansen. "I never heard of any Angelica living in Tyler. What kind of name is Angelica? She sounds like a floozy."

"She's somebody from Bonneville, I suppose. Or Madison, perhaps."

"A man like Joe Santori ought to be content with a local girl," Inger snapped. "Not getting his jollies out of town."

"Don't be crude, Inger," said Martha Bauer. "Rose, can't we arrange a few accidental meetings between Joe and Susannah?"

"They meet every day in my kitchen," said Rose. "I don't know what else we can do."

"A kitchen's not very romantic."

"Well, he's coming to my Christmas party."

"Is he bringing Angelica?"

"I don't think so."

Martha Bauer said, "Would Susannah quit her job at the television station so she could come back to Tyler and marry Joe? I don't think he's the type to give up his work for a woman."

"But Susannah's a big star!"

All the ladies began arguing about working wives after that, and the discussion became very lively. Rose had her doubts that either Joe or Susannah would give up their work for love, but she didn't voice her worry. Modern couples managed with all kinds of arrangements nowadays. Why, some wives and husbands lived on opposite coasts and got together only on weekends.

"Well, we'll just have to make sure Joe meets Susannah under the mistletoe," said Inger in her loud voice. "But don't leave them alone together, Rose. We saw what happened the other night when they were parked right outside our front door. These young people today! They don't have any morals."

Though she'd known Inger for fifty years, Rose was outraged, and snapped, "Susannah's morals are just fine, Inger!"

"But we saw them—"

"You shouldn't have been snooping, you old busybody! What they do in private—"

Martha Bauer patted Rose's arm soothingly. "Don't get so angry, Rose. My goodness, your blood pressure! Inger is just picking a fight. Like always."

"Nobody says terrible things about my granddaughter and gets away with it!"

"Rose, please! Don't get so angry. It can't be good for your health."

"Yes, we're worried about you," chimed in another friend. "You don't look well. Let's talk about your party instead. We're all so excited about coming! Judson Ingalls has arranged for us all to ride over in his big car."

Rose was easily diverted into discussing her Christmas party, but her friends were right. She didn't feel especially well, and after a while she excused herself early and telephoned Susannah for a ride home.

"What's the matter?" Susannah asked at once, sounding very worried.

"Nothing's the matter," Rose said into the telephone receiver, despite the fact that her heart was thumping so hard it hurt. "I just don't feel like listening to a bunch of old biddies this afternoon."

"I'll be there in a few minutes."

"There's no need to rush. Not if Joe's there with you."

"Joe isn't here," Susannah said firmly. "I believe he had work to finish at the lodge today. He says the Ingalls family has finally sold the place and he has to hurry with the job."

"He'll still be able to come to our party tomorrow night, I hope?"

"I think so," said Susannah. "Just wait at Worthington House, Granny Rose. I'll come inside to get you."

"You don't have to treat me like an invalid," Rose said, but Susannah had already hung up the phone.

Rose went home and slept for the rest of the afternoon—something she never did. When she finally woke, Susannah was doubly worried, so Rose made an effort to act as if everything was normal during their light supper. But she felt groggy and went to bed early, telling herself she had better get over the flu—if that was what she had—before the party. Since Joe's men had finished the kitchen that day, Susannah spent the evening cleaning up the mess and putting the cupboards and drawers in order.

The next day, of course, Rose had no time to think about her health. She wished Susannah happy birthday and shared an extra large banana-nut muffin with a candle in it. Susannah opened her gifts—a pretty gold pendant and a collection of old family photographs that Rose had painstakingly labeled and mounted in a handsome album.

"Oh, it's wonderful, Granny Rose!" Susannah had tears in her eyes. "I've always wanted to sit down with you to learn about the family. Thanks so much for taking the time yourself!"

Rose was pleased that Susannah found the album so precious. It was important to pass along family history, Rose felt. She was glad Susannah felt the same way.

Side by side with Susannah, Rose spent the morning working in the kitchen. In the afternoon, they mixed the punch, set out glassware and napkins, arranged a few extra chairs in the sitting room for the elderly guests and chose the music that would play on the stereo during the party. A dozen phone calls interrupted their preparations, but Rose didn't mind. She loved the excitement.

At six o'clock, she dashed upstairs to change her clothes. In her haste, Rose realized that her heart had begun to pound with excitement, so she sat down on her bed for a moment's rest and promptly fell asleep.

She woke an hour later with Susannah gently shaking her shoulder.

"Granny Rose, are you sure you're up to this?"

"Oh, my heavens, what time is it? I must have dozed off!"

"It's seven o'clock." Susannah looked lovely in a red wool dress with her gold pendant around her neck and her fair hair loose around her face. With a worried frown, she said, "Judson Ingalls just arrived with a carload of your friends. Shall I tell them you're still dressing?"

Rose scrambled off the bed. "It will just take me two shakes to get ready, Suzie. Can you entertain everyone until then?"

"Of course," said Susannah, turning toward the door. But she hesitated and looked back. "Granny Rose..."

Rose waved her hand to hurry Susannah out. "Don't slow me down, darling. I've got to get dressed. Where's my slip?"

By the time Rose had put on her clothes, combed her hair and applied her lipstick, the party was in full swing. The house looked lovely and smelled like Santa's kitchen. Susannah was merrily greeting guests at the door, while soft carols played on the stereo.

Rose arrived downstairs just as Joe Santori stepped in the door, looking quite handsome in a sport coat. Little elves with hammers decorated his tie. Rose saw Susannah give the tie a familiar tweak and make a joke, and Joe laughed, bending close to give her a kiss and wish her a happy birthday. At the last instant, she turned her head to prevent him from kissing her on the mouth. Joe smiled and kissed her lingeringly, anyway. Susannah's eyes were full of pleasure when she raised her gaze to Joe's. For an instant, the two of them were completely unaware of the rest of the world.

Then Rose launched herself off the bottom step, crying, "Merry Christmas, Joe! I'm so glad you could come. Do I get a kiss, too, or must I trap you under the mistletoe?"

Joe tore his gaze reluctantly from Susannah's and laughingly gave Rose an obedient kiss. "Merry Christmas, Rose. I hope your kitchen is open for business tonight."

"Thanks to you and your men, it is. Thanks for helping me out so quickly, Joe. I won't expect the rest of the renovations to be so speedy."

Joe said, "My crew's finishing up out at Timberlake—we lost the job with the Ingallses—so I'll be back here tomorrow morning, if you like."

"What do you mean, you lost the job with the Ingallses?"

"Liza says they've sold the lodge."

"Great heavens! To whom?"

"Edward Wocheck."

"Eddie—! Why would he want to buy the old lodge?"

Susannah frowned. "Granny Rose, I told you about this when we were baking the other day. Don't you remember? I spoke with him at Worthington House."

"When were you at Worthington House?" Rose asked in confusion.

"We saw Edward Wocheck at Worthington House the night we took the tree over there," Joe explained. "I guess he wants to turn the lodge into some kind of resort. He's sent a bunch of plans to the town council, and if they approve his ideas on Monday, the lodge will no longer belong to the Ingalls family."

"How sad," Susannah murmured. "Timberlake was kind of an ancestral home for them, wasn't it?"

"Too many bad memories now, I think," Rose said idly, still worried about her memory lapse. "It's just as well. I'm sure Eddie will allow the Ingallses free run of the place, if they want it. He and Alyssa Ingalls used to be very close."

The final sale of Timberlake proved to be the biggest topic of conversation at the party. In the dining room, townsfolk crowded around Judson Ingalls when he finished filling a small plate from the buffet table and began to speak about selling his property. The other guests made appropriate responses to his comments, and Rose was relieved that nobody asked him any uncomfortable questions.

Except for one person. Fortunately, crotchety Inger Hansen was in the kitchen when she said loudly, "I wonder if Judson's selling the place to cover his tracks."

"Hush, Inger!" Rose turned from the oven where she was removing a tray of hot toast points. "Keep your voice down. I won't have you making a scene tonight!"

"It's not a scene if it's the truth," snapped old Inger, selecting a plump apricot cookie from the plate waiting on the counter. Munching it, she said, "A lot of people are saying that Judson killed his wife—the police proved that was her body they dug up last summer, you know. He's probably unloading Timberlake so he can take his money and run off to South America!"

"Don't talk nonsense, Inger." Rose hastily left the kitchen, hoping that Inger wouldn't spread such awful gossip if she didn't have anyone to talk to. Maybe the old biddy would eat all the apricot cookies and make herself sick.

But as Rose pushed through the swinging door, she nearly collided with Liza, Judson Ingalls's granddaughter. The tall young woman looked especially lovely in a short, loose-fitting dress over a pair of skintight bicycle pants. It was an outfit more suited to a cosmopolitan party in a big-city high-rise, but Rose was rather pleased that Liza had chosen such an outré ensemble for that evening. She lent a certain sophistication to the party.

But from Liza's expression, it was obvious that she had overheard Inger's thoughtless talk. Seeing her stricken look, Rose said quickly, "Don't listen to Miss Hansen, Liza, dear. You know she's not right in the head."

Liza swallowed hard. "But it's what everybody's saying, isn't it? That my granddad killed his wife."

"Liza, don't think about the past. Just put it out of your mind. You've just married a very sweet man, and—"

But Liza shook her head. "I can't forget the past. I wish I could! But the police investigation is digging into the whole awful business. I'm so afraid! I just... It's..."

Rose set down her tray of hot canapés and took Liza's arm. She guided the tall young woman into an alcove before the other guests noticed her momentary loss of composure. For an instant, Rose feared that Liza was going to burst into tears.

"There, there, sweetheart. It's not so bad...."

Liza gathered her poise and managed a halfhearted smile. "I'm not myself these days. I never was the most stable person in the world, but this has really sent me over the edge! I just . . . I'm afraid for my grandfather, that's all. I don't want him to go to jail. Not now. So many things are finally going right for our family. . . ."

"Judson won't go to jail," Rose said firmly.

"How can you be so sure, Mrs. Atkins?"

"Because I've known him a lot longer than you have, young lady. And I knew Margaret, too. I'm sure he didn't kill her. Why, he loved her very much! She just wasn't right for him, that's all."

"Did you believe she'd disappeared?"

Unwillingly, Rose shook her head. "No, I never believed that. Margaret wasn't the type to just vanish and start a new life somewhere. She would've come back to town to show off. No, I suspected your grandmother had come to a bad end, Liza. I'm sorry, dear."

"But if she was murdered, who did it?"

"Oh, there were lots of possible suspects around in the old days. She ran with a very wild crowd. Perhaps one of her beaux decided to kill her when she refused to divorce Judson."

"Would you recognize some of her boyfriends?"

"Well, they've all aged, I'm sure, and—"

"No, no," said Liza. "I brought those old photos I told you about."

Remarkably, Liza began to rummage in her handbag and came up with a packet. Rose accepted the handful of fragile old photos and stepped closer to the light to examine the faded faces that looked up at her. "Why, yes," she said softly, gazing at many of her old acquaintances and letting the memories swim up in her mind. "Here's your grandmother," she said to Liza, pointing to one picture. "Wasn't Margaret a beauty? She looked very much like you, dear."

Liza pointed to one of the men standing by Margaret's chair in the photograph. "Who's that?"

"Roddy," Rose said promptly. "I forget his last name, but he was one of Margaret's friends from Chicago. A wonderful dancer and quite a card player, I recall. He and Margaret were... well, very close."

Bluntly, Liza asked, "Was he her lover?"

"I'm not sure," Rose said uneasily. "But probably. My dear, Margaret had many friends. If you'd like me to keep these pictures for a while, I'd be happy to try to remember the names. But I didn't know Margaret intimately. I don't know who killed her, if anyone did. I only know it couldn't have been Judson. He's a kind man. And he loved her."

Liza shivered. "Then maybe there's a killer still on the loose in Tyler."

Rose gave the young woman a small smile. "I'm sure there are a great many secrets floating around Tyler, my dear. Some of them are best left buried."

"And that's what Chief Schmidt was doing," Liza murmured softly. "He was stalling the investigation. Sometimes I wonder if Granddad asked him to take it easy."

"That's possible," Rose replied, for she knew Judson Ingalls and the police chief had been good friends for many years. "But the chief may have been doing Judson a favor, you know, without being asked."

"What's going to happen now that he has retired?"

With a sigh, Rose said, "Your guess is as good as mine, Liza. I doubt that Brick Bauer and the newly appointed head of the Tyler police substation will be as easygoing as Paul Schmidt has been over the years."

"Maybe Granddad *is* in a lot of trouble." Liza hugged herself to suppress more shivers of fear. Half to herself, she said, "I've got to do everything I can to protect him."

Fondly, Rose patted Liza's arm. "You'll have a lot of help, my dear. Everyone in Tyler respects your grandfather."

"Everyone respects him, but not everyone likes him," Liza reminded her. "He's made a lot of enemies over the years."

"Please don't worry," Rose urged, handing her back the photos. "Everything will turn out all right."

Liza sighed. "I wish I could be sure."

She walked away, leaving Rose wondering for a moment if the answer to the mystery could lie in those photographs. She wished making the Ingalls family troubles go away could be as easy as looking at some old faces, but suspected many more months would pass before all the answers were unearthed.

Rose allowed the problems of the Ingalls family to slip from her mind as she entertained her guests for the rest of the evening. She enjoyed chatting with friends and neighbors, and she even met a few new people.

One new addition to Tyler was Nora Gates's husband, the handsome Byron Forrester. The two had married after a whirlwind romance, and half the town expected the couple to split up once the first blush of romance wore off. But Nora and Byron appeared to be proving the gossips wrong. If anything, they looked more deeply in love than anyone Rose had ever known. Approvingly, she noticed that they laughed together a great deal. A marriage based on laughter was surely the best kind.

Rose surprised Nora and Byron when she slipped into the pantry for another bottle of wine and found them there. The newlyweds pretended to be admiring the collection of preserves Rose stored on the narrow shelves, but she knew at once that she had nearly caught them kissing. They joked their way out of that potentially embarrassing position.

Then Rose asked Nora, "Don't you teach piano to Gina Santori?"

"Why, yes," Nora replied. "I do. She's very musical."

"She comes from a musical family, I'm told."

"And she's quite an athlete, too. I'm very proud of her." Nora smiled. "But I'm curious. Do you know if she ever got a date for the Tinsel Ball?"

With a laugh, Rose asked, "You knew about that, too?"

"Yes, but I didn't dare give her any advice on the subject. She's a stubborn kid."

"Susannah played matchmaker, and Gina is going to the dance with Lars Travis, the paperboy."

"Good choice!" Nora declared, applauding. "He and his brother Ricky take lessons from me, too. Let's hope he and Gina have a wonderful time."

At that moment, a chorus of voices called for Nora. The most accomplished musician in Tyler was summoned to the piano, and she graciously allowed herself to be dragged into the sitting room. Cracking a joke, she seated herself at the instrument and easily played a few bars of a popular Christmas carol. Voices soon joined in with the words, and the room swelled with the harmonizing of friends and neighbors.

As she sang along, Rose looked around the room at the faces of the people she knew and loved so well—Judson Ingalls, Susannah, the members of the Quilting Circle. Even Joe Santori and Liza Forrester—they were all men and women Rose had come to think of as family. They were part of Tyler, part of her. It was a joy to see them all gathered in her home and raising their voices in thanksgiving.

This is the most wonderful night of my life, Rose thought, standing back to study each face. Seeing Susannah's expression as she met Joe's gaze, noting the way Liza Forrester slid her arm around her grandfather—Rose felt a swell of happiness that life in Tyler was proceeding peacefully.

"Joe!" cried someone when the last strains of the carol died away. "Let's hear Joe sing!"

At once, all the people in the room began to coax Joe to sing for them. He refused with a modest laugh at first, but eventually Susannah persuaded him to entertain everyone. After a short consultation with Nora at the piano, Joe good-naturedly sang a funny, upbeat version of "Jingle Bells" that caused everyone to laugh. But then Nora played the opening bars of "Ave Maria," and Joe could hardly refuse to sing.

The song, always dramatic, began with soft and poignant phrases, which Joe carried off almost effortlessly in his beautiful baritone. But gradually, the tune's power and reverential words called upon his upper range, and the room fell into a hushed silence as Joe closed his eyes and released the full power of his voice. The familiar tune rang out, filling the house to the rooftop and sending shivers through Rose as she listened. Gathered around the piano, the rest of the guests also listened in awe as Joe reached the climax of the song. The words hung in the air as if suspended, then Joe allowed his voice to die into a worshipful whisper. The final note quivered in the air, exquisitely emotional.

As if one person, the guests swallowed hard and burst into applause. Joe accepted their praise with an endearingly shy grin, and then he forced Nora to stand and take a bow. They gave each other a fond hug, then Nora sat down once again and really rattled the keyboard with a ragtime version of "Rudolf the Red-nosed Reindeer." The crowd was soon rocking along with her, their faces suffused with the feeling of well-being.

Despite the noise, Rose managed to hear the doorbell ring. Surprised that a guest would be arriving so late, she worked her way through the crowd toward the door. In the entry hall, she bumped into Susannah and Joe, standing hand in hand.

"I heard the doorbell," Susannah said to Rose. "Who could be coming at this hour?"

"We'll find out in a minute," Rose said. "First I must tell Joe how wonderful that was. Your voice is magnificent! I had no idea you were so accomplished."

"Oh," he said mildly, "I'm just an amateur."

"He's too modest," Susannah protested, eyes shining. "Isn't he, Granny Rose?"

"Modesty is just one of his many good qualities," Rose countered, taking both their hands in hers so that they made a small family circle under the chandelier. "I think you ought to snap up this man, Suzie, dear. Before he gets away."

Susannah blushed. "Granny Rose..."

"She's lovely when she blushes, Joe, don't you think?" Rose appealed to him laughingly. "Surely prettier than any other lady in your life."

"Granny Rose!" Susannah cried, embarrassed at the merest reference to Joe's girlfriend, Angelica.

"Susannah is the loveliest woman I've ever met," Joe agreed without missing a beat.

"And isn't it lucky that you're standing under the mistletoe?" Rose inquired.

Joe laughed and said that it was, then swept Susannah into his arms. Without protest, Suzie slipped her hands up his chest, clinging to him as if she'd already had some practice at that, and in another moment they were kissing. They made such a charming picture, too—an attractive couple embracing beneath the mistletoe and surrounded by Christmas decorations. They were so perfectly matched that Rose found herself entranced by the sight of her granddaughter so lovingly gathered in a man's arms—even when the doorbell sounded impatiently again.

With a chuckle, Rose turned away, saying, "I think I know what Santa's going to bring you two."

Joe and Susannah laughed softly, but didn't break apart, and at that instant Rose opened the front door to the guest who had been standing irritably on the porch. For a split second, Rose didn't recognize the man.

Then Susannah made a queer sound in the back of her throat and hastily stepped out of Joe's arms.

"Roger!" she squeaked.

"Roger?" Joe repeated. "Who's Roger?"

"Good heavens," said Rose, clapping her hand to her mouth. "What terrible timing!"

Roger Selby, the manager of Susannah's television station, stepped into the house amid a flurry of snowflakes. His brow looked thunderous, and he stomped the snow from his immaculately shined wingtip shoes with the air of a man finishing an arduous journey.

With a resounding thunk he dropped a fine leather valise on the floor.

"Roger..." Susannah began, but couldn't say more.

"Who the hell is Roger?" Joe demanded.

"The man who won't let you flush your career down the toilet, Susannah."

CHAPTER ELEVEN

SUSANNAH WAS thunderstruck. "Who said anything about flushing my career?"

Roger was nearly as tall as Joe and even more imposing in his elegant clothes. He gave Susannah a lofty look and said, "I had my suspicions, Susannah, so I came to make sure you haven't been brainwashed in this little town."

"I have not been brainwashed!"

"No? Then what was all that nonsense on the phone the other day? You were rambling on about your life, Susannah. It worried me. And you didn't return my call yesterday or this morning concerning the Easter-basket segment."

"I've been busy!"

"Looking after your sick grandmother?" Roger asked archly. He glanced down at Rose, who looked like the picture of health. "That's the most feeble excuse in the book, Susannah. I've never seen a fitter-looking woman than your grandmother. Hello, Mrs. Atkins."

Rose, with a fierce look in her eye, managed to make a liar out of her granddaughter without saying a word.

Roger turned back to Susannah. "Our trip to the Caribbean was very important. The substance of the whole next season hangs in the balance. When you canceled, I began to worry about you. Now I'm even more dismayed."

Susannah fought for composure. "Roger, you needn't have made this trip. There's nothing to worry about."

"Really?"

"The show's very important to me. It's been my whole life." Conscious of Joe standing nearby and her grandmother's narrow gaze, Susannah added, "It's not the *only* thing in my life, of course."

Roger's frown grew more intense. "What do you mean by that? I don't like to see your energy diluted."

In a deep growl, Joe said, "She's a woman, not a machine."

"And who," Roger asked, "are you?"

Hastily, Susannah said, "This is Joe Santori, Roger. He's a—a friend."

"A friend," Joe added, "who recognizes the importance of family and a hell of a lot of other things. Susannah came to Tyler to see her grandmother again. I think that's more important than getting sunburned while you talk about recipes and household hints!"

"Our show is not about recipes and household hints," Roger began, flushing red at the implication that their program was lightweight. "It's much more than that. Why, we—"

"Now's not the time to discuss the merits of 'Oh, Susannah!,'" Rose intervened. "Roger, since you're here, why don't you join the party? My friends are all fans of your program. I'm sure they'd love to meet the producer."

She took Roger's arm and guided him forcefully into the parlor, where a few of the guests had already fallen silent when voices began to rise in the hallway. Susannah realized they had made a scene, and she was embarrassed on her grandmother's behalf.

Joe caught Susannah's arm before she could follow her grandmother and Roger back to the party. He spun her around to face him. "Did you mean what you just said?" he asked, voice low. "That your show's the most important thing in your life?" His expression was tense.

"I didn't say that."

"But you meant it," he insisted, "didn't you?"

"Look," Susannah whispered, trying not to prolong her embarrassment, "I can't escape the fact that I *am* Oh, Susannah, Joe. Of course the show's important to me. A lot of people depend upon my doing a good job."

He released her arm and took a step backward. "I thought you had changed this week. I must have been kidding myself."

"I haven't changed," Susannah agreed. "Maybe I've recognized a few things, but I—I can't give up being Oh, Susannah. Not for Granny Rose. Not," she said meaningfully, "for anyone."

"Why not? If it's ruining your life, trapping you into a corner—"

"I can't turn my back on success, Joe."

He gave a snort. "Success! You're being smothered, Susannah. This week, I've gotten to know the real you. And I think it's a damned shame you're going to let this guy walk in here and drag you back to—"

"He's not dragging me anywhere."

"Oh, no? Just why do you suppose he's come?"

"To make sure I'm still part of the team, I suppose."

"To make sure he hasn't lost his star player," Joe said bitterly. "He can't get along without you, so he's come to take you back before we poison your mind."

"You make me sound weak," Susannah snapped. "I'm not easily influenced by anyone—not you *or* Roger. I have to think about all the people involved with 'Oh, Susannah!' before I make any rash decisions, Joe. I can't quit my job on a whim."

"I thought," he said, "that I was more than a whim."

Susannah felt her face grow hot. "Let's keep our perspective, shall we?" Her voice hardened. "You and I have never discussed a relationship of any kind, let alone one that required me to leave my job and—"

"We've reached a lot of conclusions this week, Susannah. Maybe we didn't say the words, but don't deny you haven't thought about the possibilities."

"The possibilities are rather limited, considering your circumstances, Joe."

His frown deepened. "What circumstances?"

Before she could think straight, Susannah blundered ahead, saying angrily, "I had to hear about your friend Angelica from your *daughter.*"

Joe's face went blank. "Angelica?"

"Yes, Gina told me all about her."

"Gina told you?" Joe asked, his gaze narrowing.

At the mention of his daughter's name, the pieces suddenly came together in Joe's mind. Susannah's reluctance to let their relationship grow. The sly remarks from Mrs. Atkins about "any other lady" in Joe's life; he'd assumed she was referring to Gina herself.

"She *does* exist, doesn't she?"

What's that kid doing to me now? he asked himself. Heaven only knew what kind of lies might spring from

Gina's fertile imagination if the circumstances were right.

Seizing Susannah's arm once more, Joe asked, "Just what exactly did Gina tell you?"

"Nothing that should have surprised me," Susannah replied, endeavoring to look calm. "After all, you're an attractive single man. I'd be a fool to assume you didn't have a . . . a—"

"A lover?"

Susannah colored. "A friend, I was going to say. Is it true?"

Joe wanted to blow up then and there. But not in Rose Atkins's house, and not before he confronted his daughter. He squelched his temper, suddenly aware that many of Rose's guests were shamelessly eavesdropping from the parlor.

Joe lowered his voice. "We have a lot of things to set straight, Susannah." With a supreme act of self-control, he said, "But not now. I don't want to spoil the party. And I have something to take care of first."

"People are starting to whisper," she agreed, glancing toward the parlor. "We'll discuss this another time."

"But it can't wait long, Miss Suzie." Joe pulled her around again until he could look deeply into her eyes, and he didn't give a damn who was watching from the other room. "I care about you, Susannah. Don't pretend you don't understand. I've fallen in love with you."

She stared at Joe, her expression full of conflicting emotions. For an instant, she couldn't speak.

So Joe decided to take full advantage of the moment. *Let her be good and rattled,* he thought. Swiftly, he pulled her close and kissed her fully on the mouth, even forcing her lips apart for a long, hot, penetrating kiss that should have sent her senses reeling. And judging by the dazed expression on her face when he set her back down on her feet again, the kiss had done exactly that. Susannah put a shaky hand on a chair to steady her balance.

"My goodness," she whispered, blinking.

"Think about that," Joe said darkly, "when you go to bed tonight."

He left the house then, without bothering to say good-night to Mrs. Atkins or to retrieve his topcoat. After turning up the collar on his sport jacket, Joe walked home. Anger at Gina kept him plenty warm enough.

Once in the house, he marched up the stairs to confront his daughter. But Gina's bedroom door was closed, and no light shone from beneath it. So Joe proceeded to his own room, stripped off his clothes and climbed into bed to seethe.

Women! They could drive a man crazy. Joe never pretended to understand the intricate moods of his daughter. He couldn't guess what had prompted her to create the story of Angelica. Jealousy? Or had she taken an instant dislike to Susannah and decided to drive her away?

The telephone rang about an hour later. Joe was still wide awake and ruminating on the fairer sex. He picked up the receiver on the first ring.

"Joe?"

It was Susannah's voice—a little breathless and hushed. "Did I wake you?"

"Who can sleep?" He relaxed into the pillow again, holding the receiver to his ear. "I've been thinking about you."

She hesitated for a moment, and Joe envisioned her face—probably troubled, but lovely just the same. She said, "I haven't had a chance to do much thinking yet. But I can't leave things hanging this way until tomorrow. I put my grandmother to bed—"

"How is she?"

"Tired," Susannah admitted. "Granny Rose went straight to bed as soon as all the guests left." Her voice changed. "I'm even more worried about her than ever, in fact. She forgot Inger Hansen's name tonight, Joe."

"Have you spoken with the doctor?"

"No. It's not really my place, is it? She has promised to see him right after Christmas."

"Is that soon enough?"

Susannah sighed. "I hope so. I can't force her to do anything, Joe. She's an adult with free will and...well, dammit, she's so stubborn. I hate fighting with her."

"I know," he murmured.

A short silence ensued, then Susannah whispered, "You know a lot of things, don't you?"

"Not everything," he said, matching her tone.

"Joe, I..."

"Yes?"

Susannah was silent for a long time. Then she said, "I wish my life were simple, but it isn't. I can't give up everything just like that."

"I'm not asking you to give up anything. I just want us to be together."

"But that means I have to give up everything else," she argued reasonably. "Unless you want to move to Milwaukee."

"I can't do that. Gina's home is here in Tyler. She needs some stability, and this is the best I can do for her."

"I know. But my work is in the city. And I can't conduct a relationship on weekends. I work then, too. Roger needs me—"

"He can't control every minute of your life. And he does, Susannah. He doesn't even want you to take time to see your grandmother. He's afraid of losing 'Oh, Susannah!' "

With another sigh, Susannah said, "I'm beginning to see that. But what can I do?"

"I'll tell you what. You can start by—"

But she laughed. "That was a rhetorical question, Joe, not an invitation for you to take charge of my life."

"But—"

"I'm not your daughter or one of the elderly ladies you manage to control with your combination of charm and bossiness. I'm not giving up 'Oh, Susannah!' I can't. I just have to find more balance in my life. And I have to do it myself, not at your command."

"Susannah..."

"I won't have you running my life."

"Roger does."

"He tries," she admitted. "But he also accepts the fact that I have a mind of my own. I'm not sure you do."

"I'm starting to realize it."

She laughed lightly, but didn't sound amused. "I just wanted to tell you how I felt. I'm sure we'll talk again. But for now..."

"Susannah—"

"I've had enough for one night," she said, cutting off his argument kindly. "Let's think things over before we continue this discussion."

"I'll be over first thing in the morning."

"No, don't do that. Roger will be here. I need to get a few things straight with him, all right?"

Joe had work to finish at Timberlake, anyway. "All right," he agreed. "If that's what you want."

"You see?" she asked, a smile in her voice. "You're getting better already. Good night, Joe. Sweet dreams."

It was five minutes before Joe realized he hadn't settled the matter of the imaginary Angelica. But the more he thought about it, the more Joe realized that Angelica was a problem Gina had created. She should be the one to resolve it.

IN THE MORNING, Susannah faced Roger over breakfast. Naturally, he came downstairs freshly showered and dressed casually—as casually as Roger Selby ever dressed. His wool trousers were neatly creased and he wore a cardigan sweater over a starchy button-down shirt.

He was astonished to find Susannah still in her bathrobe.

"Oh, excuse me," he said, faltering in the doorway. "I'll come back when you're decent."

"For crying out loud, Roger, I'm perfectly decent!" Susannah made space on the cluttered counter for the coffee maker and plugged it in. "Come in and sit down. I'll get you a muffin."

"Do you have any bran cereal?"

"Of course," she said patiently, guiding Roger by one stiff arm to the table. "Now, sit. I'm sorry about the mess. Granny Rose and I were too tired to clean up after the party last night. I guess we have our work cut out for us today."

Roger seated himself in one of the comfortable kitchen chairs and proceeded to look completely *un*-comfortable. He wasn't accustomed to chatting with women in their kitchens. Roger much preferred to conduct business from across the neatly arranged expanse of his office desk. But he made an effort at conversation by asking, "Where is your grandmother this morning? I didn't get a chance to thank her for her offer of a room last night."

"She's still in bed. I checked on her a few minutes ago, and she's still sleeping." Frowning at the thought, Susannah busied herself at the kitchen counter. "She looked terribly exhausted by the end, don't you think? I'm very worried about her."

"Actually, Susannah, I didn't come to Tyler to discuss your grandmother's health. It's your career that's on my mind."

Susannah withheld a sigh of resignation. She knew there was no avoiding the discussion to come. But she didn't want to suffer through one of Roger's patented "career-plan strategies." He could go on for hours talking about the future of the television station and Susannah's vital role in it.

She set a place at the table for him, then dished him up a bowl of bran cereal and poured skim milk over it. Setting the bowl in front of him, she said firmly, "I know what you're going to say, Roger. But for once, will you let me have the first word?"

Roger looked startled. "By all means."

Susannah sat down across from him and propped her chin in her hands. "Look," she began, "it's not that I don't appreciate everything you've done for me in the past, Roger. I have you to thank for my success."

It wasn't quite true, but Susannah was feeling generous and wanted to butter up her boss.

While Roger ate his cereal, she continued, "But I'm starting to think I need to make some drastic changes in my life, Roger. I'm not happy in Milwaukee."

"Not happy!"

"I feel as if I'm going through the paces, that's all. I'm not living my life anymore. I'm letting you and 'Oh, Susannah!' guide it."

Frowning, Roger said, "You're blaming me for a personal problem?"

"No. I'm sorry if it sounds that way. I meant that my life hasn't felt very full. And I feel as if my time is starting to run out. Can you understand that, Roger? I want to *have* a life before I miss my chance."

"What do you mean?" Roger had raised his spoon to his mouth, but he froze, milk dripping onto the table, as shock set in. "You're not leaving 'Oh, Susannah!'?"

"No," she said at once. "I'm not. At least, not yet. But I have to cut back, Roger. I can't be consumed by the show every waking minute of my life. I want more."

"More what?"

Susannah lifted her hands helplessly. "Family. Friends. And passion! Passion for something other than ratings and time slots."

Roger put his spoon back into the bowl. "Do you feel passion—" he stressed the word distastefully "—for that big fellow who was here last night?"

"His name is Joe."

"How appropriate," Roger said, allowing an unpleasant smile to flicker on his mouth. "And he's some kind of mechanic, your grandmother tells me?"

"He's a carpenter, Roger, and don't be condescending, please. Just because a man works with his hands... well, Joe may not have the ability to schedule television programs like you do, but he's very talented in other ways."

"Now who's being condescending?"

It was impossible to argue with Roger. He used every trick in the book. If he wasn't being manipulative and making Susannah feel guilty, he was turning the tables so it was impossible for her to do likewise. Susannah sighed, hoping to hang on to her temper for once.

"I'm not going to argue the good qualities of Joe Santori. Why, I've only met the man recently. But he's helped me come to a few conclusions about myself, Roger. I've got a lot to give, and I can't go through life just giving it to a television audience."

"What's your plan?"

How like Roger to expect a plan when Susannah had only started thinking about the problem. She said, "I don't have one yet. But I'd like to phase out of 'Oh, Susannah!' Maybe do the show only a few days a week. Maybe I could get a cohost to take some of the load."

"Cohost?"

"Someone like Josie, for instance. She'd be good—maybe better than I am."

"She lacks the homey quality you have, Susannah."

"She could learn. She's got a future, Roger. You know that as well as I do because you hired her."

Roger eyed her solemnly. "You want to quit."

"No. Maybe." Susannah shook her head. "I'm not sure. I'm not too old to have children. Maybe someday I'd like to—"

"Good Lord," Roger said. "I should have known it was your biological clock ticking. I thought you hated children."

"I don't hate them. I just don't know how to handle them. But I can learn. I'm starting to see that. All I need is a chance."

"How will you support yourself if you stop working for me?"

"I'll manage. I have an idea."

Roger looked interested. "Tell me about it."

Roger might have been a little unfeeling when it came to his programs, but he had a very sharp head for business—especially when it came to self-promotion and public relations. And he had been her closest friend and colleague for a long time. So Susannah took the plunge and told him all about her book idea. She poured coffee for both of them and talked for nearly half an hour. Roger made a couple of astute observations and suggested a particular agency that specialized in booking talent for talk shows.

"You could do the whole circuit once your book is ready for distribution," Roger said. "I could make a few calls to get you on the national programs, if you like."

Susannah wasn't surprised that Roger would be willing to help promote her book. He was a pro. But it was a revelation to learn that Roger, who had always been a commandeering boss, didn't hold a grudge after all.

A quick wave of friendship for him caught Susannah unawares. It tugged at her heart and brought an involuntary smile to her face.

"What are you thinking?" Roger asked, seeing her expression.

"Nothing," Susannah said, leaning across the table toward him and impulsively covering his hand with her own. "Just...thank you. You've been a first-rate boss and a first-rate friend, Roger."

"And this Santori fellow?"

"What about him?"

"Do your plans for the future include him?"

"I'm not planning a future with Joe Santori," Susannah said. "But he wouldn't be a bad choice if I were. Joe's a good man, Roger. Kind and hardworking and . . . well, I don't mind saying he's sexy as hell."

Roger smiled sadly. "That sort of thing passes, Susannah. At a certain age, sex becomes unimportant."

"Maybe to you," Susannah shot back.

He looked surprised. "What does that mean?"

"I'd just like to give sex a chance, that's all. I feel as if I've missed out on something because I really haven't let my hair down all these years."

"And your carpenter is a sexual athlete, is he?"

"Don't be crude, Roger."

"Sex aside, you have to admit the man has nothing to offer you, Susannah."

"You hardly know him!"

"Can you list one good quality?"

"Certainly. He's got a sense of humor, and his singing voice is magnificent."

"Great. He can entertain you with singing telegrams."

"He's also very generous, sweet and gentle, yet he . . . well, he challenges me. He makes me look at things differently. We enjoy the same things—music and movies and . . . just plain people, I guess. But he's got a different perspective, and I like it."

Roger gazed at Susannah steadily. "Have you told him that?"

"No," Susannah admitted. "I suppose I should."

JOE HAD a terrific row with his daughter and came perilously close to forbidding her to attend the Tinsel Ball that evening.

"You can't go through life lying just for the fun of it! And lying to Susannah Atkins, of all people! If it hadn't been for the Atkins family, you'd be sitting at home tonight, the laughingstock of all your friends! And the way things look right now, you might be locked in your bedroom tonight, anyway—tonight and every night for the next four years!"

For once, Gina was chagrined by her own behavior. Her voice was barely a murmur. "I'm sorry, Dad."

Joe ran his hand through his hair in exasperation. "You're only sorry because I'm threatening to keep you away from the dance tonight."

"No, really." Gina's large dark eyes were liquid with pain and humiliation. "I'm sorry I told Susannah that stuff about a girlfriend."

"Why did you do it?" Joe demanded. "Why would you make up such a story about me?"

Gina's head drooped, and she couldn't meet his eye. "I dunno," she mumbled.

"Just to embarrass me?"

"No, Dad. I never meant... It just slipped out, I guess. I don't know why. We've been talking about Mom a lot lately, and... well, suddenly there was this really pretty lady in our house asking questions about you. I was afraid."

"Afraid?" Joe felt his anger drain out as if a plug had been pulled. "Afraid of what?"

Gina crumpled onto the sofa and curled up, hugging her knees against her chest. She couldn't meet her father's gaze. "Afraid you were going to forget about Mom, I guess."

"Gina, honey..."

"I mean, I know she's dead and you miss her. That's not the problem. Before she died, Mom said you should get married again. But I didn't want another mother. I still don't."

"A mother isn't somebody you replace, Gina. Neither is a wife. If I got married again, I wouldn't be erasing your mom."

Gina's head snapped up. "Then you *are* thinking about getting married?"

"No! Not this minute, anyway. But someday, maybe. If the right woman came along, I suppose."

"Is Susannah Atkins the right woman?"

Joe hadn't expected such hard questions from his daughter. For a moment he was at a loss for words. "I don't know," he said slowly. "I've only known her a short time."

"Well, she's okay," Gina said gruffly. "If you had to marry somebody, I guess it could be her. She's not exactly the motherly type, is she?"

"She's herself," Joe said.

"She doesn't try bossing me around," Gina noted, adding darkly, "and she'd better not start."

"I'm sure she'd have mixed feelings about dealing with you at all, young lady, after what you've done."

Again, Gina's expression was contrite. "Did I mess things up for you, Dad?"

"Would you be happy if you did?"

"N-no," Gina murmured. "I didn't mean to hurt you."

Joe softened with love for his daughter. Despite her troublemaking tendencies, she was still the best thing in his life. "You didn't hurt me, Gina. You caused some trouble, but nothing that can't be fixed. But *you* are going to do the fixing, my girl."

Gina looked startled. "Me? What am I going to do?"

"You're going to get yourself over to the Atkins house before the dance and explain everything."

"Oh, Dad!"

"I'm one hundred percent serious, Gina. You can't lie whenever it suits you and get off scot-free. You're going to tell Susannah that you lied, and then you're going to apologize."

"Dad!" she cried in anguish.

"I've been too easy on you," Joe said resolutely. "I've mended your fences in the past, but this time you're going to take care of it yourself. Maybe the experience will teach you a lesson that will end this lying business for good."

"You're mean! I'll be so embarrassed!"

"Good," Joe shot back. "Now go call Lars and tell him there will be a slight detour before the dance tonight. He can drive you over to the Atkins house to show Mrs. A. your dress. She told me last night how much fun she had helping you shop for it. The least you can do is visit her before the dance."

Gina surprised him by saying, "I already planned to do that, Dad."

Satisfied that he'd done his fatherly duties, Joe worked the rest of the day. He drove to Timberlake Lodge to check on the final renovations, then hurried back to the house to shower and dress.

All day he thought about what Gina had said—about marrying again. Could a woman like Susannah Atkins be happy as the wife of a simple man in a small town? Or was she cut out for the more glamorous life of a television personality?

Joe suspected he'd find out soon. The evening, he thought, promised to be very enlightening.

CHAPTER TWELVE

ROSE WAS SURPRISED to open her front door at six-thirty on Friday evening and find Joe Santori standing on her threshold. He looked more handsome than ever to her, and the glimmer of light in his eyes made her smile.

"You're a vision tonight, Mrs. A.!" Joe gave Rose a hard kiss on her forehead and presented her with a bunch of flowers—mostly red carnations with a jaunty plastic Santa in the middle.

"My land! Where did you get flowers in the dead of winter?"

He grinned and stepped into the house, thoughtfully closing the door behind himself. "At the supermarket. They certainly don't match your beauty tonight. Is that a new sweater?"

"This old thing? Heavens, no!" But Rose was pleased nevertheless. Joe always made her feel young. "What are you doing here? Certainly you're not coming to look at the plumbing?"

"Nope," said Joe. "My charming daughter will be here any minute to explain. Gina and Lars Travis have gone over to his parents' house to take some pictures before the big dance. But they'd like to drop in here to show off Gina's dress—and make a few apologies."

"Apologies for what?"

Joe lifted his palms. "My little girl has an active imagination, Mrs. A. She's been known to create a story when she sees a situation she doesn't like. I'm sorry to say that she led Susannah astray."

"About Angelica?"

"Oh, you heard that, too?"

"Yes, we thought..." Rose hardly dared to hope.

Cheerfully, Joe said, "There *is* no Angelica. She doesn't exist. Gina saw Susannah getting too close for comfort and thought she'd try keeping us apart by making up a girlfriend for me."

"Oh, Joe!" Rose's heart leaped. "Then you and Susannah... I mean, if something wonderful has truly happened between you two..."

Joe clasped Rose's arms fondly. "Something wonderful has certainly happened, Mrs. A. I've fallen pretty hard for your granddaughter. You'd better get a big stick if you want to keep me away from her."

Joyously, Rose cried, "Oh, Joe, there's nothing I'd like more in the world. What a wonderful Christmas this is going to be!" She pulled him down and gave him a big kiss, laughing. Joe was one of the most appealing men she had ever known—full of vitality, strong-willed yet good-humored. "Susannah's very fond of you, too, Joe. I hope you know that."

He winked. "I think I do."

"Joe, can I ask you something?"

"Sure. Anything."

Suddenly not sure why she wanted an answer, but needing it just the same, Rose asked, "Will you promise to take good care of my granddaughter?"

The laughter died out of Joe's eyes, and he frowned. "Why are you asking that now, Mrs. A.?" Full of concern, he asked, "Is something wrong?"

"No, nothing's wrong. I just . . . I want your promise, Joe. I've looked after Suzie ever since she was a little girl. She's not as strong as she looks. Inside, she's vulnerable, Joe. She needs family around her, and when I'm gone—"

"Don't," Joe urged reprovingly. "You shouldn't say things like that. If you're truly not feeling well, let's take you over to the hospital for a—"

"No, no. I'm being practical, that's all," Rose said, mustering a smile for him. "Will you promise?"

Joe's dark gaze searched hers for a long moment, but he nodded at last. "I promise. She's become very precious to me, Mrs. A."

Rose smiled and felt as though a weight had been lifted from her shoulders. She patted Joe thankfully and changed the subject before the moment turned maudlin. "Thank you. Now, how about an eggnog?"

"Sure. Or I could make you one of my grandmother's eggnog cocktails. She used to claim it was the only drink that could tame my grandfather on Christmas Eve. Want to try one?"

Rose smiled at Joe. She liked him very much. He was just the person she would wish for her granddaughter. "It sounds dangerous."

"Actually, it's sneaky. The secret ingredient creeps up on you."

Rose giggled, thoroughly enjoying Joe's high spirits. "How can I resist?"

He took her hand and wrapped it around his arm. "This way," he said, drawing her toward the kitchen.

They were laughing together over the blender when Roger made his entrance into the kitchen, catching Joe with one of Rose's frilly aprons tied loosely around his waist. Roger froze in the doorway, clearly amazed to see a man dressed so ridiculously.

"'Evening, Selby," Joe called cheerfully. "Want a cocktail?"

Stiffly, Roger said, "No, thanks, Santori. Susannah and I are going out shortly. I like to keep a clear head when I get behind the wheel of a car."

"Going out? Where to?"

"The Heidelberg. I'm told we'll find the best food there."

"Well, I'm partial to Marge's Diner, myself, but there's no accounting for taste. I can't tempt you with a cocktail, huh? Well, that just makes more for us, right, Mrs. A.?"

Roger cleared his throat. "I've just met your daughter, Santori."

Joe stopped pouring. "Gina's here?"

"Yes, she just arrived with a young man. Susannah's chatting with them in the sitting room."

Rose appealed to Joe. "Should we join them?"

Joe finished pouring some of the eggnog potion into a fluted glass, and shook his head. "Gina has a few things to tell Susannah in private. We'll let them hash it out, okay?"

Roger looked alarmed. "What's going on? Maybe I'd better..."

Before he could leave the kitchen, Rose seized his arm and drew him to the table. "It's nothing to worry about, Roger. Have a drink. Loosen up, for heaven's sake."

"I'm sufficiently loose," Roger said, casting a worried glance at the door, but taking the cocktail automatically. "I don't think Susannah should have to cope with the problems of a teenager who—"

"Oh, there's no problem," Rose sang, exchanging merry glances with Joe. "No problem at all, in fact. Drink up, Roger, dear."

Roger sipped the cocktail suspiciously, then choked as the liquor in it stung his throat.

Lars chose that moment to peep into the kitchen. "Uh, Mrs. Atkins?"

"Lars! Don't you look handsome tonight! Step into the light and let me have a good look at you!"

The lanky teen edged nervously into the kitchen, looking like a cross between a penguin and a well-dressed stork in his evening clothes. His long hair had been painstakingly combed back from his face and was held in place by some concoction that smelled suspiciously like strawberries. Lars played nervously with his hands and couldn't seem to decide if he wanted to look in any direction but the floor. Finding himself in the presence of his date's father seemed too much for him.

"Very handsome indeed, Lars," Rose pronounced. "Joe, find the boy a soda pop from the refrigerator."

Joe casually grabbed a bottle from the fridge and passed it to the teenager. In an obvious effort to ease Lars's nerves, Joe asked, "So, what do you think about the playoffs, Lars? Who's gonna win this year?"

The boy's face brightened. "Oh, Oakland looks as good as ever, sir," he said eagerly. "But Dallas isn't bad."

"Dallas?" Joe snorted. "They can't play on anything but their home turf! What do you think, Selby? Got an opinion on the playoffs?"

"Uh," said Roger, "I don't feel team sports are politically correct."

Lars and Joe looked at each other and burst into laughter. Rose tried to smother her own giggle, but she failed miserably and began to laugh, which was how Susannah and Gina found them a moment later. Susannah had her arm around the girl's shoulders, and Gina, looking shy for once, was obviously happy to have made her peace over the Angelica issue.

Susannah had eyes only for Joe. It was impossible to miss the electric glance that passed between them, Rose thought. The kitchen nearly sizzled with it. Susannah's face was shining, and Joe seemed to freeze for a long moment, his face wreathed in a grin.

But Rose and Lars were still laughing. Seeing their hilarity, Gina asked, "What's so funny?'

"Never mind," said Rose, still amused but hating to see anyone made a fool of. "Gina, darling, you're so pretty tonight! You'll be the belle of the ball."

Gina's shy smile of pleasure—along with a sharp push from the toe of Joe's boot—prodded Lars into crossing the kitchen to Gina's side and saying, "Maybe we'd better get going, Gina."

"Sure," said Gina. "But one thing before we go. We, uh, we want to thank everybody for all your help. Susannah, and Daddy, and Mrs. Atkins—thanks a lot for everything."

Rose found herself enfolded in Gina's arms, and she clung to the girl for a moment longer than she needed to, just to enjoy the hug of a grateful teenager on her way to one of the most memorable nights of her life. How many times had Rose seen the young Susannah off on dates like this one? A funny wave of déjà vu swept over Rose.

Next, Gina kissed her father, who squeezed her back with a fond grin. Susannah had moved to his side, and Rose suddenly noticed what a handsome family group they made.

When Lars cleared his throat and again said they'd better be going, Roger looked relieved, and muttered something about a dinner reservation. Everyone decided to leave at the same time, so the gathering of coats, boots and car keys was noisy and full of laughter. Joe waited in the doorway with Rose, and they watched adults and teenagers sort out their belongings.

Going out the door, Roger said, "We'd invite you along, Santori, but Susannah and I have business to discuss."

"That's a shame," Joe said, feigning solemnity. "Is that the only way you can have dinner with such a pretty lady, Selby?"

Roger managed a weak smile. "Hmm. Good night, Mrs. Atkins. We'll be back early."

Susannah was next, studiously avoiding Joe's eye and hugging Rose quickly. "I hate leaving you alone again, Granny Rose. . . ."

"Don't start that again, Suzie!"

Joe slipped his arm around Rose. "I'll stay with her, Miss Suzie. We're going to drink eggnog and play poker. What do you say, Mrs. A.?"

"I say I hope you cleaned out your bank account today, buster, because I'm a crack poker player."

Susannah looked reassured. She touched Joe's arm, glanced up into his eyes and said softly, "Thank you."

"Good night, Mrs. Atkins!" Gina called, leading everyone down the snow-dusted porch steps.

"Call the restaurant if you need me," Susannah said over her shoulder as Roger propelled her out into the evening air.

They left, piling into their vehicles, and Rose found herself alone with the crestfallen Joe, who watched the cars depart through the window.

"You look like a kid who didn't get the red bicycle for Christmas," she said to him.

Joe grinned sheepishly and admitted, "I hate like hell seeing her go off with him tonight."

"Well, do something about it."

"Like what?"

"We'll think of something," Rose said firmly.

And they did. Maybe two heads were better than one, for between the two of them, they came up with a plan that sounded foolproof.

Joe laughed and agreed to try, though not without expressing worry about leaving Rose alone for the evening. She brushed him off and sent him on his way, wishing him good luck and happy hunting. He gave her a hearty kiss and rushed out the door with coattails flying.

Rose waved to him from the doorway. Then she closed the door and was alone in her cozy home.

Maybe I'll just go to bed early, she told herself, sagging wearily against the doorjamb.

But at that moment, her gaze fell on a small handbag left on the hallway chair. It was Gina's, no doubt, and full of lipstick and hairspray and all those vital necessities a girl needed for her first formal ball. Rose snatched up the purse and hurried to the door. If she was quick enough, she could catch Joe before the truck pulled away. He could take the purse to Gina.

She yanked open the door just as Joe's truck began to pull away from the curb.

"Wait!" Rose shouted, but her voice was carried away on the wind.

The porch steps were slippery, but she hurried down them and dashed out onto the sidewalk. Her thick sweater was not warm enough to protect her from the biting winter wind, but she kept going and held the purse over her head, waving frantically. "Wait! Joe! Gina's purse!"

The truck reached the corner and paused for the stop sign. Rose ran after him, but Joe pulled away without noticing the old woman in hot pursuit. Disappointed, she faltered to a stop beside the Morgan family Christmas display. A lighted reindeer stood attentively in the yard. Rose leaned on an antler to catch her breath.

And that was when the pain hit her like a freight train. She cried out as a weight slammed into her chest, knocking her to the snowy ground. The reindeer toppled with her, and she fell over the stiff plastic legs. Her knees cracked through the crust of snow, then Rose sprawled in the snow, unable to draw a breath for the agony in her chest. The pain felt like fire, and it spread quickly to her neck and left arm.

"Oh, dear," she gasped, clutching the reindeer and trying to right herself.

Not now. Not like this. She fought to take in enough breath to call for help. *Not at Christmas,* she thought. *Don't let me be sick for Christmas.*

The reindeer slipped from her grasp and Rose crumpled into the snow. Very quickly, the fiery pain swelled up again and engulfed her.

SUSANNAH SAW the pretty white lights of the Heidelberg glowing as they approached the restaurant. Roger pulled under the decorated canopy to drop off Susannah before parking his fancy car.

"Are you sure you want to do this?" he asked, seeing her hesitate with her hand on the door handle.

She managed a smile. "Joe will look after Granny Rose."

"She'll be fine," Roger assured her. "And since we didn't get our trip to the beach, I really need to discuss those program segments with you, Susannah. We can get some of that out of the way over dinner."

"Roger," Susannah said on impulse, "can't we just have a pleasant dinner together?"

He looked surprised. "Of course. And we can talk business at the same time."

Susannah withheld a sigh. For Roger, business *was* pleasant. With a thrill of surprise, she realized that until lately, she had felt the same way. But now, at least, she could differentiate between work and play. That was a start, she supposed.

She got out of the car and went into the restaurant while Roger found a parking slot. She gave her coat to the attendant, who made a fuss about "Oh, Susannah!" until Roger arrived. Then he took her arm and spoke persuasively to the hostess, who led them into the crowded restaurant. The room, attractively decorated for the holidays with garlands of greens draped around the fireplace and windows, looked even more dramatic at night than it had at lunchtime, Susannah noted. Each table was lighted by a beribboned candle. A graceful tree glowed in the middle of the room, decked with ornaments that had obviously been made by elementary school students out of construction paper, glue and glitter. Beside the tree was a large, impressive, red-cushioned chair, obviously the seat saved for Santa Claus. Susannah ran her fingertips over the carved back of the imposing chair as she passed by.

Roger always insisted on a prominent table. It was his way, Susannah realized, of showing her off to the public. The hostess took them to a table close to the Christmas tree. Susannah was aware of the stir her appearance aroused, because many Tyler citizens murmured as she sat down. A few waved to her from across the room.

"See?" Roger asked, sitting down across from her. "Isn't it nice to be recognized by the public?"

"Yes and no," Susannah replied, burying her nose in the menu. For some reason, she didn't want to be Oh, Susannah tonight. It was nearly Christmas, after all.

Roger must have sensed her mood, because he snapped his menu closed and said, "Let's celebrate, shall we? I'll order some champagne and we'll toast another year of 'Oh, Susannah!'"

Susannah knew her smile was weak. "That sounds nice, Roger."

Even before the champagne arrived, Roger plunged into his planned discussion. He had decided to expand the horizons of the "Oh, Susannah!" program and wondered if Susannah would like to try conducting segments on family health matters twice a week.

"We'll get a local doctor for you to interview in the studio," Roger said, enthusiasm glowing in his face. "Each week you can talk about a different topic—childhood illnesses, women's health problems, the sort of things our audience will find informative."

"Sounds fine," Susannah said distractedly. She frowned at the menu and wondered if it was written in hieroglyphics. It made no sense. Her head was swimming.

"Do you like the idea? I've been interviewing doctors all week. I think I've found one who'll be just great. She's got a lot of pep and will look fine on camera. Besides, she can turn a good phrase and—"

"So you've already made the decision?" Susannah asked.

"Well . . . no. Your opinion counts, too, Susannah."

"Why do I need to interview the doctor? If she's so great, why can't she do her segment by herself?"

"Because the show is 'Oh, Susannah!,' that's why. We need you on camera all the time, Susannah."

She sighed and listened to Roger with only half an ear while he explained the rest of his ideas.

"We've also found a veterinarian who could come in and talk about pets. He says he can bring in puppies or kittens—even snakes, if we want. He'll talk about training and feeding and all that kind of thing."

"I won't hold snakes, Roger. I hate snakes."

He nodded. "We'll get around that, I promise. Then we've been interviewing a guy who is an expert in gadgets."

"Gadgets?"

Roger leaned forward, his eyes alight. "Right. He's a little weird, but he knows all the latest developments in technology. Computers that run your household, gizmos that make life easier... Why, he showed me the television of the future! It's got three screens and a modem hookup so you can do your banking or shopping simply by—"

"Roger, I don't know anything about computers."

"You don't have to! The computer weirdo can do all the talking!"

Susannah put down her menu. "Then why do you need me?"

"I told you," he said patiently. "Because the show is 'Oh, Susannah!,' not—"

"But what you're describing *isn't* 'Oh, Susannah!,' Roger. I do cooking and crafts and entertaining. I'm not Regis Philbin or Kathy Lee Gifford. I'm not Geraldo or Sally Jessy Raphael, either. I'm me."

"But to get a broader audience—"

"I'm unique the way I am now. You want to turn the program into something that everyone else does."

"Susannah, it's time to grow."

She laughed. "That's what I've been telling you, Roger!"

He frowned. "I don't understand."

"I want to grow, too. But growth for me doesn't include a broader television audience. I'm ready for some personal growth."

"We can do both," Roger said earnestly, "by expanding the horizons of the show, Susannah. Wouldn't you like to know more about medical matters? Or—"

"Or computers? Or snakes? No, Roger, I want to know more about *me.*"

"But—"

"Look, Roger, why can't you expand the program without me? If you really want to change the focus of the show, why don't you use all these wonderful people you've found and let me be one of the crowd?"

"The show is called—"

"I know what it's called. But names can be changed."

"We don't want to lose you, Susannah."

"Maybe not..." She smiled. "You wanted to talk to me about all this at the beach, didn't you, Roger? You wanted to get me alone, wear me down and make me agree to all your new plans."

"That's not it at all." But Roger turned a charming shade of pink. "I wanted your input."

"But you'd already made the decision."

"Don't be angry, Susannah."

"I'm not." Susannah found herself flushing with excitement. "I'm really not angry. I'm happy, in fact."

"Look, we certainly do want you to continue to anchor the show. You're the mainstay, Susannah. You're the glue that holds everything together."

"Josie holds everything together. She's the brains behind the scenes."

"But you're the personality *on* the scene. Not just for the audience, but for the crew and staff as well. We need you, Susannah. We're prepared to make a lot of changes in your contract to make you happy. It's up for renewal in three months, you know."

"Yes, I know."

Roger heard Susannah's tone and looked at her for a long time. "I'm not sure I like the look in your eye."

Contract renewal time. It was always a good chance to make some changes. Susannah laughed and picked up her menu again.

"Why are you laughing?"

"Because I'm happy, of course."

"But... but—"

"Don't look so worried, Roger. Look, here's the champagne you ordered."

"Suddenly I don't feel like drinking it."

Roger looked positively glum while the waitress planted the champagne cooler by his chair. She pulled the bottle out of the cracked ice, ready to pop the cork, but Roger waved her off. "I'll open it in a moment," he said.

"Fine, sir. Are you ready to order?"

"Not yet," he said. "Give us a few minutes. Susannah..."

But he was prevented from continuing their conversation by the arrival of Santa Claus.

"Ho, ho, ho!" The powerful voice boomed across the restaurant, causing heads to turn and laughter to break out.

The tall, red-coated man stepped into the restaurant, waving merrily. He headed for the chair in the middle of the room, shaking hands with a few of the men and kissing the hands of ladies along the way. He caused quite a stir. His white beard almost ended up in someone's soup, and his gleaming black boots left a trail of snow across the carpet. But everyone in the restaurant responded with good cheer.

From the lounge came the sound of someone playing "Here Comes Santa Claus," on the piano. Everyone clapped and a few people began to sing as Santa made his way across the room. The jolly fellow used the sleeve of his red coat to polish the bald head of one of a group of local businessmen, causing more laughter.

Susannah watched the fun, smiling. But when the white pom-pom on Santa's red hat fell over his face and he blew it out of the way with a noisy puff, she gasped. Then she laughed, too. "Oh, no!"

Roger looked around at the commotion. "What's going on?"

Santa made his way across the room, working his audience like a pro. At last he reached the table where

Susannah and Roger sat, and he struck a pose with his fists braced on his hips. "Ho, ho, ho!"

Susannah smiled up at him and patted the pillow that was his belly. "Merry Christmas, Santa."

"Merry Christmas to you, Miss Suzie," said a familiar voice. Joe's dark eyes gleamed from behind the spectacles, and he grasped Susannah's hand. "Have you been a good girl this year?"

"Oh, yes, Santa, a very good girl."

"Then come with me," he intoned, "and we'll discuss your Christmas list."

Roger's mouth gaped as Susannah was swept out of her seat by Santa Claus, who also made a grab for the champagne bottle and made off with both prizes. He led Susannah to the big chair beside the Christmas tree and made a show of bowing and inviting her by pantomime to sit. The restaurant diners laughed and clapped, so Susannah graciously curtsied and sat primly in the big chair while Santa knelt on one knee before her and popped the cork on the champagne. A waitress appeared at his elbow with two glasses, and Joe poured. He handed one to Susannah, who accepted it with a bow of her head.

No one in Tyler would let Joe Santori get by without singing a Christmas song, and the pianist soon played the opening chords of "I'll Be Home for Christmas."

Joe groaned laughingly and tried to refuse.

"Please sing," Susannah encouraged, too softly for anyone else to hear.

He kissed her hand. "How can I say no to you?"

So he sang the old favorite—half for his audience, but mostly for Susannah. The lyrics were poignant, but Joe's voice made them even harder on the heartstrings. He soon had the whole room enraptured, and Susannah felt as if her head were already swimming from the champagne. There was nothing more romantic, she decided, than a handsome man pouring out his soul in a song.

He must have seen how deeply she was affected by the tune, because he held her hand tightly. For the final verse, he pulled off his beard and smiled into Susannah's eyes so winningly that surely no one in the room could doubt his feelings for her.

When the applause began, Susannah said, "That was wonderful."

He leaned close and kissed her cheek. "You're wonderful."

The audience aahed, and Susannah blushed, touching Joe's cheek with her fingertips and wishing they were alone.

The applause died away and the patrons of the restaurant went back to their meals, leaving Joe and Susannah to look longingly into each other's eyes.

Then Roger harrumphed nearby and Susannah shook herself as if coming out of a magic spell. "Oh, Roger..."

"Never mind, Susannah," he said. "I can see your mind isn't on business tonight."

She got hastily to her feet. "I'm sorry, Roger."

"No, you're not." He allowed an unhappy smile. "But that's okay. I understand. We'll talk another time."

"But our dinner?"

He patted Joe on the shoulder. "I think you've found a more entertaining dinner companion. I'll go back and see your grandmother. Good night, Santori. I enjoyed the song. You've got quite a gift."

"Thanks," said Joe, faintly surprised. When Roger had departed, Joe said, "The guy's got more class than I first thought."

"I think he's come to the same conclusion about you."

Joe grinned. "Have you?"

"You're a classy guy, Joe Santori." Susannah smiled. "And you've got courage, I must say. Waltzing in here in that getup..."

He pretended to look wounded. "You don't like my suit?"

"It's perfect for sliding down chimneys, but for dinner..."

"Nobody's going to mind," he declared, and climbed to his feet. He pulled Susannah off the red cushions and drew her to the table Roger had just vacated. He handed Susannah into her chair once more and quickly slid into the seat next to hers so he could be close. He said, "You look so beautiful tonight, I hated to see it wasted on Roger Selby."

"Roger's not as bad as you think."

"Maybe not. But I was damned jealous."

Joe wanted to do nothing but sit in his chair and admire Susannah's beauty. She looked wonderful, her simple wool dress set off by a long pendant that drew his attention to her breasts. She was easily the prettiest woman he had ever known. With his voice turning husky, he said, "I wanted to be with you tonight, Susannah. Did Gina tell you the truth?"

"About Angelica?" Susannah's face began to shine and she leaned toward him. "Yes. I had my suspicions, especially after you mentioned you'd been having trouble getting the truth from her. But...oh, Joe,

I was so worried you were already committed to somebody else."

"I'm only committed to my daughter," he said, adding cheerfully, "the lying little pest."

Susannah reached out and touched his cheek. "Don't be hard on her, please. She did it for love, you know. I think she's afraid of losing you."

"I'm beginning to see that," Joe admitted, covering Susannah's gentle fingers with his own hand. "I'm beginning to see a lot of things more clearly now, in fact. Susannah, I've fallen hard for you."

She smiled. "Is that what you call it?"

"This isn't the time or place to say more," he replied, and was unable to stop himself from adding, "I want to be alone with you, Miss Suzie."

"We are alone."

"I mean *alone,* not in a room with a hundred people. I want to take you home to my bed, Miss Suzie," he clarified, his quiet voice laced with desire, "and make you mine."

Damning their audience, Joe leaned closer yet and pressed his lips against hers, searing Susannah with a kiss meant to tide her over until he could do the job properly. Susannah's mouth tasted warm and sweetly of champagne, and her hands tightened almost imperceptibly on his shirt as he deepened the kiss and teased her delicate tongue. *I want to be alone with you now,* he thought, and she gave a small affirmative moan as if in answer.

Joe released her gently and enjoyed her slow blink of languorous pleasure.

Susannah felt like a woman in a dream—a wonderfully perfect dream.

I'm in love with him, she thought. *This is what love feels like. I can't think straight. I can't possibly make polite dinner conversation—not tonight.*

"Suzie," Joe murmured as if reading her thoughts, "let's get out of here."

"And go where? Roger will be at Granny Rose's house."

Joe took her hand and said very seriously, "Come to my house, Suzie. Come home with me tonight."

"Gina?"

"She's at the dance. And Lars is taking her to a friend's house to spend the night afterward. We'd be alone, Susannah. All night."

CHAPTER THIRTEEN

JOE'S HOUSE WAS QUIET, with only one lamp burning in the hallway. By that light, Joe helped Susannah off with her coat. He hung it in the closet and led her by the hand through the kitchen, where he stopped long enough to pull a bottle of chilled wine from the refrigerator. Carrying two long-stemmed glasses upended through his fingers and the bottle in the crook of his arm, he guided Susannah directly upstairs.

"You're not giving me any time to get nervous, are you?" she asked, hesitating on the threshold of his dark bedroom.

"You're having second thoughts?"

"No." But Susannah stopped in the doorway and watched as Joe put the wine on the nightstand and proceeded to the small Victorian fireplace where a log had already been laid. He opened the flue, lit a match from a tin box on the mantel and set the tinder on fire. A moment later, a small flame sprang up, warming the room with a soft glow. Joe used the same match to light a single candle on the mantel—an act that was surprisingly sexy in a man his size.

He blew out the match and tossed it into the grate. Turning to Susannah, he put his hands into his trouser pockets and smiled. "You *look* like a woman with second thoughts."

"This is the first time I've done this in...well, a long time."

"In this day and age, I guess that's a good thing. Abstinence has been the best way to stay healthy. I had my annual physical checkup a few weeks ago, and I'm clean, too."

"Heavens, I wasn't asking—"

He laughed. "I know. Don't look so mortified."

"I suppose even people our age should be careful."

Joe crossed the carpet to her and took Susannah's hands in his own. "Don't start on the 'people our age' thing, all right? You'll get me worrying about my performance before we get our clothes off."

She mustered a smile. "I can't imagine you worrying about anything."

He drew a circle on her cheek with one finger. "I worry about a lot of things, Susannah. One of them is making you happy."

"I'm happy when I'm with you," she whispered, hardly trusting her voice to speak any louder. Suddenly she was very nervous indeed. Alone with Joe in a restaurant or a snowy sleigh or even his truck late at night was one thing. But alone in his bedroom, his easy chair piled with magazines, a dirty shirt and a paper bag from the pharmacy, was quite another. His bed was a huge four-poster with a bright quilt on top—a product of the Quilting Circle, if Susannah was any judge of quilts. He kept four pillows on the bed, all trimmed with white lace. He had left a set of headphones on the bed, too, and the cord stretched to a CD player on the dresser. Joe liked to listen to his music at all hours, it seemed.

The intimacy of the place was overwhelming for Susannah. Glancing around the room where Joe must have lain dreaming about his wife, Susannah felt like an intruder.

Voice subdued, Joe said, "I won't push you tonight if you'd rather not go through with this, Susannah."

With a rush of gratefulness, she said, "I—I guess I'm a little uncertain, that's all. We've talked about your wife, but—"

As if guessing where her thoughts had traveled, Joe said, "She never lived here, you know. I came to Tyler after she died."

"But—"

"We can talk about Marie, if you like." Joe pulled her to the bed and sat down on the quilt, drawing Susannah beside him, thigh to thigh. "I know I've allowed my wife's death to shape the way I am now. I'm bossy and overprotective and a lot of other things—maybe to make up for the way things happened with Marie. I always felt as if I could have helped her."

"Joe, don't beat yourself up."

"I know, I know. I shouldn't feel guilty, but I do, and I overcompensate sometimes. But getting to know you, Susannah, has taught me that I can't be the one who makes all the decisions."

"She was such a big part of your life."

"Yes, and that part's not over—not while Gina's still here. But I'm ready to start again, Susannah. With you."

"Are you sure?"

"Are *you* sure?"

She smiled. "Of course. I trust you."

"Even though you haven't known me long?" He brushed her hair back from her shoulder so he could see her expression better.

"I feel as though I've known you forever. We clicked, almost from the first."

"Despite a few complications along the way."

"But I've felt comfortable with you all along," Susannah insisted, resting one hand uneasily on his knee. "It's my own feelings that upset me. I'm at such a crossroads, it seems. I'm afraid."

"Of living?"

"Maybe." Susannah took a breath. "You're so full of vitality. You take risks and enjoy every moment. You're like Granny Rose that way. I wish I could be like that, but I..."

"You can be like that." Joe leaned closer. He nibbled her earlobe and murmured, "Let me into your life, Susannah."

"What if I bore you?"

He laughed softly. "Not a chance."

Anxiously, Susannah staved off his hand before he could touch her and asked, "What if I'm not good enough? What if I can't please you?"

"Don't talk nonsense," he said.

"Joe..."

"Shut up," he said amicably, already unfastening the top button on her dress. "There's just one thing you need to know."

"What's that?"

"I love you." He kissed her mouth and whispered again, "I love you, Susannah."

Her heart turned over at the sound of his melodic voice rolling those three wonderful words out, and she kissed him back, lifting her hands to his face to make the kiss last forever. As the first dizzying sensations of desire washed over her, she was hardly aware that he finished unbuttoning her dress. He pulled it from her shoulders slowly, as if unveiling a treasure. Then he sat back and warmed Susannah with his gaze.

"You're so lovely, Suzie. Sometimes I feel like a big ox when I'm with you."

She loosened his tie and began to unfasten his shirt. His jacket came off first, then the shirt, and finally he was bare-chested. Susannah kissed his cheek first, then his neck before moving down his chest. She swiped her tongue naughtily across his flat male nipples, conscious that his breathing stopped and his grip tightened on her. His skin was taut over hard muscle—evidence of the labor he performed every day. Caressing him first with feathery touches, Susannah soon moved to unfasten his belt.

Long minutes later, Joe looked more like a Roman god than ever before in the golden glow of firelight. Seeing him in his beautiful natural state, Susannah suddenly wanted to be naked, too. She forget to be shy about her body, and didn't care if Joe found the dimples on her knees. Together, they stripped off the rest of her clothing and then fell across the bed, entwined and feverish.

"Darling," he murmured. "Do you know how much I want you?"

"If this is any indication," she whispered back, touching him, "it's no secret."

"Oh, God, don't do that or we'll be finished before we start!"

"Do you like that? And this, maybe?"

Joe groaned and rolled over, pinning Susannah to the quilt and forcing her to stop the caresses that were almost too much for him. He began to kiss her all over, trailing his mouth along her skin as if enjoying a rich dessert. "You're so beautiful, Susannah. So sexy. I can't believe I've waited this long to have you."

"It's been agony for me, too," she said, slipping her fingers into his thick hair and arching her back to meet his kisses. "Do you know how close I came to asking you to drive us to Milwaukee?"

"Milwaukee?" He lifted his head and stared at her. "In heaven's name, why?"

"Because we could have used my apartment. My bed. We could have been alone and—"

He feigned anger. "You witch, why didn't you say so? You mean we could have been making love all week?"

"Well, it's more than an hour away by car and—"

"It would have been worth the drive, don't you think?"

Susannah gasped as he caressed her with new intimacy. "Oh, yes," she sighed.

His smile was wicked and he coaxed her body with gentle, rhythmical fingertips. "Have you truly wanted me?"

She smiled through lazy-lidded eyes as he increased the tension by running his left hand over her skin and following the caresses with his lips. "Yes." She could hardly breathe, let alone speak, but she forced the words out. "I couldn't admit it, though—not even to myself—until just a few days ago. I thought I was past all this nonsense."

"Nonsense?" He nipped her earlobe.

"I did. But now I... oh, Joe, please don't stop doing that." She shuddered with pleasure, closing her eyes at the tide of sensations that washed up from within. Instinctively, she wrapped her legs around Joe's lean hips, and he settled against her with a hungry growl. "Oh, Joe."

There was little talking after that—just a cry or a moan that communicated everything they had to know. Susannah felt as if the fire had leaped up and consumed them. The flickering light bathed Joe's body in an unearthly glow, and her own flesh felt as if it might burst into flame at any moment. She gave herself up to the delights Joe introduced, wantonly begging for more when he teasingly withheld his favors and brazenly prolonged his wait when he growled his readiness to take her completely.

At last they became one flesh and, absurdly, Susannah found herself weeping and laughing with the wonder of their union. Joe whispered sweet nothings in her ear, tenderly rocking until her mind was deliciously full of nothing but exquisite pleasures. When her climax came, it shook Susannah to her very core.

"Oh, Joe, I love you!"

The words drove him over the edge of sanity. A mad moment later, Joe exploded in a tremendous shudder of joy. Exhausted yet rejuvenated in spirit, they clung to each other, sharing a heartbeat and a long, liquid kiss.

A lifetime later, they were properly tucked into the bedclothes together and sharing a glass of wine. As the cool liquid eased down her throat, Susannah wondered if she'd ever felt so content. So satisfied. So loved.

"I adore you," she murmured to him, nestling her head on his chest and trailing her hand down his belly. "I may never get enough of you, Joe Santori."

"We have a long time to find out," he replied, toying with her hair and drinking deeply from the wineglass. Then he set the glass on the nightstand and pulled Susannah under the covers again for another bout of erotic caresses. Afterward, they lay talking for hours. Joe spoke about Marie again, and Susannah listened carefully. He had grieved, she realized, but she felt he was right—Joe *was* ready to start again. The fire burned low and the bottle on the nightstand slowly emptied, and Susannah felt as if she'd never been so close to another human being before in her life.

At last, Susannah peered at the alarm clock beside the bed. "It's after one o'clock. I should go home."

"Spend the night," Joe urged.

"We may not get another chance like this for a long time," she murmured, drawing whorls in the crisp hair on his chest. "But I shouldn't stay."

"Your grandmother will be shocked."

"You might be surprised where she's concerned," Susannah said with a smile. "She's very fond of you. But just the same, I think I'll go."

Joe agreed and kissed her once more, then climbed out of bed and pulled Susannah to her feet.

They were dressing when the doorbell rang downstairs.

Joe straightened abruptly from pulling on his boots. "Who in the world?"

Gina, Susannah thought. *Something's happened to Gina.*

She didn't say that, but she could see the same thought on Joe's face. He left the room without a word, still shirtless, and clattered down the steps to answer the door.

Hastily, Susannah finished dressing, then tiptoed to the top of the stairs. She was astonished to hear Roger Selby's voice in the downstairs hall.

"She's here, isn't she?" Roger asked, his voice strained and awkward sounding.

"Hold on, Selby. What's the problem?"

"I need to see Susannah," Roger stated brusquely. "There's been an accident."

At the word *accident* Susannah started down the stairs immediately. It was suddenly not important that Joe was half-dressed and she herself was on the second floor. Any fool could see what was going on.

"Roger, what's wrong?" She clutched the handrail for dear life. Her imagination was already boiling with possibilities and she said, "Has something happened to Granny Rose?"

"She's had a heart attack," Roger said curtly.

Susannah felt her heart freeze, and she sat down abruptly on the steps, too dizzy to stand.

Joe clutched Roger's coat as if ready to punish him for being so cruel. "Blast you, Selby, cut the dramatics and tell us everything before I wring your neck."

"There's no need for threats, Santori. While you two have been cozying up here doing God knows what, your grandmother, Susannah, has had a heart attack. One of the neighbors found her in a snowbank and called an ambulance. She's at the hospital."

"She—she's alive?" Susannah could barely whisper.

"For the moment," Roger said. "Come on, Susannah. I'll take you to the hospital."

She felt as if she were swimming in Joe's dark eyes, but it didn't help the pang of guilt. Nor did the pressure of his hand on hers or the quick kiss he gave her temple to tell her that he understood. There was no need for words. Joe grabbed her coat from the closet and helped her into it. Roger opened the front door and waited, letting a blast of cold air into the house.

Susannah rushed into the night.

She endured an interminable ride to the hospital with Roger, who summarized the situation as best he could.

"You'll have to speak to the doctor for the whole story," he said. "They wouldn't tell me much. I've been scouring the whole town trying to find you tonight."

Susannah flushed. If only she'd known Granny Rose was so sick!

Roger dropped her off at the front door, and Susannah rushed into the hospital alone while he parked the car. The intensive-care unit in Tyler's hospital had only three beds, and Granny Rose was the sole patient. The nurses were sympathetic and kind.

"She's resting now," the head nurse explained to Susannah outside the room. "The doctor's been checking on her every hour, and we watch her monitors like hawks."

"Thank you. May I go in?"

"We can bend the rules, I think." The nurse smiled reassuringly. "Don't wake her."

"Is she..." Susannah was almost afraid to ask. "How bad was it?"

"The doctor who admitted her should give you that information. But at your grandmother's age...well, it didn't help that she spent so much time in the snow. The results of hypothermia in a patient her age—"

"What was she doing outside?" Susannah cried. "I left her in the house. I can't imagine... Oh, I should have stayed at home tonight. I should have...oh, dear."

The nurse patted Susannah's arm. "Don't let the guilt eat you up. You couldn't have prevented anything. And we're taking good care of her now."

Susannah nodded and tried to pull herself together. Then she went into the hospital room to sit with her grandmother.

In the big bed, Granny Rose looked appallingly small and her face papery. An obscenely fat plastic tube had been fastened to her nose, and a bottle of some medication was dripping from an IV stand into her thin arm. Susannah choked back a sob at the sight.

But she didn't waken her grandmother. She tiptoed to the edge of the bed and sat down in a stiff plastic chair. Then she began a long vigil—of watching Granny Rose breathe and trying not to cry.

Please don't let her die, Susannah prayed. *She's such a vibrant woman. She's still so young—young at heart. Don't take her yet. I'm just learning the lessons she tried to teach me.*

The night crawled along, and Susannah's only company was the equipment that monitored her grandmother's life. The beeps sounded terribly weak. The thin liquids that seeped into Granny Rose's arm seemed inadequate. Susannah's fear grew as the hours stretched into a dim winter morning.

The doctor arrived at 6:00 a.m., and it was Jeff Baron, Liza's brother. He knew Rose well indeed. He spoke with Susannah in hushed tones.

"I won't kid you," he said softly. "Your grandmother has had a severe heart attack. Has she been under unusual strain lately?"

Susannah nodded miserably. "We've had a busy week."

"Getting ready for Christmas, I suppose?"

"Yes, but she saw Dr. Phelps. He was going to give her more tests."

"She's had some severe arrhythmia problems, I understand. Well, that sort of thing can escalate into a heart attack if left untreated."

"Why didn't he treat her, then?"

"I'm betting Rose refused the drugs so she could be on her toes for Christmas. She's a remarkable woman for her age, but this kind of condition should have been treated right away. Now, well, things aren't good."

"What are you saying, Jeff?"

The young doctor sighed. "I won't make promises, Susannah. Let's see how she manages this morning. We'll be able to make more accurate predictions after she's had some time to stabilize."

But Susannah could see Jeff wasn't hopeful. Left alone again with Granny Rose, Susannah sank into the bedside chair and began to cry. She couldn't help herself, and the tears flowed so forcefully that she began to hiccup, too.

That was enough to wake Granny Rose.

Susannah saw her grandmother's eyes stir and open, and for a long moment, Rose stared at the ceiling of the hospital room. Then she forced her gaze to travel slowly to Susannah, who leaned forward.

"Good morning," Susannah whispered through her tears.

Rose swallowed with difficulty and tried to speak. But she was very weak, and her voice wavered. "What happened?"

"You've had a heart attack," Susannah explained, then found she couldn't say more. She grasped Rose's hand and held it.

Rose closed her eyes. "Damn," she muttered.

Susannah laughed and hiccuped again, but her face was covered with tears. "Oh, Granny Rose!"

Rose lay quietly for a moment, as if marshaling her strength. Then she opened her eyes again and whispered, "It was stupid. I was running."

"Running! Whatever for?"

"Gina," Rose said. "Gina's purse. Forgot it."

Susannah patted her hand. "Don't talk about it now. Save your strength. Just rest. We want you to get better."

"Joe," Rose whispered.

"He—he's not here. Roger brought me."

Rose's brow twitched weakly. "Roger..."

"Roger Selby. He's been very kind, Granny Rose. He brought me here last night, and I think he's still waiting outside. He's worried about you."

Too weak to stay awake any longer, Rose closed her eyes. Softly, she said, "Hogwash."

CHAPTER FOURTEEN

THE MORNING CRAWLED as only mornings in an intensive-care unit can. Susannah spoke with the day-shift nurses who came in often to check Rose. But mostly she watched her grandmother and silently prayed. Rose slept fitfully and woke once, but her mind had begun to wander and her few words made little sense.

Exhaustion was seeping into Susannah's bones, and her own brain was starting to function poorly. She dozed in her chair and found herself swimming in memories of the happy times she'd spent with her grandmother. It was Rose who had taught the young Susannah how to bake wholesome breads and make clear, tart jellies. She had coached Susannah at her sewing machine and taught her how to drive a car. They had gone berry picking every summer together and sneaked up to the lake to skinny-dip on hot August nights.

Rose Atkins had been more than a mother, more than a friend to Susannah. She'd been both—and more. A confidante, a soul mate, a cheerleader. She'd been Susannah's toughest critic. And her biggest fan. Over the years, she had called Susannah with great ideas for her television program. She'd given her advice on her love life and her career—but only if asked. She had loved Susannah unconditionally. And Susannah loved Rose back just as fiercely.

What will I do if I lose you? Susannah asked silently, allowing herself some time to think selfishly at last. *How can I be me if I don't have you behind me, Granny Rose?*

Susannah sat forward and tried to talk to her grandmother. "Granny Rose? Please don't leave me. You're a fighter. You can get well if you try, I know you can. Don't you want to take our sleigh ride this Christmas? And what about New Year's Eve? We've got to drink ginger ale and play cards, just like always."

But Rose didn't waken. Her heart seemed to grow weaker, in fact. The unsteady beat on the monitor became slower and more erratic as the hours plodded along.

In the late afternoon, Jeff Baron came in again, as he had several times during the day. He stood beside the bed and read the nurses' notes, then examined Rose gently. Then he called to her. "Rose? Rose, can you hear me?"

With an effort, Rose attempted to rouse herself. She saw Jeff's face above her and she waved weakly with two fingers of her right hand.

Jeff tried to coax the elderly woman into answering his questions, but her watery gaze traveled to Susannah. In a feeble voice, she croaked, "Joe?"

"He's not here right now, Granny Rose."

"Yes, he is," Jeff said, straightening from the bed. "You mean Joe Santori? He's been waiting outside since last night. Would you like to see him, Rose?"

Against her pillow, Rose's head made the barest movement of assent. The doctor went out into the hall and called, "Joe? Would you come in for a moment, please? Rose would like to see you."

Joe ventured cautiously into the sickroom, still wearing the clothes he'd hustled into last night and looking unshaved. With a start, Susannah realized he must have arrived at the hospital shortly after she had and remained outside the room all through the night and day. A rush of love for him swept through her.

The sight of Rose in the bed must have shocked him, Susannah could see. He couldn't hide his surprise at how ill the elderly woman looked. Susannah realized she had gotten accustomed to Rose's pinched white face, but Joe was seeing it for the first time. He looked quickly at Susannah, communicating a question, but she lifted her hands helplessly.

Taking a deep breath, Joe slid into the chair beside the bed and grabbed both of Rose's hands in his large ones. He bent close, mustering a grin. "How are you doing, Mrs. A.?"

Rose blinked. "Not so good," she whispered. "I'm dying."

Susannah gasped, and Jeff Baron reached for her arm and squeezed it, silencing her.

To his credit, Joe didn't argue. Bluntly, he said, "I'll look after Suzie for you. You know that."

Rose managed a small smile. "Love?"

"I love her very much. She's stubborn on the outside, but she's the sweetest woman I've ever known. I want to marry her and keep her here in Tyler, where she belongs."

That answer seemed to please Rose very much. Her gaze held his for a long time, shining.

Then Rose sighed and closed her eyes. "Suzie?"

Susannah rounded the bed so she could lean close. She kissed Rose's cheek to let her know she was there. "Yes, Granny Rose?"

"Roger."

"What about Roger?"

Quite clearly, Rose said, "Don't let him talk you into anything you don't want to do."

Joe laughed. "You tell her, Mrs. A.!"

Rose smiled, but she looked very tired. She seemed to grow smaller, and her chest barely moved as she breathed. Softly, she said, "I love you both."

Susannah put her head down on the bedclothes and wept, unable to hide her grief. For the first time she forced herself to face the truth. She stood on the edge of life without her grandmother. The woman who had been proud and fiery all her life was ready to let herself be carried into the next world. And there was nothing Susannah could do to stop it.

A long time passed—perhaps an hour or several—and neither Joe nor Susannah moved from the bedside. The doctor and nurses moved quietly in and out of the room, but there was nothing more they could do. Rose did not wake again.

In the evening, Rose Atkins died peacefully.

Susannah was strangely happy to be with her at the moment her spirit passed from her body. And she knew it clearly—that Rose was no longer with them, even though her body remained behind.

For Joe, the moment Rose passed away brought an odd relief. He was glad to see her go so quietly. He had not been at the hospital when Marie died. That long-ago morning, he'd taken an hour to go home to check on Gina, and when he returned to the hospital, Marie was gone. He had been haunted by the guilt of letting her die alone. How many times had he wished he could live that hour over again? He had wanted to comfort her. But watching Rose, he realized the dying didn't need the kind of comfort he'd assumed they did. Perhaps Marie had waited until he was gone before she let go of life. Perhaps she'd wanted to be alone.

But Rose seemed at peace when she gave up. Joe hoped Marie had been just as relieved to die.

At last, he got up from the bed and drew the sheet over Rose's face. The nurses had come in, but it was up to Joe to help Susannah to her feet and hold her while she cried. She clung to him weakly, and he realized she was too tired to function.

"Let me take you home," he said, wiping the tears from her cheek with his finger.

Susannah nodded, but she seemed unwilling to leave yet. Joe put his arm around her and guided her into the hallway.

Gina was there, still waiting in the chair she had taken when she arrived at the hospital earlier that day. She stood up awkwardly. "Dad?"

Susannah hesitated.

Gina stepped forward, her face blurred with tears. To Susannah, she said, "I'm sorry. The doctor just told me that she died. She was... I really thought she was neat."

Susannah smiled weakly. "Me, too. Thanks, Gina."

"I'm going to take Susannah back to her house," Joe said. "You want to come along?"

Sometimes his daughter surprised him, all right. Gina looked very mature at that moment. She nodded. "Sure. Maybe there's something I can do."

At the Atkins house, Susannah unlocked the door and went inside first, so she was the one who found the note from Roger Selby.

She opened it with shaking fingers and read the message aloud. "'Susannah, I've been called back to the station for a meeting. We'll discuss your new contract next week. I hope your grandmother feels better. Roger.'"

"He's a jerk," Gina said.

"Gina!" Joe reproved her automatically.

"No, it's okay," Susannah said, folding the note again. "Sometimes he is a jerk, Gina. But not always."

Joe helped Susannah up to the second floor, where she undressed and climbed into bed without much coaxing. He tucked her under the blankets, aware that she had fallen asleep almost instantly. Joe kissed her forehead and left the room.

"She sure looks beat," Gina said when he went downstairs again.

"Rough night," Joe agreed, running his hand through his hair.

"For both of you," Gina noted. "Why don't you sack out on the couch for a while, Dad? I'll make some phone calls. Somebody ought to let Mrs. Atkins's friends know what happened. A lot of them stopped in at the hospital today."

"You can handle that?"

Gina nodded solemnly. "I think so. I'd like to give it a shot."

Joe realized he was so tired he could hardly think. So he nodded and staggered into the sitting room. He flung himself across the sofa and fell asleep in no time.

FOR SUSANNAH, the funeral arrangements and visitations were almost as painful as her vigil at the hospital. Fortunately, Joe stood by her side and helped make all the decisions.

"Wait an extra day," he advised Susannah. "You don't want to have the funeral on Christmas. Rose would want you to wait, I'm sure."

Susannah agreed. Granny Rose would have hated the idea of spoiling everyone's holiday.

At the house, between the sessions at the funeral home, Susannah felt as though Rose's home was under siege by her grieving friends. Susannah received their hugs and tears, and she found it comforting to talk with all the Tyler folk who were going to miss Rose. The kitchen was soon crowded with foods of every description, and the refrigerator bulged with casseroles.

Gina proved to be very organized, and she kept lists of what neighbors brought which dishes, to make the thank-you writing simple. Gina also answered the phone and was the one who broke the news of Rose's death to Roger Selby when he called. He told Gina to express his sentiments to Susannah, rather than talking to her himself.

Susannah was glad to have Gina and Joe around, for they were sources of support and comfort. Joe was never farther than an arm's length away, and Susannah drew strength from him.

But then it was Christmas Eve, and Susannah knew she couldn't ruin everyone's holiday by keeping them by her side. She also felt the need to send the others home so she could be alone in the house for a while.

Joe protested, holding her fast in his arms. "I don't want you to spend tonight by yourself." He had once again slept over the night before—in the room Roger had used.

"I have to do this! Go home and spend Christmas with Gina," she urged him. "I'll be fine."

She insisted, and soon Joe had to obey. He drove Gina home, and Susannah took the phone off the hook. She turned off the downstairs lights and retired to the second floor to spend the evening alone. It might have looked like a sad way to spend Christmas Eve, but she felt it was the best way to say goodbye to her grandmother.

Susannah sat in Rose's bedroom and began to go through old photo albums and the stacks of scrapbooks her grandmother had kept over the years. Rose had saved all kinds of things that chronicled her life—pictures, newspaper clippings, tickets from plays, the programs from banquets, musicales, weddings and funerals. A great many of the bits and pieces Rose had saved represented Susannah's accomplishments. Every scrap of publicity the television station had ever sent out seemed to have found its way into her grandmother's hands.

Susannah had hoped to brighten her own spirits by looking through Rose's things, but she found herself deeply saddened that night.

Rose's passing seemed to have come at such a turning point in Susannah's own life—a turning point she had hoped to celebrate with her grandmother. Instead, it had marked the end of Rose's life. And perhaps the beginning of Susannah's.

She went to her bed late that night and slept fitfully. In the morning, she awoke and could hardly believe Rose was gone. The fact hit her again like a bulldozer.

But at last, Susannah dragged herself out of bed and dried her eyes once more. She showered and dressed for church, thinking she might feel strong enough to go later in the morning. In the kitchen, she made a cup of tea and chose a muffin from the enormous array of baked goods left by friends and neighbors. The house was very quiet. It hardly felt like Christmas.

At ten o'clock, the doorbell rang.

Although she was tempted not to answer, the visitor was insistent and rang the bell twice more, until Susannah steeled herself to open the door.

"Good morning," said Joe, standing on the porch in his parka and scarf. His smile brimmed with love and concern. "You have your phone off the hook."

Susannah summoned an apologetic smile. "Yes, I have. I needed some time."

"Feel better today?"

"No," she admitted. "Worse, in fact."

"You should have let me stay last night."

She shook her head. "No, I—I needed to let a lot of emotion out. Would you like some breakfast?"

"I've already had mine," he said. Then, "I've brought you something."

"Oh?"

He stood back, revealing the vehicle that stood at the curb in front of the house. Rather than his pickup truck, Joe had come in the bright red sleigh, complete with Bessie harnessed to the traces. Holding the horse's head was Gina, looking stunned to find herself standing in the snow with a bridle in her hand.

"Oh, my heavens!" Susannah exclaimed, clapping one hand to her mouth. She felt a fresh wave of tears well up in her eyes. "Oh, Joe. How did you—?"

"You told me about your family tradition," he reminded her. "Get your coat. We're going for a sleigh ride."

"I can't. I can't go through with it."

"Yes, you can," he soothed, guiding her inside and locating her coat in the closet. "Traditions aren't supposed to die with family members. You're supposed to keep them going."

"But—"

"Don't argue. Rose would want this."

He was right, of course. No one had reveled in family traditions more than Rose herself. As Susannah stepped off the porch and walked toward the sleigh, she had the uncanny feeling that her grandmother was watching from somewhere. Along with Susannah's parents and the family members who had started the tradition long ago, Rose was certainly smiling at the sight of Susannah climbing into the sleigh on Christmas morning.

"Here you go, Dad," said Gina, handing over the reins. "Drive carefully."

"Come with us, Gina," Susannah urged.

"Not this time," the teenager replied. "I'll go next year." She winked. "When Dad's better at driving the horse!"

Joe laughed and bundled Susannah under the blanket. Then he gathered up the reins and clucked to the mare. In an instant, they were off, gliding down the snowy street.

"When did you learn to drive a sleigh?" Susannah asked, when she could trust her voice.

"An hour ago." Quite cheerfully, he said, "Mr. Vaughn had me practise all over his fields. He says I'm terrible, but that Bessie knows what she's doing. I figure if we get into trouble, you can take over."

As the sleigh skidded along the street and took the corner with care, Susannah snuggled close to share his body heat and said, "You're a sweet man, Joe Santori."

"When did you figure that out, exactly?"

She smiled, feeling as though her heartstrings had just been plucked. "I'm not sure, exactly. But I'm convinced of it now. Along with all your good qualities, sweetness is probably the best."

"What about my superior bedroom skills?"

Susannah didn't answer that, and Joe glanced down to find out why his light remark had fallen so flat. Susannah struggled to control herself before the tears began anew. Joe made a noise in the back of his throat and drove out of town, away from the prying eyes of the Tyler citizens who were already out on the streets and heading for church. He pulled the sleigh into the nearest empty field, then gave Bessie her freedom. The horse stopped moving and dropped her nose to find a blade of grass in the snow.

Turning in the seat, Joe said, "What's wrong, Susannah?"

She shook her head and couldn't look at him. "I still feel guilty."

"Guilty?"

"About the night we spent together. If I had gone home... if I hadn't let myself enjoy those hours with you..."

Joe's breath made a hissing sound in his teeth. "Don't, Susannah."

"I can't help it! If I'd been at home with her, she'd be alive today."

"How can you be sure of that?"

"I can't—I just—I feel as if I let her down, Joe. For my own pleasure."

Joe sat for a long moment, then said firmly, "Do you think Rose would look at it that way? If given the chance to go out with a friend and spend the kind of night we spent in each other's arms, what would her choice be? Would Rose have stayed at home herself?"

"I don't know."

"Yes, you do. Rose grabbed her share of life wherever she could find it. She wanted the same for you, Susannah."

"But—"

"And she wouldn't want you to feel guilty this way."

"I miss her!" Susannah cried out.

"Of course you do. Just don't let guilt get mixed up with your grief. I'm sure Rose would be the first to tell you how wonderful it was that we found each other—that we made love with the kind of intimacy and intensity we shared. She'd be happy for us, Susannah."

"I can't be happy."

"I know that. But it will come again. Time passes. We'll find a way to remember Rose without feeling sad."

"Do you really think so?"

"I'm sure of it." He lifted her chin, and a glint of a smile had already lightened his face. "After all, wasn't Rose one of the happiest human beings on the face of the earth? She was funny and caring and...damn, I just hope we can live up to her expectations."

Susannah smiled ruefully. "What do you suppose she'd expect of us?"

Joe leaned close and kissed her lightly on the mouth. "Well, first of all, I think she'd expect us to get her affairs taken care of as soon as possible so we can start planning a wedding."

"Joe!"

He laughed. "All right, all right, I won't press the issue today. It's unfair to take advantage of a woman when she's been weakened. But I will marry you, Susannah. If you'll have me."

"Is that a proposal?"

"Yes. I love you."

"I love you, too." She touched his face and met his dark gaze with her own. "But it will be awfully complicated. My job..."

"We'll make a home here in Tyler, just as Rose would have liked. You can do whatever you want with the television station—stay in your job or cut back to part-time, whatever makes you happy. We'll make it work. But eventually, you're going to write your book and become nationally famous, and I'm going to find a way to raise a teenage daughter without going crazy."

"There you go again—being the bossiest man on the planet."

He smiled down at her. "Will you marry me in spite of my faults?"

"Yes. I do love you, Joe."

His arms tightened, and his voice turned husky. "I'm so glad to hear you say that, Susannah. I love you with all my heart."

She kissed him that Christmas morning, with the feeling that she was going to be kissing Joe Santori on many more Christmas mornings to come. Then Joe turned Bessie around and drove back into Tyler, the town filled with friends and neighbors who would welcome yet another happy couple into the community.

And now,
an exciting preview of

BLAZING STAR

by Suzanne Ellison

the fifth installment of the
Tyler series

When Karen Keppler gets the police captain's job that all of Tyler thinks rightfully belongs to Brick Bauer, Brick has a hard time pretending he's a loyal subordinate to a woman who is exquisitely beautiful . . . and hard as nails. He can't change jobs: his whole life is keeping the peace in Tyler. But he's falling in love with a woman who absolutely refuses to have an affair with a man under her command—even though it's obvious that she can't live without him.

And now...
an exciting new novel

BLAZING STAR

by Suzanne Ellison

the third installment of the [illegible]
Tyler series

When Lucas Klippert gets the police captain's job that all of Tyler thinks rightfully belongs to Brick Bauer, Brick has a hard time accepting he's a loyal subordinate to a woman who is [illegible] and [illegible]. He can't change jobs; his whole life is [illegible] the [illegible] in Tyler. But he's falling in love with a woman who absolutely refuses to have an [illegible] with a man under her command—even though it's obvious that she can't live without him.

CHAPTER ONE

BRICK BAUER PARKED his old black pickup outside the main gates to the Schmidt farm, then hurried up the long gravel walkway that led through the dark to the house. It was already after eight, and he hoped the chief's retirement party would be in full swing by now—the bigger the crowd, the less conspicuous his token appearance was likely to be. A half hour or so ought to do it, just long enough to say hello to everybody who'd be sure to notice if he lacked the courage to show up here tonight. All week he'd felt like a bug in a specimen jar, and he had no intention of spending the next week the same way.

Since last Monday, Brick's name had been on the lips of every housewife who had her hair done at Tisha Olsen's Hair Affair, every cop who hung out at Marge's Diner and every old codger who was living out his sunset years at Worthington House. Nobody had dared to spread rumors at the Kelseys' boardinghouse, but Brick figured that was because his Aunt Anna had threatened to take a spatula to the backside of any of his fellow boarders who so much as mentioned that he'd been passed over for promotion, let alone that a *woman* from the other end of Sugar Creek County was going to take the helm instead of him.

The worst of it was that Brick still wasn't sure how it had happened. He'd been Chief Paul Schmidt's right-hand man at the Tyler Police Department for the past six years, and back in college he'd been engaged to Paul's daughter, who was supposed to be making one of her rare pilgrimages home for the party tonight. Granted, Brick and Shelley had parted painfully, but nobody could blame him for that. It wasn't his fault that Shelley had decided that being a big-city microbiologist suited her better than marriage to a hometown cop. She still hadn't married; she claimed she never would.

Brick was single, too, but it wasn't because he didn't want a family. He just hadn't found his lifetime mate yet. He'd actually grown a bit weary of searching, but his Aunt Anna still spent a good deal of her time trying to find him the perfect wife. Her latest candidate was the new boarder who was moving in tonight.

Aunt Anna and Uncle Johnny had zipped off to Milwaukee at the last minute to put their daughter Kathleen on a plane for Switzerland, conveniently leaving Brick as the resident family member to greet the newcomer anytime after nine. He wasn't holding out any hopes that he'd want to get particularly chummy with the new boarder, but he was pleased that he had such a good excuse to leave the party early.

As he pocketed his key and marched up the gravel walkway, Brick spotted a pair of long, magnificent female legs moving at a good clip in front of him. At once he found himself checking out some impressive curves that not even the stylish wool coat could conceal. Brick knew every woman in the retiring police chief's life—there weren't many—but for a moment he had trouble placing this one. The confidence of that saucy walk made him question his own memory; besides, there was something different about the hair.

Shelley always wore her hair long and loose, the way he liked it. Tonight it was wrapped in a classy chignon, but it was still dark and thick and tempting. In fact, in the moonlight, it looked even more silky that Brick remembered it. *Shelley* looked more silky than he remembered her! Womanhood had been good to her. Not only did she move with more compelling grace than she used to, but she'd put on a little weight, too... in all the right places.

As Shelley approached the porch where they'd exchanged fervent kisses so many times, Brick felt an odd sense of déjà vu. Was it possible that he still had deep feelings for her? Was that why he'd never really found another woman to take her place? Was that why she looked so good to him—better than ever—after all this time?

As December's first tiny snowflakes began to fall, Brick remembered how Shelley had looked the first time he'd kissed her snow-sprinkled nose, when she was nineteen. She'd giggled ever after when he'd called her Snowflake. Oh, it was all over and done, but those had been special days, and he still had special memories. He imagined that Shelley might, too.

Suddenly Brick realized that he didn't want to greet her for the first time in years under the gossip-mongering eyes of every busybody in Tyler. Whatever they had to say to each other should be said alone outside.

He jogged the last few yards between them, reaching Shelley just as she pushed open the chain-link gate at the edge of the porch. Because she seemed to be rushing, Brick reached out with a friendly arm to encircle her waist, about to say, "Hey, Snowflake, you never used to be in such a big hurry to go inside when I took you home."

He got as far as "Hey, Snowflake" when the most amazing thing happened. Shelley grabbed his elbow, jammed her hip into his leg and flipped him straight up and over the gate. Twisting sideways as he struggled to find his feet, Brick came down hard on the protruding edge of the chain link. Raw steel ends clawed his jaw and shoulder, shredded his best suitcoat and bloodied a fair amount of skin before he hit the ground on his side. Gasping for breath, he rolled flat on his back before he caught a good look at his assailant's face.

She wasn't Shelley! In a dizzying rush Brick realized that this classy brunette was a total stranger. She was beautiful; she was curved in all the right places; she was pulling out a .38 Smith & Wesson from underneath the left side of her coat.

"Don't move a millimeter," she threatened in a dry tone that rivaled Dirty Harry's. "Touch me again and you're going to lose a vital portion of your anatomy."

"Lady, I wouldn't touch you with a ten-foot pole!" Brick grumbled, realizing even in his confusion that fear, not malice, was the reason she'd reacted so violently to a simple touch. This stunning female had clearly been trained in self-defense. She'd also lived with the threat of urban crime or else watched too many cop shows. He wouldn't be surprised if she tried to make a citizen's arrest for...well, for whatever it was she thought he'd tried to do to her.

"I'm a police officer and I thought you were an old friend," Brick explained, too dizzy to sort everything out. His voice sounded odd and hollow. "Sorry if I frightened you. Now may I get off the ground?"

To his surprise, the woman did not immediately accept his explanation. She didn't even look embarrassed. In fact, on closer examination, he decided that her beautiful gray eyes looked more fierce than frightened. Sternly she ordered, "Show me your police ID. Slowly."

Brick was too angry to be scared, but he didn't like the way she kept that gun trained on him. "Good God, you could shoot somebody with that thing, lady." He dug out his ID and pushed it a few inches toward her. "Do you have a permit for that piece?" He didn't ask her if she knew how to use it; it was obvious she knew all too well.

She barely glanced at his identification, unreadable in the darkness, before she barked, "What's your badge number?"

Not his name, his badge number. A curiously eerie feeling, worse than the pain now coursing through his back, began to steal over Brick. How many women were so well versed in self-defense, handled a side arm like a pro and instinctively asked a question like that? Now that he was getting a grip on his equilibrium, he realized what all the signs pointed to.

His assailant was a cop.

She was also a rare beauty; she bore no resemblance to the woman who'd gotten his former partner killed. This lady wasn't a tiny thing, but she wasn't a husky bruiser, either. She looked to be five foot nine or ten, sturdy but slender, with high, sculpted cheekbones and infuriatingly well-curved lips. Even in his current situation, Brick found her femininity hard to ignore. He didn't want to think about the effect she'd have on him if she ever traded in that scowl for a dazzling smile.

Brick told her his number, then added darkly, "Lieutenant Donald Bauer, Tyler Police Department. Go ask my chief. He's inside."

"Lieutenant Bauer," the husky voice countered, "Chief Paul Schmidt is now retired and the Tyler Police Department he ran for seventeen years no longer exists. You now represent the Sugar Creek County Sheriff's Department. Archibald Harmon is your regional commander and Captain Karen Keppler is taking charge of the Tyler substation." She sheathed the gun in a shoulder holster he hadn't noticed underneath the thick coat. "Commit that information to memory, Lieutenant. You may be called upon to use it again."

That was when he knew for sure. Brick felt his face flushing a furious red in the darkness, grateful she couldn't see it but certain that she knew his face was hot. He was not a man who was easily embarrassed, but he knew that only a miracle would save him from the whole damn town's discovery of his humiliation.

It was bad enough that the brunette was a strikingly beautiful woman who'd gotten the better of him. Under any circumstances, Brick would have hated lying here on the ground, dizzy and wounded, with a looker like that leaning over him. Knowing that *she* was the one who'd hurt him, knowing that *she* was his new boss, knowing that *she* had stolen the job that was rightfully his and would lord it over him—*lady* it over him!—as long as she lasted in Tyler... it was just too damn much.

Incredibly, the brunette had the unmitigated gall to offer a hand to help him up. Brick ignored it. Still steaming, he struggled to stand up on his own, but when his wobbly knees gave out he plopped back down on the ground.

"I'm Captain Keppler, Lieutenant," the beauty informed Brick, still towering over him. "Sorry about the misunderstanding. Are you injured?"

Brick tried to swallow his fury as the front door opened and he heard Paul Schmidt call out, "We thought we heard somebody out here. Glad you found the place all right, Captain." Then, after a sharp breath, "What the devil—"

"Lieutenant Bauer had a little accident," his new captain said bluntly, her husky voice devoid of humor or concern. "He's bleeding."

The next few minutes were a nightmare for Brick. Paul instantly called out, "Somebody get George Phelps out here!" and rushed over to his side. "Brick, what happened? Are you all right?"

Brick had to steady himself on the gate as he tried—and failed again—to stand. His spine felt battered and his scraped jaw stung. Blood dribbled down his chin to the gravel.

By this time half a dozen people had bounded out of the house. Through the din of worried friends and coworkers, he recognized a few voices: Judson Ingalls's, Janice Eber's, and—it was inevitable—Shelley's.

She sounded just the way she used to when he'd gotten hurt playing football. "Brick! Oh, Brick! You're bleeding! Let George take a look at you and—"

"Oh, for Pete's sake!" he burst out, ready to strangle the whole lot of them. He was fully upright now and his head was finally clear. "I'm fine, but my suit's a wreck and Aunt Anna wants me to meet some damn boarder at home by nine o'clock. I just dropped by to say hello to Shelley, goodbye to the chief and to meet

Captain Keppler. I guess I've done all three, so if you don't mind—"

"It won't seem right without you here, Brick," protested Zachary Phelps, a former chief of police, a fellow Kelseys' boarder and a member of the town's council. The tone of his voice said more than his words: Zachary was still feeling guilty for having voted to merge the Tyler Police Department with the Sugar Creek County Sheriff's Department, even though he'd explained to Brick in detail why the town's financial situation demanded it. Brick was certain that neither Zachary nor anybody else on the Council had ever believed that the regional commander would bring in outside talent to run Tyler's law enforcement in the wake of Paul Schmidt's retirement. As Zachary studied Karen Keppler in the dim porch light, Brick read the same dismay on the old man's face as he was sure Zachary read on his own.

"Brick, I thought we'd have a chance to talk," Shelley said quietly, so quietly that probably no one but the nearby captain could hear. "I haven't seen you in years."

Brick gave his old flame a quick glance, trying to remember why he'd wondered if some seed of love for her still lingered within him. Oh, she was still pretty...though she'd cut her long, black hair. But she was a stranger, a woman who'd chosen the big city and the scientific world over anything Brick could offer, and he knew that his earlier momentary fantasy had had nothing to do with her.

Kindly he said, "I'll call you, Shelley. Maybe we can have lunch sometime before you go."

"That'd be nice, Brick," she replied, but he saw nothing but "for old times' sake" in her eyes.

He saw something different in the eyes of Captain Keppler, who still stood tensely over him. Calculation, assessment . . . disapproval that did not bode well for a police officer under her command.

By this time George Phelps, head of staff at Tyler General Hospital and Aunt Anna's boss, had pushed his way through the gathering crowd. "Everybody get back!" George commanded, like Moses parting the Red Sea.

They did pull back, but they didn't disperse. Impatiently Brick snapped, "There's nothing wrong with me a dab of Bactine won't cure, George. If you want to help, just get all these folks to stop gawking at me, would you?"

George seemed to get the picture faster than anybody else. Then again, he was a doctor, and he knew when blood was serious and when it was just as embarrassing as hell.

His eyes were sympathetic as he called out, "Okay, everybody, Brick's fine. Let's go back inside."

Before Brick could thank him, Captain Keppler asked in a businesslike tone, "Are you feeling strong enough to drive, Lieutenant? I can ask one of the other officers to take you home."

"I can take care of myself, Captain," he snapped. If she'd been a man, he would have been hard-pressed to keep from decking her. But he'd been raised to be gentle with women; he'd been raised to obey his boss. Still, he wasn't used to the raging fury that was strangling him at the moment. It was something new and terrible, a beast he knew he must learn to subdue. A beast that drove from his heart the slightest interest in getting reacquainted with Shelley, lauding his old boss or kissing up to his new one.

Reluctantly Shelley said good-night, then turned back to the house. Her father shooed a couple of other men after her. Captain Keppler, rebuttoning her coat, had the nerve to look downright pretty as she brushed past Brick without another word and followed them inside.

While the sound of laughter from the house drifted out to his still-red ears, Brick limped out to his truck. On the street he ran into two more late arrivals from the substation—Sergeant Steve Fletcher and tubby Orson Clayton—but he ducked into his truck before they could see that he'd been roughed up. Tomorrow would be soon enough for them to start their ribbing.

By the time he turned on the ignition, the scrapes on Brick's jaw were beginning to clot over, but his backbone was hurting worse than ever. He'd broken up barroom brawls with less pain and certainly with less humiliation! By morning every damn soul in Tyler would know how Brick Bauer had been bested by the new female captain who'd been hired instead of him. The gouges on his face would heal a lot sooner than the scars on his pride.

KAREN STAYED at the party longer than she'd intended, not because she was enjoying herself—she wasn't—and not because she thought courtesy demanded it. It was Paul Schmidt's moment of honor, which in a town this size meant that most of his fans and foes were likely to make an appearance. Karen wanted to study those people with great care... particularly the ones who'd been an important part of Schmidt's life for the past forty years or so.

At the top of the list was Judson Ingalls. Everybody kowtowed to him as though he owned the town. Ditto for his elegant blond daughter, Alyssa Ingalls Baron. Ingalls also had a niece named Janice Eber, who seemed sweet and unassuming, but Karen wasn't taking anything at face value. The doctor was a Tyler fixture, as was the lady who owned the diner and the flamboyant one who cut everybody's hair.

And then there were the other cops. Lieutenant Bauer—why did they call him Brick?—had only lived here since high school, according to Karen's information, but his relatives had lived here for generations, and that might be highly significant. Both Alyssa and Janice were Bauer's aunt's close friends. The fact that he had some sort of relationship with Schmidt's daughter might also prove important, and not just because it had provided the catalyst for his unfortunate first meeting with Karen.

If only that handsome man had been able to read her mind! If only he'd guessed how terrible she felt about embarrassing him, how frightened she'd been by the way he'd lunged at her, how his virility had unnerved her even after he'd quelled her fear by revealing that he was a cop! She'd done everything in her power to fool him with her tough-as-leather facade, and she hoped she'd succeeded. She would need a full set of armor to run the Tyler substation—not to mention carry out Commander Harmon's secret assignment.

Everything Karen had heard about Brick Bauer—and everything she'd read in his file—caused her to believe that he was a man of powerful convictions, keen loyalties and devotion to his fellow police officers. Under some other circumstances, Karen would have looked forward to working with such a man. Commander Harmon had given her the impression that he truly hoped she wouldn't find any black marks on Bauer's record—he'd even confessed that he still had high hopes for the lieutenant's career. But Harmon was a diligent cop, if a chauvinistic one, and he had a reputation as a man who upheld the letter of the law no matter who got in the way.

Karen had glowed when he told her that she'd earned the same reputation since she'd moved from Milwaukee to Sugar Creek.

Living under the same roof with Bauer would certainly make it easier to ascertain which hometown loyalties bound him, but after their inauspicious meeting, Karen knew that their domestic situation was going to be a strain on both of them. The knowledge did not dishearten her. She'd devoted her life to the badge and she had police work in her blood. From birth her father had urged her, "Make your old man proud," and she'd devoted her life to that goal. His death in the line of duty had only strengthened her determination.

Karen's courage, however, did little to squelch the butterflies in her stomach as she rang the doorbell of Kelsey Boardinghouse, a beacon of cheery light in December's nighttime gloom. The wreath-bedecked door swung open on the first ring, which surprised Karen. The sight of the man who opened it surprised her, too.

He was wearing low-slung jeans, thick socks without shoes and a Green Bay Packers sweatshirt. Droplets of water clung to his freshly washed short black hair; droplets of blood oozed from three deep gouges on his face. His blue eyes sparkled with fun and his square jaw was softened by deep dimples when he smiled. It was the sort of smile that could make a woman forget everything else in the world.

Karen found herself wrestling with her memory.

"Hi, there! I'm Brick Bauer, Anna Kelsey's nephew," he greeted her cheerfully, reaching for the suitcase in her hand. "She asked me to roll out the red carpet and give you the grand tour. Did you have any trouble finding the place?"

Karen stared at him, wondering if Bauer had dual personalities. What a joy to find him so forgiving, so friendly, so...*so damn male.* With a jolt she realized that the man's dimpled smile was triggering an unexpected female response within her, one she ignored a good deal of the time and always suppressed with policemen. Karen had an uneasy hunch that she was safer with this man when he was angry, but it seemed cowardly to go out of her way to make him mad.

As it turned out, such subterfuge was totally unnecessary. The instant she stepped into the lighted hallway, the smile vanished from Brick Bauer's face. A shell-shocked look stilled the magic of his dancing eyes.

"Your aunt's directions were quite clear, Lieutenant," Karen said neutrally, firmly holding the suitcase handle. "I can carry my own things, thank you."

Karen wasn't sure why it hurt her to see Bauer change so drastically before her eyes. She didn't know this man and couldn't afford to like him. But she'd been spellbound by his delightful greeting when he'd assumed she was an utter stranger; now he was smoldering because he realized they'd met before.

"Captain Keppler?" His tightly controlled tone could not conceal the fury that now raged in his eyes. "My aunt didn't mention her new lodger's name. I didn't realize that the new police captain would be—"

"Invading your home?"

His lips tightened at her bluntness. Karen almost regretted the harsh words, but she knew that surprise and anger often drove people to reveal things they'd normally keep well hidden. If Bauer had any secrets, she wanted to find them out for Commander Harmon right away. She also wanted to clear the air about their respective positions. Sooner or later, they were likely to have it out over the way she'd been brought in to take the job he'd expected. Better to do it in private than in front of the men. They'd all be on his side. One to one, she had a better chance of victory.

"Captain Keppler, you are free to live wherever you like. I was just . . . startled to realize you were the new boarder. My information was incomplete."

He said the words like a police detective who knew his stuff. Karen wondered how he'd managed to uncover so little in his investigation of the body found at the old Timberlake Lodge, recently purchased by Edward Wocheck.

So did Commander Harmon.

"I don't like to advertise my private life, Lieutenant," Karen told him. She didn't need to add the obvious: she'd deliberately avoided revealing the nature of her job to chatty Anna Kelsey when they'd made arrangements on the phone. "I don't have much off-duty time, but when I do, I want it to be all mine."

"I feel the same way."

"Good," she said stoutly. "Then we have something in common."

Bauer glanced away. He was fuming, she was certain, but trying to show respect. Karen had to admire him for it—even more than she had to admire his massive shoulders. Still, she couldn't afford to let his hidden anger smolder.

"We have something else in common, Lieutenant. We both wanted the job I came here to do."

His harsh gaze swung back on her. "Captain, I'm doing my damnedest to be courteous to you. Why the hell are you baiting me?"

"I don't want you sandbagging me when we're on the job, Lieutenant Bauer," she told him truthfully. "I came here to run the Tyler substation to the best of my ability, and I'll do it—with or without you. But as long as you remain here, we'll have to work closely together. If you've got something to get off your chest, I'd rather deal with it right now."

When he stared at her for a long, bitter moment, Karen had a sense of what it would be like to be a criminal collared by this man. He was a good six feet tall, his body a solid wall of muscle that looked as if he maintained it at a gym. Karen was used to dealing with all kinds of cops and all kinds of criminals. She was rarely intimidated just by a man's physical strength, but this big guy had her struggling to keep her breathing even. She knew he would not be easy to control, physically or mentally. She'd flipped him over that fence only because he'd been oblivious to danger. She knew she'd never take him off guard again.

With slow, measured anger, he shut the door behind her. "On behalf of my aunt and uncle, welcome to Kelsey Boardinghouse, Captain Keppler," he said as tonelessly as a robot repeating a coded message. Coldly he turned away from the door and began to limp toward the back of the house, speaking as she followed. "Breakfast is served at seven o'clock. Dinner is served at six. There's a refrigerator and microwave you can use yourself as long as you clean up. The living room is for everyone. So is the phone. The den is my aunt and uncle's private space. Only the family goes in there."

He started climbing the back stairs, two at a time, and Karen found it hard to keep up with his long, angry stride while dragging the heavy suitcase she'd refused to let him carry. He took half a dozen steps down the hall, then dug into his pocket. "This is the key to the front door. This is the key to your room." He dropped the keys in her palm, being careful not to touch her skin. Then he opened the door to her room and gestured for her to go inside.

With relief, Karen saw that the room was well-kept and charming. On the old four-poster lay quilt, hand-pieced in yellows and blues. It matched the curtains. There was a small desk and a tallboy chest of Early American style. A chestnut-and-rust braided rug covered most of the shiny hardwood floor.

Before Karen could comment on the welcoming vase of flowers and the note she spotted on the nightstand, Brick marched over to the far door and pulled it open, revealing an equally quaint bathroom. "This is the bath. You share it with the lodger on the other side." He opened the far door a crack as if to illustrate his point, but Karen couldn't see much of the other bedroom.

When he took a stiff step and grimaced, Karen felt a sharp need to offer another apology. It was obvious that his scrapes and bruises were bothering him. As the secret investigator who might bring about his downfall, she couldn't afford to show much mercy, but as a human being who prided herself on her quiet compassion and tact, Karen found it hard to keep from showing concern.

"Any questions?" he asked brusquely, interrupting her thoughts.

Will you always hate me? Will all the other Tyler cops hate me, too? Will I ever see those incredible dimples again?

Aloud she said, "No, Lieutenant. Thank you. Good night."

"Good night," he said stiffly, his cautious movements revealing his pain as he edged through the far bathroom door.

It took Karen a moment to realize the significance of that simple act. *He's the boarder who lives next to me!* she realized in dismay. *We'll be sharing meals and the same bath.*

As she juggled the memory of his anger with the realization that such proximity would make it easier to uncover Bauer's secrets for Harmon, Karen closed the door between her room and the bath, locked it carefully, then read the note beside her bed. It started personally,

Dear Karen,

I'm so sorry we were called away tonight, but we'll be back in the morning to fix you up with anything you need. In the meantime, you can count on my nephew to make you snug as a bug in a rug.

Isn't he adorable? He's Tyler's finest police officer and single, too. I'm sure you'll have plenty of time to get acquainted. We're so glad to have you with us. Just make yourself to home!

Anna Kelsey

Karen fought back a lump in her throat. Mrs. Kelsey would never know how much it meant to her to know that one person in Tyler actually welcomed her. The officers she'd met at the Schmidts' had made it clear enough that they'd all been hoping Brick Bauer would be their new captain. And Bauer himself—why the hell did he have to be so handsome, why the hell had he greeted her with that dimpled smile at the door?—was probably already making devious tactical plans to oust her.

Wearily she began unpacking all she'd need for the first few days: her uniforms, a warm robe, jeans, sweatshirts and sturdy barrettes to clip her waist-length braid flat against her head whenever she was on duty. At the bottom of the suitcase Karen found the one sentimental item that followed her everywhere: an eight-by-ten glossy of her father in uniform, taken shortly before his death. He was smiling, as he'd so often smiled in life, and she felt his faith in his only child buoy her now.

"I'll do it, Daddy," she vowed softly. "I'm going to make you proud."

She touched his beloved face through the cold glass, then she placed the frame on top of the desk, took her gun out of its holster and laid it on the nightstand near the flowers. Quickly she took down her hair, shed her heels and peeled off her panty hose. She was standing in her bare feet, still wearing her slinky black dress and empty shoulder holster, when she heard a knock on the adjoining bathroom door a moment later.

"Yes?" she asked as she opened it uneasily. Karen wasn't used to such domestic proximity with a handsome, hostile stranger. *Maybe he's come to clear the air,* she told herself hopefully.

Belatedly Karen realized that she truly didn't want to go to bed in a strange place with her housemate and second in command furious with her, whether he was guilty of a cover-up or not. There was a fifty-fifty chance this man was innocent of any wrongdoing, and besides, a skilled police officer ought to be able to maintain civil relations with another cop without divulging any secrets. Surely she'd displayed enough strength for one night! Now maybe she could set things right.

But the minute she found herself face-to-face with that square, bloody jaw and those blue eyes dark with rage, Karen knew it was way too late for reconciliation.

"Captain Keppler, there's something I think you should understand," Bauer stated baldly, his great size seeming to fill the room. "I'm damn proud to be a Tyler cop, and that's never going to change. If you can't stand to work with me—" his tone grew nearly feral "—*you're* the one who'll have to move on."